KILL THE WILLING

KILL THE WILLING

I FEAR NO EVIL™ BOOK ONE

MARTHA CARR
MICHAEL ANDERLE

DISRUPTIVE IMAGINATION

Thanks to the JIT Readers

John Ashmore
Peter Manis
Kelly O'Donnell
James Caplan
Sarah Weir
Joshua Ahles
Paul Westman

If we've missed anyone, please let us know!

DEDICATIONS

From Martha

To everyone who still believes in magic
and all the possibilities that holds.
To all the readers who make this
entire ride so much fun.
And to my son, Louie and the wonderful Katie
who remind me all the time of what
really matters and how wonderful
life can be in any given moment.

From Michael

To Family, Friends and
Those Who Love
To Read.
May We All Enjoy Grace
To Live The Life We Are
Called.

S hay Carson wondered which one was dumber - returning to New York when she was supposed to be dead or kidnapping a man while driving a sports car. The bright red Porsche was fast enough, but if her target resisted at all, the poor baby might end up damaged. Kidnapping really seemed like more of a sketchy, window-less van kind of activity.

Not that the vehicle choice mattered that much, she supposed. The Porsche wasn't even her car, but it did seem like an asshole move to rent a car, and a Porsche at that, and then trash it. Though if all went well, there wouldn't be an issue, and even if there were, it'd be the poor fictional redhead, Abigail Johnson who would have to deal with the fallout. At least Shay wasn't such a bitch that she stole someone else's identity for the job. Manners, even while on the job. It was important to maintain standards.

Wish I had my Spider, but it's not like I wanted to drive all the way back to L.A. from the opposite coast.

A quick check out the window indicated her target

hadn't stepped into the street yet. The timing needed to be perfect. Her previous recon suggested very little foot traffic this time of night. All she needed to do was get the man in the car, and the dark of the early evening and her tinted windows would do the rest to conceal her snatch and grab operation. Even if someone spotted her, her fake plates, auburn wig, and oversized sunglasses would be enough to lead the police or any other dangerous and interested men down the wrong path.

The door to the office building swung open and her target stepped out. A young man, twenty-four, a little on the scrawny side, and handsome enough in that kind of generic Connecticut white-bread-wealthy-family way. Not really her type, but she could see the appeal.

Jefferson Peyton Coolidge. It's been a while.

Shay chuckled. It'd also been a long time since she thought much about his full name. The man tended to go by his middle name, derived from his mother's maiden name, another white bread custom.

The full name screamed money, unlike her name, Shay Carson.

"Look at you," she snickered to herself. "You shouldn't have played at being independent. Too late now, though."

Peyton made his way down the street toward a crosswalk. He took one step off the curb as Shay gunned her engine, the Porsche speeding toward the man. Her target froze, his eyes widening. The car screeched into a halt right in front of him.

Shay leapt out of the car before the man even registered that he wasn't becoming a new hood ornament. She yanked hard on Peyton's arm, threw open the passenger door, and shoved him in. Only respect for the car's paint job kept her from jumping over the hood to get back to the driver's seat. Still, a quick and successful kidnapping. Took seconds from start to finish.

"Wha...what is going on?" Peyton asked, his head turning side to side in a frantic effort to understand what the hell just happened.

Shay peeled out and took a hard right. "Put on your seatbelt." She yanked off her red wig and glasses and tossed them at Peyton's feet, revealing her dyed blond hair.

The man stared at her, his brown eyes wide. "No, no. This isn't happening. I... you're *dead*. I went to your funeral!" He gasped. "Oh crap. Are you a ghost? Wait... you're driving a car. You're a revenant? Shit...*please* tell me you didn't get mixed up with necromancers before you died, Shay."

"I'm not dead, idiot," Shay said with a smirk, making a hard left across oncoming traffic, flipping off one of the drivers that honked. "And I appreciated the flowers at my funeral. That was a nice arrangement you put on my casket. Very sweet, touching... *almost.*"

Peyton stared at her, his mouth unable to form any more words for a solid minute. Shay didn't mind, it gave her a chance to concentrate on the road and check for any vehicles or worse, drones, that might be following them. The skies and roads were clear of anything suspicious.

"What's going on?" the man finally managed. "I... don't understand why you're here, and why I'm in your car."

Shay slowed a bit, checking her mirrors. There was no reason to attract NYPD attention with something as stupid as speeding. Save it for something more fun.

She glanced over at him before returning her attention to the road. "First of all, just to be very clear, I faked my death. I decided I needed a new life... that didn't involve killing people." She frowned. "Well, at least not killing people all the time. A line of work that doesn't list killing people in the mission statement, for money or otherwise."

Peyton nodded slowly, his face still scrunched up in confusion. "So, you're not a hitman – woman – whatever - anymore?" He gave her a side long glance. "At least not on purpose."

"Nope. I was tired of that shit for a lot of reasons. Lucky for you, I still keep my eye on a lot of sites related to my old job, if only to watch out for anyone coming after me. You'd be surprised how easy it is to stay under the radar once everyone thinks you're dead and they stop looking for you." She winked and rested her hand on the bottom of the steering wheel, easily maneuvering the car. "I was doing my regular check on those sites and found out there's a hit out on *your* stupid ass, so I decided to save it. Your ass, not the hit. Lucky for you I can use an IT guy and you don't annoy me to the point of wanting to kill you."

Peyton let out a long sigh. "I didn't know there was a hit out on me," he rested his arm on the side of his door, tapping the leather. "But I guess I'm not surprised either."

"Oh?"

"You know me." He shrugged. "I'm an information guy. I was digging around when some new clients contacted me about working for them."

"Criminals?"

"Depends on whether you think breaking the law makes you a criminal or just financially motivated." He

4

slunk down in the seat and started to put his foot up on the dashboard till he saw the cold look come across Shay's face. At the last second, he crossed his leg and sat back up.

"Good move. May not be my car, but it's still a Porsche. Have some respect." Shay cut across to a side street where she could get around the traffic.

She ignored the honks this time.

"I thought I could handle them, but I found some information that links several members of Congress to a bunch of different organized crime groups. Mafia, Russian mob, Harriken, even a couple of problem Elves that might be involved with some shady Oriceran groups. I was planning to bank it for later use." Peyton turned to look out the window as they drove. "I think I fucked up. There's a chance I trusted the wrong guy when I was confirming things, and I..."

"What?"

"I guess I thought my family would protect me even if I don't ever see my brother and sister anymore. They've been my get out of firing range free card for a while."

"Looks like that card just expired on you."

Peyton looked down at his hands. "So, you think me turning up that information is what got the hit put out on me?"

"You were the keeper of secrets for a lot of dangerous people. The word is a lot of them think you're about to leak that information. The second that rumor got out there that you'd possibly leak anything? They wanted you dead. This shit isn't a game."

"I never thought it was a game."

"Sure."

Shay glanced at Peyton and considered telling him she'd found evidence there might be more to the hit than worried gangsters, something more personal, but decided it'd be too much, too soon. Shock still covered Peyton's face, and she could tell he was having trouble processing it all.

"No one wants you to burn their poor honest congressmen," she offered instead.

Peyton snorted. "People taking money from organized crime are honest?"

"You don't get it, do you?"

"What?"

"The actual definition of an honest man."

"What's that? I figure criminals have their own kind of honor, but that's not the same thing as honesty."

"Not exactly. An honest man stays bought once you bribe him." Shay took a deep breath and shook her head. "I warned you about this. You can't roll around with this kind of scum and not end up in the mud. I always told you that you should stay the fuck away. It doesn't matter if you're one of the best when it comes to research. All it takes is for you to learn the wrong thing, and then you're not only a liability, you're *the* liability. Like now."

Peyton frowned. "I used to help you, and you're not exactly a saint."

Shay wagged a finger at him. "If you were smart, you would have stayed away from me, too. But lucky you, I turned over a new leaf, and I'm helping your ass."

"Lucky for me, you need me." He eyed her, "You're really not a killer now?"

Shay looked over her shoulder and easily maneuvered

the Porsche in between a semi and a Subaru, cutting in and out of lanes. She loved the way the car responded to her touch. Just like a good piece of artillery or the right man. Well balanced and responsive. "I don't kill people for money anymore. I'm not gonna say I never kill anyone."

"They should put up a statue of you and give you the Nobel Peace Prize."

Shay chuckled. "Yeah, you're just as mouthy as I remember."

Peyton shrugged. "What's the plan here?"

Shay changed lanes. "Long-term, I'm snagging you back to L.A. with me, where I can hide you safely for a while. Set you up with a project I have in mind."

"And short-term?"

The ex-hitman gave Peyton a feral grin. "I *kill* you and collect your bounty."

"Don't move," Shay said, slathering red moulage makeup on Peyton's forehead. The fake wound would look real enough in a picture as long as she gave everyone a reason to believe what they were seeing. "You're gonna get this shit on the sheets, and I don't want to have to pay an extra cleaning fee to the hotel."

"You're really worried about some cleaning fee?"

"Hey, some of us didn't grow up in rich families."

Peyton snorted. "I know how much money you made in your old job. You have to have a pile stashed somewhere."

"Doesn't mean I still don't appreciate the value of a dollar. Now stay fucking still."

"It's so weird that you came this prepared to fake someone's death."

"You forget, I've had practice, and isn't that the Girl Scout's motto? Be prepared?"

"Fuck you. I was a Boy Scout. We had it first."

Shay grinned. "Not that I was ever a Girl Scout." She resisted the urge to slap Peyton upside the head to stop his fidgeting. "I said stop moving, damn it. Do you want me to really kill you or just fake kill you? Because, you know, I'm sorely tempted by the first."

"You know, Shay, you're just as angry as I remember you. Maybe even angrier. I would have thought fake dying would have made you a little more chill."

"I'm only angry because you won't stop moving. What are you, five years old? Stay still for two seconds. I'm only trying to save your fucking life here. *Sorry* that it's such an inconvenience."

Peyton muttered something under his breath. "I still don't get this. You're going to save me by making it look like you shot me in the head?"

"Yes. It's not that damned hard to understand."

"I think I have a new nickname for you: Angry White Bitch."

Shay snorted as she added in some texture and additional color to the growing headshot wound on the man's forehead. "I have a nickname for you, too. Clueless."

"I'm not that clueless. I stayed alive all this time, didn't I? And that's dealing with all these dangerous people and swimming around in the middle of their shit. You would not believe the information they pass back and forth."

"You never took this shit seriously. You did it for kicks."

"That's not true."

"Yes, it is, and anyway, you did survive, but it wasn't you. It was that family of yours that kept you alive, until they didn't want to anymore."

Peyton jerked away from her, scowling. Shay fought her natural instinct to palm strike the man's nose after his sudden movement. Then the makeup wouldn't be necessary to make him look dead.

"What do you mean?" he asked.

"First of all, get the hell back here, so I can finish." Shay narrowed her eyes at him. "Second, I think the whole corrupt Congress scum thing is a convenient excuse to get you out of the way. I think your family pushed this. This isn't the first time you've stumbled onto big info that was not in your purview, but this is the first time people decided they needed to kill you for it."

"Wait, you think my family wants to get me out of the way?" The man scooted back toward Shay.

"Come on, you're not that dumb," She lifted her brush. The death wound needed only a few final touches.

Peyton sat, rigid as a statue as Shay finished her work. "I'm not... that's a bit much, don't you think, trying to get me killed?" His eyes searched her face for an answer.

Shay finished her moulage application and shook her head. "Connect the dots, Peyton. Your father was a king-maker before his stroke. He amassed a fortune and isn't much longer for this world. We both know your brother and sister would like to get you out of the way so they can inherit everything. That's a lot of money. Shit, I've killed a lot of people for far less than that, and that money also has a lot of influence that can go with it. Power and money.

Add in some sex, and that's what makes the world go around."

Peyton shook his head as Shay grabbed his chin and held it tight, making the final touches..

"I don't know if I can believe they would come after me like that. No. I refuse to believe it. Why do you even think it's them behind all of this? Gangsters can want me dead for knowing their secrets without my family being involved."

Shay rose and nodded toward the bathroom. "I already have the fake blood all set up in the bathtub. Go in there and just rest your head in the open spot so I can get photographic proof of blowing your brains out with a nice low-caliber pistol. Glad I didn't decide to kill you with a fake shotgun. That shit would have been a lot more annoying."

"You're dodging the question." Peyton stepped toward the bathroom. "You always were good at that, Shay."

She shrugged a single shoulder. "I can only tell you what it smells like to me and what information I found. It doesn't matter if you believe me or not. The end result is the same. There's a serious hit out on you, and you have to leave, or you'll end up dead for real. Even if you try to go back for your inheritance after your father finally dies, you'll just end up buried right next to him."

"Not saying you're wrong, but I'm also not saying you're right, either."

Shay gave him a cold stare. "Whatever. Don't really give a shit as long as you do what I say. I'm risking my life coming back here to help you out. Not exactly how I wanted to spend my Friday night."

Peyton entered the bathroom. "And it's not like I ran off screaming now, is it?"

Shay followed him into the bathroom and waited for Peyton to lie down. "Stay still while I get a few pics." She lifted her phone and took pictures from a few different angles. "Okay, I'm done."

"You're seriously going to get money off fake-killing me? Won't that lead to you getting caught alive?" Peyton sat up in the red-splattered bathtub. He looked like a country club zombie. "That is the part I find more confusing than anything."

"Not at all. Not my first rodeo with aliases and fake identities. This will be easy, you see, because you've already disappeared. No corpse works out better for these kinds of people sometimes. Less disposal worries on their part. And it will keep most of the assholes off your back for a while."

"For a while?" Something approaching fear entered Peyton's eyes. "I'm not fake dying to stay above ground?"

"Stand up. I'll keep you safe if you do what I tell you."

Peyton groaned and stood.

"Bend your head over the tub so I can wash that crap out. Once we get to L.A., you're gonna have to live life even more low-profile than you do now until we make you a new life and figure out the rest." Shay carefully hosed off the sides of the tub, watching the red globs dissolve in the water. "That might take a while."

"And what I am supposed to do all day? Just sit around on my hands?"

"For now, you can put that research and IT brain of yours to use helping me out."

"Doing what? I thought you were out of the business."

Shay nodded, standing back and looking around for anything that would get a maid to call the cops. Not a good idea. "Out of the killing business. Now I have a new job. Field archaeologist."

Peyton blinked. "Huh? You're an academic now? Do they let you near students?"

The woman heaved a pained sigh and rubbed her temples. "We don't need to go into this right now. I'll explain later."

Peyton stepped out of the tub, holding up his hands. "Okay, I'm still processing everything else, whatever. I still don't know if I should be grateful or scared."

Shay grinned. "Both. For now, let's finish cleaning you up and take a ride."

2

"Where we going?" Peyton slipped into the passenger seat of the Porsche.

"I know after I died, I was really hungry." Shay started up the car as it let out a soft growl. "I figured we would get some food." She pulled out of the hotel parking lot. "There's a place about a half hour away in Union City. Great pizza, some of the best I've ever had, and that includes in NYC. Hell, we're practically already to the Lincoln Tunnel as it is. It'll be a straight shot."

Peyton's stomach rumbled at the mention of the food. "Sounds good. I was going to go get some dinner before some crazed woman kidnapped me."

Shay smirked. "Pizza's okay, though, not too low-brow for you there, Mr. Coolidge?" She spoke the name in a faux English accent.

"Hey, I'm a blue-collar worker, how can I not like pizza? I'm all about pizza and Mountain Dew. Come on. Have you seen what I'm wearing?"

"Yes, unfortunately." Shay eyed his black T-shirt and

pants decorated with red whales. "That's about the least blue-collar outfit I've seen. It's more like a wanted poster to get bitch slapped by someone." Shay narrowly missed a delivery man on a bike as he swerved in front of her. He turned and gave her the finger, smiling broadly at her. Shay gave him a friendly wave as she pulled closer to his back wheel, nudging him along. He jerked his head around and startled, banging into another car.

There, that's better than flipping them off.

"Just because you like pizza and Mountain Dew doesn't make you blue collar, Peyton."

He frowned. "What do you think I am then, if I'm not blue-collar? I work for a living, just like you."

"You don't have your name sewed on your shirt and you don't smell like grease of any kind. You're a white-collar worker, Peyton." Shay shrugged. "You're a zeros and ones guy when you slice it down to the essence. That's classic white collar. I don't know where you got the idea that you're some sort of blue-collar guy."

"Easy. Where I come from, if you don't own the company, then you're blue collar." He frowned and looked away.

Shay motioned to his clothes. "Your look is more like latent preppie on the lam with more than a heavy seasoning of hipster. Little unique for someone with your IT skills, and again, not blue collar."

"What? Hipster? Where's my man bun then? And I like the red whales on the pants. It's all retro and cool."

"This your idea of running from your family and your background? Just like playing at being an information broker?"

Peyton's face darkened. "I just like the look, okay? Whales are endangered."

"Not little red embroidered ones. Okay, fair enough. I can't help it if you want to blind people with those abominations. Just be careful who you're pointing them at."

His expression didn't brighten at her joke.

Shay didn't try and fill the tense silence. Whether or not Peyton was running from his family before, he had a damned good reason to stay away from them now.

One major lesson kept Shay alive throughout the years, and that was an understanding that a person should never underestimate the greed and ruthlessness of anyone.

Yeah, Peyton, that includes me.

The field archaeologist pulled the Porsche into the parking lot of Gino's By the Slice, her mouth already watering at the idea of downing some pepperoni pizza.

"Okay, let's go grab some pizza," Shay said.

"We're stopping to eat?" Peyton sighed and turned in his seat to look at her. "I thought we were just going to grab something at a drive-through."

Shay shook her head. "Gino's doesn't have a drive-through."

"Let me get this straight. You kidnap me—"

The woman cut him off with a snort. "Let's get one thing straight. This was a rescue, not a kidnapping."

"Felt more like a kidnapping."

"Well, it's a rescue now. It was executed as a kidnapping. Whatever, the words aren't important."

A defiant look settled over Peyton's face.

Don't do this now.

Shay sighed. "You're free to stroll back to your apartment if you want. I mean, I wouldn't advise it because there will probably be six fucking guys there ready to fill your body with bullets. But sure, you know, if you really have a hard-on for dying, knock yourself out."

"Angry White Bitch is coming back, I see."

"And Clueless never left."

"What I was trying to get at is that you *killed* me, and now we're going to have pizza in New Jersey? I thought you wanted to make a clean getaway. What if some drone flies by and gets my picture or something?"

Shay reached into her pocket and pulled out a small layered silver disc.

Peyton leaned over, his eyes narrowing. "Is that a broad-spectrum frequency jammer?"

"Yeah. Low power. We have 20 minutes to get in there, get the best pizza this side of the Mississippi, and get the fuck out of town."

The man-boy continued staring at her, utter incredulity on his face.

Shay threw open her door and stepped out. Peyton sighed and followed.

The woman walked toward the front door of the restaurant. "Look, did you really think I came all the way to the east coast just to save your scrawny ass?"

"You're serious, aren't you?"

"Maybe."

They headed inside as Shay nodded, taking a quick survey of her surroundings. Professional habit. They were hitting the place about an hour before closing, so the line was non-existent, only one old man eyeing the menu like it was written in Linear B.

"Do they have any stuffed crust here?" Peyton asked. "It's been a while."

Shay snorted. "Thin-crust NYC-style. That's the only type of *real* pizza. You fold a slice in half and eat it. None of this abomination Chicago nonsense."

"Okay. Whatever." Peyton gestured toward the napkins and plastic utensils. "I'll go grab some knifes and forks."

Shay burst out laughing. "Are you fucking kidding me?"

The old man eyed her with a frown on his face. She ignored him.

Peyton's cheeks reddened. "What?"

"I'm so blue collar," the woman replied in a mocking voice. "Here's a tip, Peyton. Blue-collar people don't eat their pizza with a knife and fork, and that's not how we roll, not if you're with me."

Shay didn't bother with a supersonic flight back to LAX. Both of them needed a little rest. Taking a redeye and resting on the plane struck her as great time management, especially if she was going to be up for giving a lecture at her day job as an adjunct professor at nearby UCLA.

The lectures were a key ingredient to boosting her profile as a field archaeologist and fed her love of uncovering the real history of the world since magic started to return.

Besides, Peyton was still adjusting to his sudden *death*

anyway, and a little sleep would help with that as well. Once again, Clueless hadn't considered he would need a fake ID once he was dead until Shay gave it to him.

Their morning arrival in L.A. soon had her back behind the wheel of her beloved red Fiat Spider, Peyton in tow as they headed toward one of her warehouses.

She controlled multiple storage buildings spread throughout L.A. to store her equipment for the different jobs and anything else she needed. A series of false names and shell companies helped keep any nosy parties from ever linking anything to her directly.

Peyton yawned as they pulled up to the medium-sized brown building. A large dark blue metal loading bay door prevented further access.

Shay pulled out her phone to bring up an app and disable the primary security on the building. A grinding noise filled the air as the door slowly slid to the side.

"You've been quiet," she said.

"Just... it's a lot to take in. I'm dead now, and I have to live in Los Angeles." He counted them off on his fingers.

Shay chuckled. "You get used to being dead after a while."

The door finished sliding to the side, and she pulled the car in before pressing a command on her app to start the door closing sequence.

Metal and wooden crates and boxes filled the high-ceiling room, and two doors led to a bathroom with a shower and a small office. The building mostly provided overflow storage to a toy company before Shay purchased it.

She exited the car and waited for Peyton to get out before speaking.

"Welcome to Warehouse Two."

"Warehouse Two?"

"I've got five of them, all for different purposes, some more important than others. It's simple, the lower the level, the less important the shit, or the easier to replace, depends on how you want to look at it."

Peyton laughed. "I only warrant a two? Ouch."

Shay ignored him to walk over to a wooden crate and pull the top off. She pointed. Boxes of 9mm bullets filled the crate. She pulled open another crate to reveal climbing ropes. A third crate contained SCUBA equipment.

"Look, you're safe here," she said, "but if someone comes here and blows up the place, then I'll have fallback places, and won't be totally fucked."

"Except for me being blown up."

"You'll die twice."

"Not funny."

"No one knows about this place. I monitor the warehouses seven different ways. I wouldn't have gone to all this trouble and then sat you down with a target on your back. You're safe."

Peyton didn't look convinced, but he also didn't bitch, so that worked for the moment.

"This is your place?" He walked closer to peer into the crates. "You live here? Or do you live in another warehouse?"

Shay rolled her eyes. "I live in a condo like a normal person."

"You're an ex-hitman who faked her own death. What's normal about any of that?"

"I didn't say I was a normal person just that I *live* in a condo like a normal person."

"Got it."

"I just don't store anything important there. This is my storage, and I'm storing you here for now." Shay pointed to one of the doors along the wall. "You can set up in there. I've got a computer all ready."

"And internet?"

She shrugged. "Create a cutout. Steal it from some of the local businesses for now so it can't be traced back to this place. I don't want anyone coming to this place to wire it up or sticking up a satellite dish. You're the computer expert. You're going to take what I did and raise it to a whole new level. It's why I saved your ass. The start of bigger things."

Peyton nodded. "That's doable. It's pretty easy for me to use a VPN and a lot of proxy servers. If anyone comes poking, I'll have them looking in Nigeria. Hell, I'll have them looking in Oriceran."

Shay chuckled. "Sounds good. There's folding cots and blankets in one of these crates." Shay looked back and forth and shrugged. "I don't remember which one."

"I have to live in a warehouse while you live in a condo?"

"For now, if you're going to stay safe and that means mostly out of sight." Shay looked away and sighed. "Peyton, I'm gonna be honest with you. It's gonna take a while for suspicion to die down, and so, yeah, it's gonna suck for you. I know because I'm dead like you. But if you stick your head up anytime soon, you will die. Do you understand?"

Peyton gave a shallow nod. "We didn't talk much about what you even need me to do. You mentioned something about being a field archaeologist now?"

Shay stared at the man, wondering how honest she should be. Feigning complete confidence might help him feel better, but they both needed to trust each other if their working relationship had any chance of succeeding.

And Shay had plans for him.

"Bottom line is I'm still breaking into the tomb raider business. I don't have much of a rep, and I need to take care of that or it's gonna be nothing but shit jobs for me." She shrugged. "Right now, part of improving my rep is locating at least seven high-profile items." She pulled a phone out of her pocket and tossed it to Peyton. "The list is on there. And keep the phone."

Peyton tapped at the phone and furrowed his brow. "These are like finding marks when you were a hitman."

"Exactly, but instead of people I plan to kill, these are items I plan to acquire."

"You mean steal?"

Shay laughed. "It's not stealing." She put up her hands and made air quotes. "It's *field archaeology*."

"Semantics."

"Stealing or whatever you want to call it, it's my new gig, and I plan to be good at it. That may take some of your skills. You're a gifted little bastard when it comes to finding that one piece of information that someone wanted hidden or everyone else forgot about but changes the game. It'll help me get a better angle on jobs and potential dangers."

Peyton took several deep breaths and nodded, working on how to tell her. "Okay, this is doable. I'm just... well, if we're going to do this, and you want it to really be secure, I'm going need a better computer than whatever piece of bargain crap you bought. We should probably get some sort of localized low-frequency jammers, some security drones, maybe some—"

"Just give me a list," Shay interrupted. "And stop wasting my time."

Peyton held up his hands. "Okay, okay. You know one thing that might help with all of this is if you explained more about what your job actually involves. Field archaeologist? Doesn't that mean you just go dig up a lot of pots and bones? What does it have to do with the list you sent me?"

Shay shook her head. "No. That's... different. A lot of people call what I do being a tomb raider. Common nickname in my new business."

Peyton shot her a confused look. "So... you raid tombs? You went from putting them into the ground, to digging them back up again. Your own kind of recycling project."

Shay rubbed her hand with her face. *Is he just screwing with me?* "Let's not start with you being that annoying." She sucked in a breath and slowly let it out. "The 1.0 version is, I wasn't lying when I was talking about not stealing. I'm not a thief. I find old artifacts, particularly old magical items and recover them from places where people have forgotten about them... or buried them and then died. Since they're dead, they don't have any use for them."

"That makes sense then, I guess."

"My business model is to research history and figure

out how history's been manipulated to hide Oriceran influence. Because where there's Oriceran influence, there's magic, and that means a lot of potential profit to be made. Once I figure out what might be a real artifact, I track down where it's hidden, and then recover it."

Peyton crossed his arms. "From tombs?"

Shay flexed her hands, fighting the urge to punch him in the neck. "From wherever. Sure, some of it is your stereotypical ancient tomb in the jungle or whatever, but a lot of it isn't like that. A lot of times it can be things like some old artifact buried under a Walmart parking lot or in a cave under a split-level three-bedroom."

"You hit up a lot of Walmarts, lately?" Peyton grinned.

"Don't make me bitch slap you. I'm still getting my business established, and the whole being dead thing hasn't helped."

"When you say you're getting your business established, that means you've done what, collected like five artifacts, ten artifacts?"

Shay looked him dead in the eye, even while dodging the question. "The key has been teaching myself to be an expert on history, the fake *and* the real. History gets rewritten by the winners, and now we know that a lot of history was crap to hide Oriceran and magic." She pointed at Peyton. "You're good at sorting crap from the truth."

Peyton eyed her for a moment, suspicion coloring his face. "I'm good at researching information, not translating ancient scrolls or whatever."

"I don't need you to understand it, just find it. Information is information, and the more important the information is, the better hidden it'll be. We're a few decades into the twenty-first century, Peyton. Even if the revelation about Oriceran and all this magical energy flowing to Earth has messed a lot of shit up, we're still a world that depends on information and computers. You can help me find the info that will lead me to an artifact. Once I find it, I sell it. Easy as that."

"You didn't answer my question before about how many artifacts you've recovered." Peyton ran a hand through his hair. "Look, I'm grateful that you saved my life, but if we're going to be working together, I can't have you hold back on me too much. It'll make my job harder."

Shay's jaw tightened, and she nodded. She wanted to glide right past her actual level of experience in her new job.

"Okay, so I've done a tomb raid. That first raid, I think I did okay."

"One?"

"Yep. One. We all have to start somewhere. It's not like I killed twenty people the first time I took a contract."

Peyton winced and nodded. "No casualties during your tomb raid? I mean, you said you're not a killer anymore."

Shay shook her head. "There were a few. It went okay, because the return on my investment was okay. I don't consider zero casualities necessarily part of the scoring for tomb raids."

"You'll still just kill anyone who gets in your way?"

She snorted. "Don't feed me that sanctimonious bull-shit, Peyton. If you weren't swimming around with scum-bags, you would have never ended up in the situation you were in." She waved a hand. "I changed jobs, I didn't change skins. I'm not going out of my way to kill people, but I'm not suddenly a pacifist, either. You understand who I am, right? You knew me from my past."

Peyton locked gazes with her. "Yeah, I get that. I also can help you with your business model. Refining it so that it's beyond what you described."

Shay shook her head. "You stick with figuring out where things are hidden and help with the necessary background information. Start with getting things set up here, and we'll see about everything else."

"Look, Shay, I really can help with this, I—"

Shay cut him with a harsh look. "I don't have time for this shit right now. I have some people I need to meet."

Peyton frowned but didn't say anything.

Shay turned to leave, before stopping to look over her shoulder. "Look, don't get me wrong about any of this. I didn't save you because I'm a good person. I saved you because you have skills I need. That doesn't mean we're best friends all of the sudden. I'm trying to make a new life for myself, and I figured you helping me out would be a nice trade in exchange for saving your life."

"Understood."

"There's food in a fridge in the office. Get me a list of groceries you need, and I can supply that, too, maybe even a bigger fridge."

Peyton gave her a shallow nod, and Shay continued walking to her car. She didn't have time for a bruised male ego.

3

Faking *a man's death one day and then having a casual brunch with two women a day later.* Shay doubted anyone else lived their life that way.

Her stomach knotted as she pushed into the small café. Two women waved at her from a booth in the back, and she made her way toward them. They represented her latest determined attempt at normalcy.

Her idea of it anyway.

When she faked her death, she got a glimpse of the path of violence she started walking in her teen years. It led her to being more than a little warped, and that was being charitable to herself. The obvious solution was to try and find some normal people to befriend. Place to start, even if she had to mislead them a little, it might help her recover some of the emotional balance she'd been missing.

It might have been the obvious solution, but it was far from the easiest.

Sure, I can fake a man's death and rescue him from imminent doom, but I can't find a few people to hang out with who I

27

MARTHA CARR & MICHAEL ANDERLE

don't want to strangle. Why the hell did I think meeting random people in a meetup group would be a good idea?

Shay slipped into a seat opposite the two women, Terry and Lisa, both bubbly bottle blondes.

"We're so sorry you had to cut out early from bowling last time," Lisa said with a smile. "You missed out on a very, very tense game. I almost got a strike."

"Sorry to hear that." Shay mirrored their smiles back at them. "I'm sure it was as nerve-wracking as being in a gunfight with a bunch of mercenaries."

Lisa and Terry laughed.

"Oh, you're so funny, Shay," Lisa said. "You have such a wacky sense of humor."

"Thanks." *Yeah, nothing but a joke. Keep believing that.*

"But we get it. It's got to be hard running around all these foreign countries doing archaeology digs. If you ever want to show us your office at UCLA, we'd love to see it. I'm sure it's so exciting and filled with ancient artifacts. Or even Oriceran ones."

Shay shrugged, the lies flowing easily now. "It's just an office. The magical stuff tends to be in the Extra-Dimensional Archaeology or Engineering departments, and not exactly in a normal newly hired archaeology professor's office. I don't even have tenure."

Disappointment passed over Lisa's face. "Oh, I was expecting it to be all, you know, like Indiana Jones or Caleb Rodriguez."

"Just a computer and desk. Really not that exciting. Real life isn't like the movies."

All strong friendships are built on foundations of mutual understanding and trust. This one is like quicksand.

Shay was lying through her teeth to her new acquaintances about who she was and what she did for a living. As far as they were concerned, she was a newly hired adjunct archaeology professor at UCLA. Okay, that was all true, but it conveniently left out a lot of pertinent facts. Like the tomb raids that took up most of her time. Remembering what to leave out kept her side of the conversation a little stilted. *It would feel so good just to shoot someone right now. Bad Shay.*

"Find anything interesting in your last dig?" Terry asked. "Like hidden treasure?"

It really wasn't that hidden. And maybe those mercenaries I had to kill counted as interesting.

Shay forced a smile. "Some evidence that may indicate a tribe was in northern Mexico earlier than we thought."

"Oh, that's interesting. How do you tell any of that anyway?"

"In this case by examining pottery and arrowheads found at the site," Shay explained. "That sort of thing."

Why am I trying so hard to lie to impress these two? How do people do this shit?

Terry and Lisa exchanged looks. "That's neat, I guess. What's your next lecture on?" asked Lisa.

"The creation of Oxford University in 1249 but not by just the English. It was really a collection of humans and Oricerans. They also later lent a hand to the Aztec civilization with the founding of Tenochtitlán in 1325."

Shay felt herself warming to the topic, ready to dive into the details.

Fortunately, the waitress came to take their orders,

offering Shay a brief respite. The awkward pain returned once the waitress left.

Terry's eyes widened, and she clapped her hands together. "So, I heard that Drake is doing a comeback tour."

Lisa gasped. "Really? I loved him when I was a kid."

"I think he's even hotter now than when he was younger. You should see the photos from the promotional tour. Seriously scrumptious abs for a man in his fifties. They say he's using some sort of special Oriceran diet."

Shay let the women's discussion of Drake recede into the background until it was more buzzing than actual speech to her.

Kill me now with a jagged ancient dagger. Small talk is torture.

Maybe Terry and Lisa would love to know the best type of gun to use depending on range, best knife for close quarters, and how to improvise a weapon when you absolutely need to kill an asshole quickly. At least I know about that.

No, instead, we're talking about Drake. Whoever that hell that is. And not only are we talking about him, but his fucking abs.

In retrospect, Shay's decision to lie about being an academic archaeologist struck her as a big damned mistake, even if it gave her an excuse for being gone for long periods. She couldn't talk about her actual tomb raider jobs without risking the truth coming out, and everyone she'd run into so far didn't seem all that interested in archaeology. Talking to an actual archaeologist would quickly expose her as a fraud.

Maybe I should start just claiming to work for the IRS or something.

Shay sighed, desperate to find something, anything, to talk about that didn't involve Drake's abs. "You know the problem these days with archaeology is that we can't trust a lot of the dating techniques."

"Huh?" Lisa said. "You mean like Tinder?"

Shay clenched her fist under the table and kept going. "More like the carbon kind. Finding out Oriceran existed changed everything. I mean, it moved magic from a stage act to something legit and altered the history of our world."

A pained look came across Terry's face as the conversation sputtered. *Not enough Drake?*

"Archaeological sites are more difficult to pinpoint a date now. Magic can throw off carbon dating, along with various other techniques. A lot of modern archaeology has to rely on more old-fashioned methods such as trying to compare layers and figure things out more indirectly."

"Really?" Lisa said. "It's weird, you know. It's like everything we know might be wrong. I don't really think about it a lot, I guess, even though they talked a bit about it in my history classes in high school and college."

Shay slapped her hand on the table, more excitement flowing through her at last. "Exactly. We thought we knew history, but what do we know? So much could be off, even more than we think, and that means our understanding of the modern world is off."

Even if she did her new job for the money, that didn't mean she didn't still love her job.

Magic was real. History was a lie. It was one of the few things that could get Shay pumped at the idea of exploring some of that. Truth a weapon in of itself, and the more she learned, the stronger she became and the more she wanted to share with her students about what she found.

"That's so true," Lisa said, bobbing her head with earnest excitement in her eyes.

Some relief flowed into Shay. The women could be led to an interesting topic other than delicious celebrity abs.

Terry nodded. "My cousin said he got kidnapped by an alien when he was younger and probed. I bet it was just a horny Elf."

"Umm-hmm. I want to date an Elf with scrumptious abs," Lisa said. "I mean they have to know some great sex magic."

Shay resisted a groan. The last thing she wanted to talk about was men, human or Oriceran.

It wasn't that she had trouble with them, not attracting them anyway. She'd always been beautiful and didn't see the point of pretending otherwise, but at the same time, that was a two-edged sword.

Men didn't want to know her. They only saw high cheekbones and curves, and that was it. A lot of them thought they could do something with her just because they were attracted.

Maybe if her early life had been different, she wouldn't get so prickly about it, but it was a decade too late for that now.

Shay gritted her teeth. *Yeah, my life was pretty fucked-up, and maybe I shouldn't even bother trying to be friends with normal people, but that doesn't change the fact that I don't want to talk about men.*

"What about you, Shay?" Lisa asked, pulling the woman out of her thoughts.

"What about me?"

"You dating anyone? You never talk about any men. Or, are you into women?" Lisa shrugged. "You don't seem the type, I think."

Shay rolled her eyes. "No, I'm into men."

"Oh, great. I totally have someone to hook you up with."

"So do I," Terry said. "Try before you buy!"

Terry and Lisa both leaned forward, hunger in their eyes.

Shay rubbed the back of her neck. The last thing she needed was the women throwing their loser cousins and friends at her. This part of the conversation wouldn't be an issue. The only thing she was better at than killing was lying.

I'll just give them my made-up ideal guy.

"I'm seeing a guy," Shay said. "I, uh, we stumbled on to each at… work, you know, um, at the college, you know?"

"Does he have scrumptious abs?"

"Oh, yeah, sure, totally. This guy, he's the Emperor of Rock Solid Bodies, pretty much. Works out tons. His face is okay, nothing to write home about it. Lots of character. Quiet guy though. I mean he can be witty, but he's usually more a man of action."

Yeah, like I'll ever meet a guy like that.

"I could use a little action with a rock-solid body," Lisa said, and chuckled.

"This guy, you know, he sees me for me, right? Not just my body and all that."

The other two women nodded.

"Oh, yeah, you definitely need a man who respects you as a person," Terry said. "And respects your intelligence."

"I guess," Shay said, "he's a little closed off, but I kind of like the challenge of opening him up."

Lisa and Terry exchanged another glance.

"When do we get to meet your man?" Lisa said. "I want to see the kind of guy who can get you to describe him that way."

"Oh, he's busy. Has a job that takes him all over." Shay shrugged. "I'm sure you'll be able to meet him soon."

Disappointment fell over the other two women's face.

Huh. Probably can't hang out with these two much longer, or they'll ask questions I don't want to answer. To hell with it. It's not even like they're all that interesting. For now, though. Ugh. Drank too much water.

"I need to hit the ladies' room," Shay said, rising. "I'll be right back."

The vapidity of her friends, if she could even call them that, struck her as she headed to the restroom. She didn't know why she couldn't find someone who didn't want to make her throat punch them.

Shay couldn't be normal friends with a man, not really, not with her issues. Men were either enemies or work contacts, even Peyton.

She understood that all too well, but at the same time, it'd been excruciating to try and find some girlfriends. Lisa and Terry represented her sixth attempt since coming to Los Angeles.

"How do normal people make friends?" Shay muttered.

The thought still haunted her when she stepped out of the restroom a few minutes later. Some business jerk in a blue suit emerged from the men's room at almost the same time.

His gaze traveled up and down her body, and he broke into a grin.

"Do I need to call heaven?" the business jerk asked.

Shay stared at him. She sniffed the air for alcohol but didn't smell anyway.

"What are you talking about?"

The man took a step forward and placed an arm beside her head on the wall, pinning her in.

Her heart rate kicked up, and she sucked in a breath.

"I was wondering if I needed to call heaven and report that one of their angels has fallen to Earth," the man said.

Shay groaned. "You should be locked up in an ultramax for that weapon of mass disappointment."

"Come on, babe," the man said, licking his lips. "I haven't seen a woman as hot as you in a long time. We could have a good time together."

"Move... your... arm," Shay said, her eyes narrowing. "Or you'll regret it, asshole."

The business jerk rolled his eyes and dropped his arm. "Suit yourself, you frigid bitch."

Shay spun on her heel and took a single step. That's when the business jerk reached over to squeeze her butt. She spun back to face him, her gaze filled with murderous intent.

The man stood there, smirking, his hands in the pockets of his suit jacket. "A body like that is wasted on a woman like you. Hey, if you're going to be frigid, can't blame me for—"

She seized his hand and grabbed two fingers. A quick bend and snap ended with the man falling to his knees. His eyes teared up, and his mouth formed an O, but only a squeak escaped.

"You... bitch," the man moaned. "You broke my fingers." Tears streamed down his face.

Shay leaned over. The corner of her mouth lifted in a sneer. "Go ahead. Get up and tell everyone that some sexy woman broke your fingers. Either people will call you a pussy, or they'll ask why it happened. Either way, you come out looking poorly, asshole."

She waved and stepped away, making her way back to her table. The man's sobs grew in volume. She sat back at her table, Terry and Lisa looking in the directions of the restrooms.

"Why is there a guy crying over there?" Lisa asked.

Shay shrugged. "Who knows? *Men.*"

4

The morning sunlight came through the narrow windows along the top of the warehouse. Shay was deep into her morning ritual, unleashing a series of vicious jabs into a black Everlast punching bag that hung from a heavy chain near the roll top door. She finished with a roundhouse kick, sending the bag sailing back.

She jumped back, avoiding the bag's return and wiped the sweat from her brow with one of her gloved hands – the fingers exposed. Sweat trickled down her belly into the top of her black lycra pants.

She was replaying the morning lecture in her mind that she had given at the university before heading to the warehouse. It was well attended despite the early hour and by the time she was finished they were on the edge of their seats. "Three schools, three original *halls of residence*, University, Balliol and Merton Colleges divided by skill levels of magic and areas of interest. A certain storyteller named Tolkien taught at Merton," she had said with a smile. "Makes you wonder…"

Hands shot into the air the moment she had signaled she was done, the students already shouting out questions. It was going to be a good day.

She punched the bag again, a smile coming across her face as the muscles across her back rippled.

Warehouse One contained a few hidden weapons – standard practice for all the locations – but One primarily served as her training facility. Technology could help a lot on a tomb raid, but it wasn't fool-proof. *In the end, the only tools I can depend on are my body and mind.* Shay wanted to make sure both were as strong as possible.

The building was conveniently located only a half mile from Pizza Coast, one of the better pizza joints in L.A. Primo pizza locations were a prerequisite for the location of any of the warehouses.

"Maybe I should have stored Peyton here," Shay muttered, giving the bag another hard jab. "Man-boy needs a little more exercise. And he needs to learn to better defend himself."

Her gaze drifted to the boxing ring dominating the center of the room. She snickered at the idea of Peyton in the ring with her.

That would be too fucking funny. At least for me. Not so much for Peyton.

A little pain in the service of personal growth would be a gift. *He should thank me if I brought him here and kicked his ass. Make sure he's around for another birthday.*

Shay unwrapped her fingers and shook out her hands. Combat training was important, but so was rapid mobility and fitness training. One of the best ways to not die was to *haul ass*.

The tomb raider turned away from the punching bag and bounded the few feet across the cement floor to a climbing wall near the corner. An obstacle course ringed the room, starting with the wall.

It was time for a few rounds through the course.

Shay easily jumped onto the first handholds, digging her fingers into the small nooks and crannies, her feet lightly touching down. She wasted no time and scurried up the wall, letting go as she let her weight fall back. At the last moment she pushed off, leaping from the top to a bar resting in the bottom rungs of a salmon ladder, the muscles in her shoulders flexing under the black sports bra.

The echo of the metal clacking on metal filled the cavernous room as she moved up each rung of the obstacle toward the sunlight streaming in along the ceiling. A slight ache hit her arms as she got to the top of the ladder, and let go with one arm, swinging out and grabbing on to the next challenge. A narrow metal balance beam connected to the ceiling by bungee cords.

The balance beam swung back and forth as she pulled herself up and got her feet under her. Shay stretched out her arms on either side, determined not to fall. The sunlight played across her wet skin as she dug deeper for more strength. *Good training for a bad day.*

Now that she was closer to the ceiling than the ground, the mats thirty-three feet below would cushion some, but not *all* of the impact.

Maybe I should start training without the mats. Talk about motivation.

Shay nimbly arrived at the end of the beam, even as it continued to sway, and jumped onto a small flat-topped pole anchored to the floor that only had space for one foot. She pushed off, immediately jumping to the next, completing a circuit of six poles with a last jump to a free-standing ledge near the wall that faced an alley. A thick blue and white rope hung underneath and Shay knelt down, going over the side as she grabbed onto the rope and rappelled to the floor.

A series of truck tires lay in front of her. She moved from tire to tire with quick feet, jumping in and out, before hitting another climbing wall.

Shay moved right up the handholds, taking her up fifteen feet to a series of chains and ropes hanging from the ceiling. Each hung too far from the other to reach without a hard swing and letting go of one to grab onto the next.

She jumped to the first chain, swinging even as the muscles of her legs were taut and grabbed the next rope without a second thought. Several more exchanges followed, including a turn in the corner of the room that forced her to push off the wall to regain her forward momentum.

The final rope brought her to another ledge connected to a wooden ramp angled down at forty-five-degrees. The ramp fed into another steeply curving ramp set up on an incline that was connected to a tall concrete block wall ten feet high.

Shay ran down the first ramp at full speed, feeling the muscles in her thighs engaging, and charged up the second, sucking in air, as she pushed off from her toes, catching the top of the wall with her fingers. She pulled herself up and rolled over the top of the wall, dropping down to the other side.

Several deep breaths followed. Pure Zen. Physical exertion *usually* worked that way for her, but it was hard to relax when someone was shooting at you or trying to gut you.

Ha ha. Maybe I should ask the next merc asshole if he'd like to dance instead.

"Let's see you do half of that, Peyton," Shay said, wiping away sweat from the end of her nose. She clapped her hands together and stretched her arms above her head. "Okay, let's do that shit a few more times."

A few hours later, Shay was back at Warehouse Two, showered and changed, staring at something so grotesque and offensive to human sensibilities she was half-convinced some sort of dark Oriceran magic must be involved in its creation.

"A *pink* flamingo shirt and... I don't even know how to describe your pants," Shay said, her gaze locked on Peyton. "It looks like some preschooler ate all his crayons and vomited all over your pants, and you didn't bother to wash them."

The man blinked and looked down, his hands held out to his sides. "I think this outfit has character."

Shay narrowed her eyes. "Wait. Where the hell did you even get those clothes? It's not like you were carrying around a suitcase when I kidnapped you. Please tell me you weren't such a fucking moron that you went shopping."

"I was bored and looked through some of the crates. Tons of clothes in them. Plus, tons of old toys. You're bitching me out for an outfit I put together from your supplies."

"Those aren't my fucking supplies." Shay rolled her eyes. "First of all, there are a lot of old crates in several of the warehouses that I haven't thrown out. That shit came from a lot of failed movies. I'm getting a clue as to why they failed. Second of all, those are *men's* clothes, so I would never wear them. Third, they are awful. Have some damned taste."

Peyton shrugged. "I like them. I had an outfit a lot like this back home. Well, back East. Guess I should stop thinking of it as home."

"How the hell did you ever hide from anyone? Shit. People can now see you from space. Darken!" The lights immediately dimmed overhead, and blackout screens fell in front of the few windows near the top. "I knew it. I can fucking see you in the dark. Lights!" The lights rose again as the screens came up, uncovering the windows.

Peyton scoffed and stomped over to a desk set up in the old office surrounded on three sides with glass. "Hey, a man has to have some small comforts after he dies."

"Whatever. You adjusting okay, other than feeding into your increasingly twisted and masochistic sense of fashion?"

"I'm fine for a man stuck in a city he doesn't know who can't talk to anyone. Sure." Peyton stared at Shay, burning curiosity in his eyes.

"What?" She glanced down, hoping that the man hadn't

decided he suddenly wanted to hit on her. She didn't want to have to beat him down.

"I heard all about it when you died, you know. Burned down house, confirmed body. They said they even did a DNA test using material from *your* teeth. It wasn't just some fuzzy pictures on some dark net forum."

"Is there a point to any of this, Peyton?"

"Yes." He nodded, rubbing the rough blonde whiskers on his chin. "You turn up here, all respectable as a professor and a badass tomb raider. How? How did you pull all that off?"

Shay chuckled. "It helps when you know someone's coming for you. It means you can plan."

"You knew someone was coming for you?"

"Oh, yeah, Natalie Leon."

Peyton's eyes widened. "Wait... I heard she retired right after your death, after collecting on the hit contract for you."

"Retirement's *one* way of putting it."

"You're saying she's dead?"

"I'm saying I killed her first." Shay grinned. "Yeah, it's pretty sweet to collect on your own bounty. That was a lot of money. Nice to know I was worth so much." She winked, her hands on her hips. "I had a solid lead that Natalie was coming for me, and I started preparing..."

The memories flowed freely into her head as if the event happened only the day before.

Shay glanced down at her watch and stood up from her

couch, shaking her head. "It's fucking rude to keep a woman waiting when you're coming to kill them. They had a new damned pizza sauce over at Gino's I wanted to try."

Her lights died.

"Huh, guess, you're here after all."

Shay smirked and flipped down her night-vision goggles. The trained killer yanked her 9mm from her shoulder holster and crouched behind her pale yellow upholstered love seat, the only noise the sound of her own shallow breathing.

A squeak from the kitchen cut through the silence. Shay spun and stood, blasting several rounds in that direction as another woman in night-vision goggles rolled away from the back door and returned fire, piercing the love seat. "So much for paying for interior decorating."

Shay pivoted behind a wall. "If you were going to kill me, Natalie. You should have just blown this place up."

"Where's the fun in that? Explosives and sniper rifles are for chickenshits."

"Why are you even here? I thought we were friends." Shay ducked.

"We are friends, and this is business. The Nuevo Gulf Cartel isn't happy with you. You killed one of their big boys not all that long ago. The money they're offering for you..." She gave a long whistle. "It's too much to pass up. You would do the same thing. Be glad the end is coming from a friend."

Several bullets blasted through the plaster wall. If Shay hadn't changed position, she would have taken three to the chest.

Should have worn a vest if I was going to get all fancy for this shit.

"Yeah, I probably would have gone after the money," Shay called back, and rolled toward the edge of the doorway. "Glad to hear that at least I'm not a cheap date."

After several more rounds pierced the wall, a faint click reached Shay's ears.

The bitch is changing mags.

Shay grabbed her phone and brought up a light app. She set the app to maximum brightness and strobe mode. She tossed it into the other room as she pulled the night vision goggles off her face.

Natalie hissed, and Shay took her chance, running into the kitchen and firing in the general direction of the other woman's voice. Something hard clattered against the tile floor.

The eerie strobe light highlighted the room in sharp relief, making the overhead fan seem as if it was moving in jerking motions.

Shay carefully walked toward the granite-topped island in the center of the room, her gun still drawn. Natalie was a tricky bitch. An arm rested on one side of the island, along with a gun several feet away. A dark pool of blood was already starting to puddle out toward the center of the kitchen. *Doesn't mean she's dead.*

The trained killer trusted her instincts and burst forward, snapping her gun down to finish Natalie. But no gun or knife awaited her, just a middle-aged assassin bleeding out from bullet wounds to the gut and chest.

"Too fucking slow," Natalie said through gritted teeth. "The second I saw even a hint of light I should have shut my eyes and pulled the damn goggles off. *Fuck*." Blood gurgled in her throat as she spit hard. "I've even done that exact shit to people before. Well, not with a damned phone, nice touch."

Shay kept her gun pointed at the other woman's head. "Do you regret coming after me now?"

The other woman let out a harsh laugh. "Fuck no. The money was too good."

"Apparently so was I."

Natalie let out a wet hacking cough. "Don't get too cocky. You're just twenty-five years younger than me. It's not luck. It's just time... and time's gonna catch up with you in the end, too."

Shay shook her head. "So, this is how it ends for you, after a lifetime of killing people? Bleeding out in someone's kitchen?"

"How the fuck else was it going to end? It's not like there's an old killer's retirement home."

"But you had money. You could have retired. Shit, you could have moved and set yourself up as some retired businesswoman or some other fairytale. Why stay in the game?"

Natalie shook her head and coughed up blood. "People like us can't leave the game, Shay." She looked up, a grin on her face despite her imminent death. "We don't do it because we have to, but because we want to. It's exciting, *a rush*, and you know it. You started earlier than I did." More bloody coughs followed as she struggled to breathe. "You put your own life... against someone... else's. Just... like... you..."

Shay pulled the trigger, finishing off her rival and

would-be assassin. She stared down at the dead body for a good minute, taking several deep breaths.

She crouched down and took a closer look at Natalie. "Damn," she whispered.

If even her friends were willing to come after her, the payout for the hit would bring every greedy asshole in the world to her door. The cartel had almost kept it quiet.

She stood back up, still holding the gun by her side. *I might miss the next callout, especially if it went wide.* She had confidence in her skills, but she didn't think she could win against the entire east coast.

Her attention drifted back down to the dead woman at her feet.

Is this what I want? To end up dead in some bitch's kitchen? Fuck that.

Shay snorted and looked down at her hands. Her conscience stopped bothering her a long time ago. It helped that most of her kills had been assholes who had it coming, including the attempted rapist fuckwad who had been her first kill.

She looked down at her gun. Killing had been the only thing she'd ever been any good at, but maybe it was time for a change. The only thing she needed to do *first* was die.

Shay glanced over at Peyton. He didn't need to know everything about her past, not yet. Trust would be earned, not given.

"Natalie came after me. I killed her. The whole thing made me understand it was time for a career change.

Even if I wanted to keep killing people, I needed to disappear permanently, so no one would ever think to come looking for me. Doing the same job in a new location wasn't going to accomplish that." She shrugged, straightening out a wrinkle in the linen gray pencil skirt that hugged her hips. "I set fire to my own house. I had a convenient bullet-riddled body to burn beyond recognition already inside. It wasn't that hard with the help of a little money to make sure DNA testing linked the body to me."

Peyton stared at her, not saying anything.

Shay shot him a bright smile. "You see. That's the difference between you and me. When my life caught up with me, I killed the bitch who tried to kill me and used her not only to convince everyone I was dead, but to earn me a payday. You, on the other hand, needed my ass to pull you out of there before you ended up floating in the East River in several pieces." She pointed at him, looking up and down at his outfit. "And I'm still trying to figure out whether me helping you out was stupid or not. Remember what I said. I'm not doing this as—"

A loud yowling echoed in the warehouse.

"What the hell was that?" Peyton said, looking over his shoulder. "You have some sort of rogue troll running around here?"

"Oh, stop wetting yourself. It's just a little alert system I set up. It's telling me I might have a possible lead on one of my jobs."

Visible relief descended on the man's face as he pressed the heel of his hand to his chest. "Or, you know, I could just hook that annoying ass sound up to your phone, so you'll hear the alert that way, anywhere you happen to be. Like someone living in the 21st century."

"Phones can get lost or misplaced."

Peyton snorted. "And when's the last time you've lost something? Come on, just let me try."

"Knock yourself out. You can check out how I've set it up on the office computer, but I have to go now."

"Wait. Go where?"

"To another warehouse. I need to get some things to verify the job."

"Let me come with you then. I can help."

Shay shook her head. "You already know too much about Warehouse Two. If I give up another warehouse's location, I'm almost asking you to screw me over."

"You did save my life, you know. I kind of owe you."

"And I just got done telling you how a good friend of mine tried to kill me over money. I haven't put it past you to sell me out to save your ass."

Peyton's jaw tightened, but he didn't say anything back.

Shay shrugged. "We'll do this a day at a time. You'll earn my trust, and then we can talk about other shit."

"You have to give me a chance if I'm going to earn it." Peyton locked gazes with her. "How do your alerts work?"

"Huh? Why do you suddenly care about the details?"

"Because I'm trying to begin planning how to make them better."

"Spiders crawling the web and the dark web, mostly. They are looking for certain combinations of information."

Something approaching interest appeared on Peyton's face. "You're better at this kind of thing than I would have thought."

"It's useful not to have to rely on others when you're killing people for a living. Makes people nervous. That means I have a lot more skills than you might think." She shrugged into her light jacket and picked up her Cambridge Satchel. "Go check out the code. You're supposed to be the fucking expert, so make it better. Prove you have a place here."

5

Only an hour had passed before Shay returned to Warehouse Two, pulling her car inside as the roll top door came back down. She hopped out of the Spider and popped the trunk, her high heels clicking along the pavement.

"Help me with this, Peyton," she said, grabbing one of two small boxes filled with electronics. "They aren't heavy. I just don't have enough hands."

Peyton moved behind the car to pick up the other box. He narrowed his eyes. "This is a quantum decrypter, isn't it?"

"Give the boy a gold star. Yeah, it's a quantum decrypter."

"That means you're trying to break through some pretty high-grade encryption."

"Well, I didn't bring it here to microwave my burritos, that's for sure." Shay moved over to the bench and set her box down. "And I have a router here that'll let me interface with the signal receiving drone I've got outside."

Despite the fancy name, the quantum decrypter in the end just looked like a small black box with a few ports. Something about that irritated Shay. She wanted her gadgets to look complicated. *Hell, they cost enough.*

She connected the decrypter to the small five-antenna gray router and pulled out her phone and started tapping away.

"What's the point of the quantum decrypter?" Peyton said. "What is it that you're trying to get access to? Something in town? A satellite?"

"Aww. You're not *just* a pretty face." Shay grinned. "Someone almost as clever as you're supposed to be helped me with this equipment. We're going to borrow a little microwave remote-sensing data from a satellite that happens to be going over an area I'm very interested in."

Peyton nodded. "Okay. That makes sense. The quantum decrypter means heavier security. Military? CIA? NSA? GRU? MSS?"

Shay snorted. "Fuck no. Part of keeping a low-profile includes trying not to encourage the government to come after me. It's just some private satellite owned by some rich douchebags who own a shipping company. Almost the same quality without risking a bunch of FBI or military kicking down my doors, let alone Russian or Chinese spy assholes."

"Okay, so now I get what you're doing, but what specifically are you looking for with this satellite?"

"Ever hear of Lake Toplitz?"

"That was the lake mentioned in your alert earlier. At least it was when I checked the computer. Something about an earthquake in the area?"

"The Nazis used it as a naval testing facility. Lot of people believe there's hidden gold there, too. The assholes dumped a lot of shit into the lake toward the end of the war."

Peyton crossed his arms and nodded. "That's what you're looking for... gold?"

"Nope. When I do these jobs, I need to get in and out. It's not exactly like a single woman working by herself is going to be able to easily transport a lot of gold. That shit is heavy, and there's only so much equipment I can get to the lake quickly by myself."

"Okay. No gold, then."

"No gold. Most of the jobs I'm looking into involve things that are a little more portable. No one's even sure there is gold there. The only thing we know for sure is that the Nazis sank lockboxes into the lake for a few different reasons." Shay brushed a strand of blonde hair out of her eyes. "Besides, if I'm gonna build a solid rep, I need to find the kind of treasures that not just any random tomb raider can find, and that means magic. Not that I'd pass up a nice jewel or something, but my business model is centered around finding magical items." She grinned. "Though I've heard there might be more than a few jewels at the bottom of the lake, too."

"What are you looking for, if it's not gold and not jewels, at least not as the main target?"

Shay smiled down at her phone.

LINK DECRYPTION 45% COMPLETE.

"The Nazis were really into the occult," she said. "Some people believe they had the Spear of Longinus at the beginning of the war, and that's why they were so successful at first."

"As in the spear a Roman stabbed Jesus with while he was on the cross?"

Shay nodded. "The very same. The higher-ups in the Nazi regime, especially Hitler, were really into occult and dark magic shit. They collected a lot of artifacts with alleged powers."

"Like they knew about Oriceran." Peyton's eyes widened.

"At least heard the stories. Too bad it was a crowd of sociopaths. Before the truth about Oriceran came out, everyone smart assumed the stories about the Nazis and dark magic were all crap, but now it's hard to act like those assholes didn't have access to some magic."

"Like the Ark?"

"That was just an old movie. And the Ark melted the Nazis at the end." Shay furrowed her brow. "Well, I think it was just a movie. Who the hell knows anymore? Maybe Spielberg was telling people the truth the entire time."

"Maybe Spielberg is an Elf or a Gnome."

She shrugged, crossing her arms, cradling the phone in the crook of her elbow. "Stay on point, Peyton. Focus. I've found some information to suggest that there could be a magical artifact, an enchanted golden eagle pin that when activated with the right kind of magic can make a person super-persuasive."

Peyton winced. "Yeah, I could see how a Nazi leader might find that useful."

Shay walked over to the large tables that served as a desk and were quickly becoming covered with Peyton's computer equipment. "I've found more than a few pictures in historical archives that show Hitler wearing something like that."

"It could be bullshit. Nazis used a lot of eagle symbolism. He's probably just wearing a pin."

Shay glanced down at her phone again.

DECRYPTION 90% COMPLETE.

"Yeah, it could be, but my gut is telling me there is a good chance I can find that pin."

Peyton stared at her. "Your gut? That's why you're hacking a satellite right now?"

"Not just any satellite. Needed one with the newer technology that can detect difference in density between water, wood and metals." Shay looked up at Peyton. "The lake is a mile long, over 300 feet deep, and over a 1000-feet wide, and there's always a chance someone else might be on their way. I need to really narrow down my search area. The scans should give me a better chance of figuring out where something interesting might actually be buried once I cross-reference it with my other info."

DECRYPTION 100% COMPLETE.

Peyton opened his mouth to speak, but Shay cut him off with a raised hand and concentrated on quickly downloading the image feed. Silence reigned for thirty seconds.

FREQUENCY CHANGED. LINK LOST.

"Damn. They caught on quicker than I planned." Shay blew out a breath. "Okay, I think I still got what I need." She pinched and tapped on the screen to magnify some of the images. "There's a lot of shit in the lake from previous expeditions. They were looking for the gold, but I've got a rundown of where they were all looking, so I can exclude them if they came up dry."

"If it was just about using a satellite to image the lake, why hasn't anyone done it before?"

"You already mentioned why. It was what tripped the alert."

Peyton's face scrunched up in concentration for a moment. The answer came to him as his eyes widened. "The earthquake?"

"Give the boy yet another gold star."

"That's getting really fucking annoying, you know."

Shay smirked. "The earthquake shifted the sediment and sunken logs at the bottom of the lake, which affected the density of the bottom of the lake layers. The particulars aren't that important. The point is the earthquake may have unearthed shit that was buried too deeply for detection until now." The tomb raider nodded slowly. "Lots of good possibilities, but I have to make my move immediately."

Peyton frowned, shifting his weight making the flamingos look as if they were walking across his pants. "You're going to fly all the way to Germany on that little bit of information?"

"Austria."

"Huh?"

"Lake Toplitz is in *Austria*."

Peyton threw his hands in the air. "Okay, you're going to fly all the way to Austria and go diving in some deep lake based off a few blobs in some satellite images and your gut?"

Shay leaned over one of the computers, typing. "Yeah,

sounds about right. Well, and a shit load of background research I've done. Did you think I wouldn't do my homework? Why the big protest?"

"Look, there's a much better business model…"

"I don't have time to debate this right now. Like I said, other people might have this information, so it's time sensitive. I have to go. *Now*." Shay spun on her Manolo heel and hurried toward the Spider.

"You should just listen to me. This is stupid, Shay."

"Says the guy who was going to get his head blown off without my help." She raised her hand and waved without turning around.

Peyton groaned as he called after her across the wide-open warehouse. "I'm only telling you it doesn't have to be so hard. You don't have to jet across the world on a few satellite images and hunches. You can work smarter, not harder."

Shay opened up her car door and slid into the driver's seat. "You're good at getting information online. That doesn't mean shit about tomb raiding. Yeah, research's a big part of it, but so are instincts. I'm the professional here, not you." She slammed the door and started up her car.

Don't get killed while I'm gone, Man-Boy.

Shay's first stop wasn't the airport, but Warehouse Three. She pulled the car inside and waited as the metal loading door closed. She stepped out of the sports car and eyed the far less impressive brown van that sat parked near the door. As much as she loved her Spider, it couldn't exactly hold a lot, and she still needed to get a decent amount of equipment to the airport.

Shay walked toward metal shelves lining the wall, eyeing the high-pressure SCUBA gear and thought over what else she would need.

Submersible drones. Definitely need a couple.

The woman stood with one hip cocked to the side, her muscular legs exposed in the short skirt, standing easily in the tall high heeled shoes. Her mind was focused on the details as she ran her hands along the yard-long finned craft. She'd need one to act as a signal relay, and one for her initial scouting. Despite what Peyton seemed to think, it wasn't like she planned to jump in the lake without taking a few precautions.

More than a few divers had gone missing throughout the decades searching the lake. Some of them buried forever under the constantly shifting and dangerous logs. For all she knew, there could also be some sort of creature in there that was awakened as magic returned in the world. She didn't want to have an underwater fight with some angry lake monster hungering for human flesh.

What else do I need? Waterproof-augmented reality goggles.

"Shit," Shay muttered, picking up some goggles. She sighed and shook her head. Great AR goggles, just not waterproof, meaning all their scanning functionality would amount to exactly jack *and* shit except at the surface of the lake.

She didn't have time to get new equipment. *I gotta go with what I have.* Any delay might end up with any decent treasure gone by the time she arrived.

I'll just have to get something better when I get back. I can still scout with the drones before I hit the lake.

Shay marched over to another shelf and grabbed an amphibious needlegun and a box of magazines. She loved the weapon, even if she didn't have much occasion to use it. Something about the flechette ammo amused her. It was like a semi-automatic gun spewing little metal arrows. Classy in a way her other guns weren't.

I knew I bought this baby for a good reason.

Shay didn't plan on getting in a gun battle under water, but at least with the needlegun she could kill someone more than a few feet way. Early on in her career as a professional killer, she'd hit upon the clever idea of ambushing a man in a pool. She'd learned the hard way just how ineffective normal guns were in water, and the little incident had almost ended with a knife in her chest.

"What else?" She tapped her lips with all the casualness of someone at Ralph's buying groceries. "Oh, underwater flares. Maybe some grenades. Just in case. Never can be sure when you need to blow someone up."

A grin split her face. This was going to be fun.

Assuming someone doesn't get there first and try and kill me. Then again, that could be fun, too.

The black rental Volkswagen Canyon truck rolled along at a good clip. Forests of spruce and pine surrounded her on both sides, broken by the occasional village or small home. The hills feeding into the peaks in the distance dominated her attention on one side.

Shay took a private plane into Austria, her equipment stored in the belly of the plane and a hefty bonus paid to the pilot. See something, don't say a damn thing.

She was already changed into her work clothes – all black and a snug fit, with her long hair tied back.

"Damn, the roads really are a lot nicer over here," Shay muttered, enjoying the smooth ride. "And the drivers are better."

Being better than a driver in L.A. or NYC is a pretty low bar to clear. Don't know how much I should be impressed. Plus, it wasn't exactly rush-hour on the mountain road.

Nah, still better. If I were in L.A., someone would have already honked at me just to be a dick.

It was a small irony that despite her speech to Peyton, Shay had ended up flying into Germany… Munich specifically. Time wasn't her ally, which necessitated a supersonic flight. The two closest airports to the lake that could handle a supersonic flight were in Munich and Vienna. The German city was actually closer to the lake, though she'd long since passed into Austria.

Not gonna tell Peyton that. Don't want him getting too smug.

Shay glanced in her rearview mirror. She'd spotted nothing but the occasional garden-variety truck or car. Every once in a while, she saw a cargo drone going in the opposite direction, but the farther she drove toward the lake, the less common they became.

Guess there can't always be killer mercenaries waiting to steal your artifacts.

She chuckled to herself, wondering if the job would be too boring without a gunfight or two. Natalie hadn't been totally wrong. There was an excitement that came with gambling with your life.

Whatever. It's not like I became an accountant. I'm about to dive into some murky-ass lake to look for some Nazi artifact. That's plenty dangerous.

Her stomach rumbled. She'd been in such a hurry that she'd skipped out on eating in any of the larger cities she'd passed through. Spending hours searching underwater on an empty stomach sounded like a terrible idea.

A review of her map app suggested the village of Grundlsee would be a good place to stop for a bite to eat. Her German might not be as good as her Spanish, but it was passable enough. Plus, she had to assume a bunch of drunk-ass foreign tourists infested the area at times, raising the chance of people having English proficiency.

Shay looked over her shoulder out the back window at the blue tarp covering all her equipment. The locals might get suspicious, or they might just assume she was there for Nazi gold in the lake like so many others and laugh in her face, just like the border guards in Salzburg when they'd asked to inspect her truck.

She'd hidden everything dangerous beneath false panels, leaving nothing more than totally legal, if conspic-uous equipment. The border guards took one look at the way she was dressed and immediately realized the implica-tions of her cargo. Their only real response was to mock her as *Fräulein Schatzjäger*, Miss Treasure Hunter.

Shay didn't give a shit about border guards mocking her. The one useful thing from the border crossing was the guards letting slip that she was the first treasure hunter they'd seen in several months. That at least suggested a lower chance of anyone getting there ahead of her, but she still couldn't discount they might have come through Vienna.

Fräulein Schatzjäger still needed to keep a low profile until she was sure. She'd run into mercenaries during her first major tomb raiding job, and she couldn't be sure she wouldn't run into someone equally dangerous. The information that had brought her here was accessible to others if they knew what they were looking for and could put the pieces together to fit the right picture.

Shay frowned as she pressed down on the gas, happy for the higher speed limits. She glanced over her shoulder to make sure there was nothing in her blind spot as she changed lanes, picking up speed.

Peyton had gone off about a better business model several times. She couldn't help but wonder what he meant by that.

What the fuck does Man-Boy know about any of this? Tomb raiding isn't the same thing as what he does. There's a different kind of research involved. This is a good business model, one that doesn't end with hits being placed on either of us.

"I know what I'm doing," she said, tightening her hands around the wheel. "I'm building a rep so I will attract major players to the buys."

Shay squinted at the road as she pulled out her phone, looking for cell service. She'd passed enough small houses and villages on either side of the road to hope at least.

Not great bars, but at least I have some.

She dialed Peyton's phone.

He answered after one ring. "Shay?"

She could barely hear him, but it was clearly him. "You're not dead, yet."

Peyton laughed. "I think I can survive a day or two without you. Hey. Wait. Were you seriously worried?"

Shay snorted. "If you get killed, that means someone's been in one of my warehouse, which means my security's been compromised. You being alive means I'm safer. That's all."

"You're just a bundle of rainbows and unicorns pouring out my ass, aren't you?"

"Fuck yeah. I'm almost to the lake. I probably won't contact you again until I'm on my way back."

"Is there some sort of protocol if you don't?"

"What do you mean?"

"What if you die out there?"

Shay laughed. "Then get my body, put it on a wooden raft, and give me a Viking funeral, along with some of the same kind of flowers from my first funeral."

"I'm serious, Shay."

"Don't worry. I already died once. It didn't take." Shay hung up the phone before Peyton could whine.

You're a big boy, Peyton. If I die, you'll figure it out soon enough.

6

No killers around so far. Well, other than me.

A quick aerial drone inspection of the area revealed no one remotely suspicious, and the only other people out on the lake were two older men on the other end. They were already pulling their rowboat out of the water and didn't look like a concealed threat.

She'd been able to roll her truck to the edge of the lake and unload all her equipment without having to deal with anything more troublesome than a stiff breeze.

It was like the universe wanted her to find treasure that day, and Shay wasn't one to question the universe.

"Your will is my command," she said, and chuckled as she got out of the black truck, stretching her legs.

She eyed a few bent pine and spruce trees near the lakeshore and the line of younger trees planted after the loggers left. The place must have been stripped bare at one point. She could see how so many logs ended up in the bottom of the lake.

Shay surveyed the area with the drone, taking one last

look around to make sure no one was nearby. But, just because no one else was there right now didn't guarantee that no one was coming. Shay decided not to waste a lot of time. *Time to go after her target.* She sent the relay drone into the dense green water, followed by her main scouting drone.

Okay, my coordinates are right, and we've got three possible spots based on that satellite data cross-referenced with my other info. This should be relatively easy.

Shay tapped a few commands into her phone and slipped on AR goggles to sync with the drone's cameras. Even if she couldn't use the goggles in the water, they'd at least make the search process with the drone a little easier.

The drone quickly disappeared beneath the surface. Shay switched on its lights and watched through the drone's cameras as it descended from the well-lit top layer of the lake.

She tensed at movement in the left corner of the drone's field of view.

Am I already too late?

Shay turned the drone to the left, hoping to get a clear view of her competitor. She didn't see a mercenary or diver. Instead, she saw a fish hurrying away from the drone.

Yeah, you better run. She chuckled to herself and took deep, even breaths. *Steady.*

The seconds passed as the drone dropped even lower. She spotted more than a few more fish, but nothing human or even humanoid. No lake monsters for that matter.

A deep darkness swallowed the drone as it hit the lower

depths, only allowing Shay to see what was floating nearby through an eerie tunnel of light via the AR goggles.

The drone closed in on the first location three hundred feet down as she activated more lights to illuminate the area.

"Come on, treasure. Don't be anno... *What the hell?* Are those...?"

She maneuvered the drone closer to the lake bed. Shay stared at the screen, unable to accept what she was seeing on the bottom of the supposedly pristine lake. Not gold, jewels, or magical eagle pins, but several large cracked open crates filled with empty beer bottles. *Environmental assholes. Nothing new.* The labels were long gone, but she could make out words embedded in the glass itself.

Stiegl? Congrats. You guys are still around. Good for you.

Shay shook her head, annoyed and switched the drone's sensors to cold thermal view. She couldn't make out anything else of interest. The beer bottles had to be from jerkwads partying on the lake and not some sort of mystical artifacts. Then again calling a Nazi a jerkwad was redundant.

Maybe I'll be kicking myself in a few weeks when I read something about how a bunch of genies were trapped in beer bottles by Nazis.

She sighed and began maneuvering the drone to the next set of coordinates.

Her heart almost leapt out of her chest as she spotted someone in a diving suit with a spherical helmet, their head down and their arm flapping behind their back. She stopped the drone's movement waiting for the other person to act. The seconds ticked by, and she realized it wasn't an arm flapping, but a torn air hose.

Shay nudged the drone forward, shining the lights more clearly on the head. She winced as the lights highlighted a fleshless skull. Whoever the poor son of a bitch had been, he'd been dead a long time before she'd shown up. The bulky diving suit dated the ill-fated attempt to the forty years prior to her attempt.

Closer examination with the drone revealed tears in the suit, and huge cracks on the other side of the helmet.

"Rest in peace, you poor bastard. Sorry it didn't work out for you, but I brought better toys."

Shay took a deep breath and moved the drone away from the skeletal diver remains to continue toward her next destination.

Unlike the accessible crates of beer bottles, a twisted mass of rotted logs rested, layered one on top of each other at the second set of coordinates, blocking any direct access to the lake bed. "A giant set of pick-up-sticks."

A few minutes of searching located a small hole that allowed the drone to slip inside. The latest *treasure* wasn't crates with empty beer bottles but a pair of rusted SCUBA tanks. Not a good sign for someone. At least this time there were no remains.

"How many people have died in this damned lake?"

Shay rubbed her neck, taking off the goggles and letting her eyes adjust once more to the daylight. The evidence piling up suggested the only thing people found in Lake Toplitz was nothing but trouble.

Her satellite data showed one more location of interest to the right. Searching the entire bottom of the lake might take days, if not weeks even with all her fancy tech, and that only increased the chance that some annoying asshole would show up with a huge team of divers and an entire navy of drones. Things had a way of happening like that when hunting for artifacts.

Shay trooped over to the truck and looked inside at a crate resting in the back that had a false bottom. Her weapons were stored inside there to avoid suspicion. She weighed her odds. A small arms defense of her site was one thing, but the area was frequented by tourists, and they tended to report things going boom to local authorities.

The harsh reality was that puttering around the bottom of the lake to find the fucking treasure could end as successfully as every other attempt had throughout the decades. Minus the lake becoming her last resting place, an important distinction.

Even worse for her chances to have a lucrative career as a tomb raider, Shay had to consider the possibility she might have interpreted the data wrong.

Damn it. Maybe my gut was off. One more thing for the list I won't be sharing with Peyton. Screw his better business model, whatever the fuck it is. I still have one decent chance.

Shay started maneuvering the drone to the last of her three likely locations. She let out an exasperated growl and walked back to the edge of the lake. "Fuck giving up," she muttered as she put the goggles back on.

She moved the drone to another location, revealing another tangle of rotted logs and vegetation, liberally covered by sediment. This time her metal scout had an easier time sliding through the logs. There was a wide access point, more than large enough for a certain sexy tomb raider to don the scuba gear and follow the drone's path if there were anything worth recovering.

Shay slowed the drone. The sunken logs formed a navigable underwater maze, but their stability looked questionable. She didn't want to bump anything and risk collapsing the whole thing, burying any treasure down there for another few decades. Minutes passed as she piloted the drone through the maze to the lakebed, turning left, a sharp right, straight ahead, left again. Her lips were pressed together in a thin line as she concentrated, taking in every detail.

"Wait... what do we have here?"

Four metal lockboxes lay half-embedded in the mud, two small, two large. The larger two were cracked open, the reflected gleam of the light on gold bars, even obvious through the AR goggles.

"This is promising. Very promising." Shay allowed herself a grin.

See, Peyton. Never doubt the gut.

Not an artifact but still gold. Even a single gold bar makes the trip worthwhile, despite what she'd said to Peyton. "One little hiccup," she muttered.

There was no convenient way to grab more than a few at a time, given their weight. Each bar would weigh twenty-seven pounds, the standard four hundred troy ounces. The two smaller lockboxes didn't appear large enough to contain any gold bars, but that only made her heart race faster and a wider grin spread across her face.

The boxes couldn't fit gold bars, but they could fit a few pieces of magical pins.

Shay kept exploring the small pocket in the log maze

with the drone to make sure she wasn't overlooking anything but there was no more to be found. "Four boxes, four chances."

She piloted the drone until it was out of the maze again, even though it took excruciating minutes. The fewer things in her way once she hit the water, the better.

The tomb raider pulled off the goggles, blinking her eyes and headed back toward the truck. It was time to put on her diving gear and grab herself some treasure.

Shay took slow, deliberate breaths as she headed toward the log maze, slowing down her heart rate and getting ready for the dive. She was going to make it out of the operation with some serious gold, and if she really got lucky, she might find the pin.

Even though each gold bar was worth over half a million dollars, it still wouldn't be enough to make her reputation in the *high-tier* tomb raider community. She *needed* that pin. The gold would be a nice consolation prize though.

Her high-pressure diving suit was rated up to four hundred feet, giving her more than enough of a margin of error since the lake bottomed out at just over three hundred. Even though the suit wasn't any bulkier than a normal wet suit, its stiffness limited her movements. She had a good hour of air in her tank, with several more tanks in the truck if she needed to make more trips.

Confidence filled her as she swam toward the entrance to the log maze. That confidence vanished as she approached where her drone had entered. She flipped her light on and off just to be sure. There was no doubt.

Shit. Seriously? I thought you wanted me to the find the treasure, universe.

The logs had shifted during her swim from the surface. She groaned and tilted her head up and down, looking for some other access point. *Nothing.* The lockboxes were there, beneath the annoying ass logs, with gold bars at the minimum, if not a damned magical artifact.

I'd take fighting off twenty mercenaries over this shit. It's not like I can kill these damned logs.

Shay swam around the logs from left to right, taking the time to carefully examine possible openings, testing the logs but couldn't find a new entrance. She floated silently in front of them, a school of small fish swimming between her and the logs as she grew calm, patiently considering the possibilities.

More than a few of the logs lay balanced precariously on the others. A simple push or two could get her access to the interior, or it could result in a collapse of wood and mud on top of the treasure.

No fucking choice. Great.

Shay took a deep breath and swam down to a spot where only a few logs crisscrossed each other. She reached over and shoved at a log. Nothing happened. *Good and bad news.* She swam down further and pushed at another log. It rolled a few inches, just enough to clear the logs it was sitting on, and sank toward the bottom, clearing a path for Shay.

Here goes nothing.

The temporary lake raider swam slowly, doing her best

not to jar any more logs with either her legs or her equipment as she entered the narrow opening. She swam down several yards, slowly rolling over and looking back up at the entrance.

I think I'd like to bleed out in a kitchen rather than die buried beneath a bunch of logs and mud.

The minutes ticked away as she continued making her way toward the lockboxes. She looked at her watch, making a note of how much oxygen she had left in her tank.

The needlegun was still back in the crate, given the lack of obvious enemies. Instead, Shay brought a mesh bag that was connected to her belt and a rogue barracuda switchblade, useful for stabbing anything with a beating heart.

Her own heart thumped hard in her chest as her head and wrist lamps cut through the murky darkness. The occasional movement of the logs sent bubbles to the surface and messed with her calm. *Slow and steady.* The situation called for less speed and more precision, no panicked movements. The passing minutes seemed like hours until she finally arrived at the lockboxes.

Shay swam over to the first of the smaller lockboxes and tried to open it. She followed that lack of success with a quick bash from the handle of her knife to the rusted-out lock. It smashed open rather easily, and she pulled the top off.

Her eyes widened as she peered into a small pouch filled with diamonds. She carefully picked it up, gently handling the worn pouch and tied it off before slipping it into her mesh bag.

Diamonds might not be my best friends, but still very good friends.

She took a few steady breaths on the respirator and turned her attention to the other lockbox. A few strikes from the knife took out another rusted lock.

Fuck Yes!

She felt a surge of what passed for joy pass through her body. Several golden eagle pins sat inside the box, no hint of tarnish or damage on them. The magical pin had to be among them.

Shay reached down as a jolt of electricity shot through her hand. She winced and yanked her hand back. The top of the lockbox glowed a luminescent red. Runes burned themselves into the lid with no obvious source of heat. Shay's eyes widened behind her mask as she recognized the symbols as Futhark, an old Germanic runic script.

What the fuck is happening?

She couldn't decipher the runes but knew enough to tell several words were completed. A bright orange pulse suddenly shot from the box. Shay reflexively threw up her arms, shielding her head. *A trap!*

Shay held her arms over her head, taking in that she wasn't vaporized by a magical trap. She put her arms down slowly and turned around in the deep water, the light from her head lamp bouncing off the interior of the maze. There was a bigger problem.

The logs all around her were shaking.

No, not the fucking logs... Shit. The trap started an earthquake somehow. Perfect. Motherfucking perfect. I'm 300 feet down about to be buried alive.

Shay glanced between her escape route and the lockbox

filled with pins. No one bothered to put a magical trap on simple accessories. She reached down again, but an invisible force and another jolt of electricity stopped her.

Her breathing grew ragged as logs above her begin to slip. If she didn't hurry, she was going to end up like the poor bastard she'd spotted earlier.

She tried to grab the edges of the pin lockbox to pull it out, but each touch only sent another nasty shock through her hand.

Damn it! You've got to be fucking kidding me.

The key to surviving any battle is to know when to stand and fight, and when you're about to get your ass kicked. Shay was tough, but she knew she couldn't win against a mountain of logs.

She swam *hard* for the exit from the wooden tomb. A huge log slid forward, missing pinning her by mere inches. The logs continued to shake. *How long will the damned earthquake last?* As if she'd willed it to stop, the main shaking ceased, but the tangled maze of logs were left even more unstable.

Her pace quickened even more, and her pulse pounded in her ears. Collapsing logs sealed off the path ahead as she swam to the side, rolling against other logs, causing another collapse that revealed a new path just behind her right shoulder.

Need to go faster. Her training kicked in and she made herself take even, steady breaths, assess the situation and then fucking reassess it again.

Shay spun to the side to avoid being crushed by two falling logs, banging against her shoulder. She spotted a way out of the collapsing logs, and kicked off, spying an opening to freedom. The lake raider just as quickly jerked to a halt at a sudden yank.

What the fuck? Is some Nazi merman trying to drown me?

She yanked out her knife and flipped out the blade, looking down. There was no merman, Nazi or otherwise. Her mesh bag had snagged on a log. She pulled against the bag, swaying in the water, but the strong mesh wasn't going to give. It was caught fast. Another log rolled away from Shay, reminding her that time was not on her side. She reached inside, grabbed the diamond pouch, and sliced the bottom of the bag away.

Her glance up confirmed her exit would be sealed in a few more seconds. She screamed into her mouthpiece as she kicked hard, stretching for the opening and clearing the space just ahead of the collapsing avalanche of logs.

Too... damn... close.

Shay took a long, deep breath and looked down at the pile of logs. Their shifting movement had kicked up sediment from the lake bed, and her lights were having trouble penetrating the cloudy darkness. It was clear no one was getting back into that mess anytime soon without the generous use of a pile of explosives.

That's enough diving time for now.

Shay lay flat on her back on the shore, her tanks and mask at her side. She sucked in the sweet alpine air and caressed the pouch of diamonds she'd managed to save.

"No other assholes are gonna be able to get to that treasure anytime soon, and even if they did, they won't be able to get past the magic trap," she murmured to herself. "Okay, no magic pin and no gold bars, but I did get some diamonds. I'll still count that as a win." She sat up and stretched. "I still think I'm gonna avoid any underwater jobs for a while."

7

Shay took a sip of her coffee as she glanced through the latest edition of the *Journal of Archaeological Research* on her phone. Conventional academic archaeology sources didn't tend to point her directly at the kind of artifacts she wanted to grab, but every piece of information she learned about archaeology and history could only help her in the future. Sometimes pieces came together that pointed Shay in the right direction that separated out were just fun facts.

"A Reevaluation of Zhuge Liang's Fire Gambit in Light of Oriceran Influence: The Possible Use of Magical Fire Artifacts in Ancient China." Shay chuckled. "What a mouthful."

She had read a lot of articles like it since her decision to devote herself to tomb raiding. To her great surprise, many historians and archaeologists were happy rather than pissed after learning that much of what they'd believed for decades, if not centuries, was made-up crap. A lot of them seemed to be overjoyed they had entire new research paths for their careers, with more than a few going on and on about their obsession with finding the *real truth*. Shay rolled her eyes at the thought.

It wasn't that Shay couldn't understand their excitement, but she would have been annoyed to have spent an entire career studying something only to find out she'd been playing make believe the entire time.

Switching jobs from killing to tomb raiding didn't require any radical changes in her thought processes or beliefs. Just no killing. Well, *less* killing.

Everyone likes a little job security.

Shay looked around the intimate little Munich street café. A handful of other customers, mostly men, worked on their meals or coffee, but no one paid her much heed. It filled her with a little relief. German men knew to keep their distance and not crowd a woman just because she was hot. Or maybe they were all gay. Whatever worked. She crossed one long leg in a dark leather boot over the other as she took another sip of the strong black coffee.

Shay had a few hours to kill before her flight and decided to get a bite to eat. After vanquishing her sandwich, she'd moved on to relaxing with some coffee while she caught up on her reading.

The small bell over the door chimed, and Shay glanced in that direction. A man in a dark suit with close-cropped blond hair stepped in, adjusting his tie as he surveyed the café, a tense expression on his face. A faint bulk disrupted the lines of his suit, both a fashion crime and an indication he was wearing a shoulder holster.

Shay resisted a sigh. She'd thought it'd been too easy for her to check out her newest target without meeting any resistance. Well, easy except for the whole almost getting buried in a watery tomb by logs. That was more than a little annoying.

Now you show up, asshole? It would have been nicer to show up at the lake where I had a more convenient place to ditch your body. Fuck, there's not even a decent seedy trash can nearby. Why do the Germans have to have such clean cities? This was always easier in New York. Hell, there were even a few convenient forgotten subway tunnels there.

Shay looked away, instead focusing on watching the man's reflection in the polished brass running behind the counter. She feigned a smile at one of the waitresses, which the woman took as a sign she wanted more coffee.

The new arrival moved to a corner table, one of the few tables where he could see the entire café and look out the window, but otherwise his back was to windowless walls.

Shay took in a deep breath and slowly let it out.

It could be nothing. Maybe the guy just likes to sit in the corner. Or maybe not.

Defensive seating. That's what she'd always called it when she still worked as a professional killer. An obviously armed man practicing defensive seating might not be a hitman, but the chance he was a local neighborhood business jerk wasn't all that high either. Coupled with the timing of her visit, she had to assume that Mr. Defensive Seating had come to finish Natalie Leon's job.

How the hell did they tag me? Where did I screw up?

Shay took another sip of her coffee, keeping her expression casual. She tapped away at her phone to activate and reverse the camera before lifting the device, so she had a clear view of Mr. Defensive Seating. She kept her phone at a slight angle, as if she were still reading the same material from before.

The likely killer accepted some coffee from the waitress with a frown, tension lines marring his face.

Shay stifled a laugh. When she'd worked the job, one thing she'd learned right away is that looking tense made you stand out and attracted the wrong kind of attention. Even an idiot could get the drop on you if they noticed you.

Surprise was one of the greatest weapons when it came to a successful kill. *Is Mr. Defensive Seating new or just bad at the job?* The thought vaguely offended her.

So, I've made him, and he doesn't know I have. Seriously, asshole, you thought you could take me out that easily? I'm insulted.

"Auf wiedersehen," said a snow-haired old man to the waitress. He'd been inside the café before Shay even arrived, slowly working on some sort of dark soup. He grabbed his cane and limped his way to the door.

Shay pulled out a few Euros and tossed them on the counter. She could finish off Mr. Defensive Seating in an alleyway, or at least somewhere without security cameras or drones, but she needed to push things along at her tempo and not his.

She hurried to the door and threw the old man a large fake smile before opening the door for him.

"Danke," he said, and stepped through.

"Bitte schön," Shay offered back, keeping the pleasant smile plastered on her face.

She spotted Mr. Defensive Seating's reflection in the glass of the window as he made his way from his table.

He'd barely had time to finish his coffee and was already standing. Any doubts she had about him being a hitman vanished.

If you were going to be this obvious, you should have just set up with a sniper rifle from a building and shot me when I stepped out, asshole.

A grin wanted to break out on Shay's face. *Excitement*, not fear, flowed through her.

Taking out a single hitman would be a nice way to maintain her practical combat skills without any serious risk. Even if her new job didn't always require her to kill, if she let her instincts rust, she'd be dead the next time a mercenary squad got the drop on her.

The old man headed up the sidewalk to the left, leaning heavily on his cane while he joined the light flow of the evening foot traffic. Shay moved the opposite direction where the walkers were less dense. Fewer people meant fewer complications. It also meant delayed police response.

Far fewer police drones patrolled the skies of Munich than she was used to in large American cities. Whether that represented German naivete or simply safer cities, she couldn't say. Considering some of the serious magic-related incidents she'd read about, she doubted the latter.

The hitman emerged from the café and straightened his tie. *Is it some sort of nervous tic? His tell.* She walked down the street for a few yards and lifted her phone as if she were taking a selfie, but mostly to check behind her, and frowned.

The hitman wasn't following her; he was following the old man.

Really? You needed to hire a professional to take down an old dude with a cane and a limp? I could hire some 12-year-old Girl Scout to take out that guy.

Shay rolled her eyes. She wasn't overly impressed with the hitman. Arrogance on her part, perhaps, but an arrogance earned through skill. Shay doubted most people could successfully assassinate *themselves*, disappear and still collect the payout.

The tomb raider slowed her pace, waiting for both the old mark and the hitman to go around the corner. *One Mississippi, two Mississippi.* She turned and hurried in their direction, maintaining a brisk walk but not fast enough to be running to avoid drawing any attention.

Curiosity fueled her now, not concern. The old man's fate wasn't hers to decide, but somehow watching a hit go down appealed to a dark part of her. The same vicious side of her soul that reveled in using her skills to defeat and take the life of another. She couldn't deny that she'd fallen into being a professional killer after finding out on her first kill – she liked it.

She'd always told herself it was more about control than enjoying the kill. *Not completely true.* She pulled her soft light wool jacket tighter against the biting wind as she slowed down at the corner.

It didn't matter, really. Shay knew how fucked up she was. In a way, the Nuevo Gulf Cartel had done her a favor by putting the contract on her life. Now, she had a chance at some sort of halfway decent human existence instead of being nothing more than a paid weapon.

Not that her soul could ever be redeemed, if there even was such a thing, but at least now she wasn't sliding farther and farther each day into becoming a complete fucking monster.

Of course, maybe my dead marks would disagree that I'm not a monster.

Shay stopped at the corner and peeked around. "Son of a bitch."

The old man now held his cane and all but jogged along without any sign of his former limp. He glanced over his shoulder and picked up the pace, hurrying away from the hitman.

Shay smirked, impressed the old man had managed to fool her.

See, Mr. Defensive Seating? That's how you surprise people, but now the guy's made you because you're so damned sloppy.

Shay jogged toward the men but kept her distance. Even fewer people walked in the narrow side streets, and it was clear the noose was tightening around the old man. She glanced around and spotted a ladder running up the side of a nearby building. After chancing another glance at the men, she ducked in an alley and grabbed onto the base of the ladder, easily scrambling up the side.

Those gym days do pay off.

Shay's muscles burned as she hit the roof of the building. She hurried to the edge to reestablish a visual on the hunter and the prey. The old man ducked into another alley.

Shay winced. If he'd stayed near other people, he might have at least had a chance. She blinked and raised a brow, her esteem suddenly rising.

The old man hurried and ducked behind a small truck

parked in the alley. He pulled on his cane, revealing a long, thin blade.

"Oh, sword cane, nice," Shay murmured to herself from her rooftop perch. She liked the idea but didn't see how a young woman like herself could pull off carrying a cane without looking odd.

The hitman reached into his coat and yanked out a pistol. He stepped around the corner into the alley. He slowed, looking back and forth, keeping his gun ready. To his credit, he moved to the opposite side of the alley from the truck. *Still, no one's looking up.*

Shay reached under her jacket, feeling the cold metal of her 9mm. She might not be able to land a shot on the hitman at this distance, but she could scare him.

He doesn't see him. She eased her finger off the trigger. *Not your business, anyway.*

The hitman turned to leave. The old man leapt up from behind the truck and charged. His pursuer spun toward him and squeezed off three rounds. Shay aimed her gun, able to get a clean shot.

The crack of the hitman's gunfire echoed in the air, and the victim slumped to the ground, his sword now useless.

His killer holstered his weapon, straightened his tie and pulled out a phone, aiming it at the dead man, presumably to take a *kill shot.* An inside joke in their trade.

A distant siren sounded, and the hitman rushed away from the alley.

Shay's heart thumped hard in her chest, and she took a deep breath. The memory of how it felt to take down a mark was hard to push out of her head.

The ex-killer licked her dry lips and shook her head.

Regular people don't carry around swords hidden in canes. That old man was another hitman past his prime... just like Natalie. Just like I would have been if I stayed in the job.

With a shudder, Shay made her way to the ladder. She had a flight to catch.

8

S hay rolled into Warehouse Two feeling pretty good. Even if she didn't snag the magical persuasion pin, it was buried under so much mud and wood that no one else would be getting it, along with the gold. Denying someone else a victory was at least part of the game, maybe even just as much as an actual win. She could always go after the rest of the treasure in the future. At least now she knew exactly where it was.

Walking away from an overseas trip with a bag of diamonds didn't exactly fall into the failure category, anyway. The diamonds weren't the highest quality according to a fence she'd stopped by on the way to the warehouse, but it would still be a good payday and help keep her knee-deep in pizza and sports cars for at least a little longer. *Might even buy Peyton a few technological toys to help the business.*

Ignoring the money, the entire mission again confirmed she knew what she was doing. Shay wasn't a killer fumbling around and pretending to be a field archaeologist and tomb raider. She was the real damned deal and now could claim the successful location of two magical artifacts.

Failure to *recover* the second artifact came with the job as far as she was concerned. Like the man once said, no plans survive first contact with the enemy. She couldn't control the logs, but there had been treasure there, and likely magical treasure. That's all she cared about for the moment.

Shay almost wanted to whistle at how impressive she was as she stepped out of her car.

Peyton emerged from the office, this time in khaki shorts and a Hawaiian shirt decorated with koala bears and eucalyptus trees.

"I..." Shay began, staring at the man's outfit. "*That* was in one of those boxes?"

"What? My outfit?"

Shay rolled her eyes. "No, your face. Yes, your outfit. It looks like you got mugged by the Australian Board of Tourism."

Peyton laughed. "No. These weren't in the boxes."

Shay narrowed her eyes. "Where did you get them, then? Please tell me you didn't go shopping when I was gone."

"Well, kind of. Not the kind you're thinking of." Peyton grinned. "This was paid for anonymously and delivered nearby."

Shay groaned. "How did you pay for it anonymously?"

"I've got a lot of cryptocurrency holdings. Bitcoin, Ethereum, lots of Trollcoin and Oricoin, too. If you know what you're doing, it's all but impossible to trace. You should really look into that, if you haven't already."

"Sounds to me like you took a risk with the life I went to a lot of trouble to save."

"Not much of one."

Shay sighed and ran a hand through her hair. "Whatever. The point is you shouldn't have left this place. It's not safe. Someone could take you out, especially if I'm not around."

Peyton shrugged. "I'm already dead, remember? You got paid for it. No one's even looking for me, and what am I supposed to do, sit here all day? It's not like you're sitting around hiding in a warehouse, and the contract on your life was worth way more than the one on me."

Shay scoffed. "Degree of difficulty to take me out... turns out they were right."

Peyton smirked. "Duly noted."

"Okay, okay, fair enough. I get it. You have cabin fever." Shay put up a finger. "But let's be smart about this. My fake death was more thorough than your death, okay? But I get it, you've been locked up in here, and you're going stir crazy. I've got a solution for that."

"And what's that?"

"We should just go out."

"Go out? After all that big speech about safety? Are you just fucking with me now?"

Shay crossed her arms. "If you're with me, you're safe, and I know I can make sure no one follows us back here. I'm only worried when you wander off by yourself. Let's go and celebrate." She grinned.

"Celebrate? Your texts were rather... uh, cryptic. You

did find something, then?" He propped his blue Vans up on the metal desk until Shay gave him a cold look that managed to send a shiver down his spine.

"Diamonds, and even gold, but there was an issue recovering everything. I only escaped with the diamonds."

Peyton nodded. "An issue? Is that code for a bunch of angry guys with guns?"

Shay shook her head. "Nope. Just man's greatest and much more ancient enemy. *Nature.* The treasure was under a pile of unstable logs, and well, they shifted, and they almost buried me. It was kind of a big fucking mess. Came close to getting buried in a bad game of Jenga."

"Wait. What? Are you saying you almost died in that lake?"

Shay laughed. "Almost dying is like being almost pregnant."

Peyton stared at her, shaking his head. "You're insane. Do you even realize that you're insane?"

"I think the word you're looking for is brave, asshole."

"If you got buried under there, no one would have known to look for you. I wouldn't have even known to contact the authorities until it was too late."

"Don't worry. If I did, I'm sure I would have been crushed to death, so it wouldn't be like I was waiting to die and praying for rescue or anything. I assume when I check out, it'll be pretty quick and probably pretty painful."

Shay opened her mouth to mention the hitman but closed it without saying anything. Following the hitman even after realizing he wasn't on her tail was an unnecessary risk. *I would have chewed Peyton a new one if he'd tried something like that. For now, it's more important that the only thing the man sees is the face of success.*

"I don't think I could swim into a pile of logs that might bury me alive," Peyton said. "Call that cowardice if you want. I call it being smart."

"Good thing you're not gonna be a field guy, then, huh?" Shay clapped her hands together. "Anyway, even if I didn't get the gold, I got the diamonds, so we can afford a little pizza."

Peyton eyed her, suspicion on his face.

"What?" Shay reached for her car keys, ready to go eat.

"It's just that I thought you didn't go there for diamonds or gold. I thought you went there for a magic Nazi pin."

Shay shrugged. "I did. And I found it. It just so happens that I valued my life more than the artifact, and I had to make some hard choices."

"I can tell you're going back there some day. Whatever. Um, glad you're not dead, I guess."

"Aww. That's sweet. Now, let's go get some pizza." Shay headed toward her Spider.

Telling Peyton the truth about the magical trap wouldn't be useful. He didn't need to be aware of any of her miscalculations. Don't tell them how you make the sausage.

The important result of the lake raid was establishing she was right about the mission. There was a magical artifact there, judging by the defenses. That established that her gut, mixed with a lot of research and some satellite hacking, was a good source of information.

Peyton headed toward the passenger side door. "I was looking around online, and I found a place that does

Chicago-style nearby. I wanted to maybe explore the California interpretation of Chicago-style pizza."

Shay halted at her door and shot him a death glare. "What did I say about pizza if you want to roll with me?"

Peyton groaned. "NYC thin crust only."

Shay grinned. "Good boy."

Shay folded up a slice of pepperoni and all but devoured it in one bite, savoring the flavor over the long seconds of chewing.

"It's good," Peyton admitted, swallowing a bite of his pizza. "I can see why you're so into this."

"Quality speaks for itself and all that."

"How did you find this place?"

"I hit Prime Pizza pretty early since the warehouse is nearby. They are known around L.A. for their NYC-style pizza. It's nice to have a place close so I don't have to worry about traffic."

Peyton took another bite before speaking. "Traffic? Come on, I know I haven't been out of my new address, but I figure it can't be as bad as New York."

Shay shook her head. "Nope. This place is terrible. One of the worst in the world." She laughed. "It makes me miss the mild-by-comparison congestion of New York. It's why a lot of people like to stick to their neighborhoods."

"Isn't that a problem for you, then? It's not like all your… stuff is in one neighborhood."

Shay winked. "Well, normal people like to stick to their

neighborhoods. I just so happen to have a lot of neighborhoods."

Peyton lapsed into silence. At first, Shay thought it was just the seductive power of the tasty pizza keeping him quiet, but the haunted look in his eyes suggested something deeper. If the man was going to work with her, then he needed to get out of the funk.

"Problem?" Shay lowered her voice, leaning across the shiny wooden table, rustling the red and white paper placemats. "Or is it something we can't talk about here?"

Peyton looked up at her and shook his head. "No... I was just thinking about how I ended up here. About what you said about my family maybe being responsible. I don't want to believe it, but it's hard to just shake it off and say it's ridiculous."

"Finally coming around, then?"

Peyton shrugged. "I know it sounds lame to bitch about growing up in a wealthy family, but I kind of feel like it screwed me."

"Oh?" Shay folded another slice of pepperoni.

"If you're poor, you know, you have to look out for each other, because you don't have the money and influence to get out of trouble, or not starve or whatever."

"Yeah, that's why poor families always look so close and loving on reality shows."

Peyton ignored the comment, wiping the grease off his hands. "But when you're rich, money and power can get in the way. At least it did in my family. It wasn't lack of money that drove everyone nuts. It was the proximity to so much of it." Peyton shook his head. "We never got along, my brother, my sister, and me. Not like our dad really gave a shit about any of us, either." He let out a long sigh. "Mom cares, she does. I think she loves us, but she let it all happen, always making excuses."

"Then why get so torn up about being separated from all of them? Even if I'm wrong, a low likelihood, you didn't like each other anyway." Shay frowned and realized she was out of pizza. "Family is a blessing and curse and all that shit."

"I never... cared like my brother and sister did. About the money. The power. Any of that shit. I just wanted..."

"What?"

"I don't know. Freedom? Control?"

"That is power."

"That's why I didn't walk the path my parents wanted for me. Not sure how I was still in line to inherit anything. Well, I was before you killed me."

"Or maybe dear old Dad was still fucking with you and wanted to make you a target to see which of your siblings could take you out first. A little test of ruthlessness."

Peyton's face scrunched up in disgust. "Sometimes I forget your old profession. Not everyone wants to settle something with a tidy death."

Shay gave a shrug and eyed another slice of pizza. "Some people call it cold cynicism. A necessary part of my old profession. Somewhat in the new one too. I call it realism. In the end though, you walked away from the empire and showed them all you have some balls. Even I can respect that."

Peyton gave a tired laugh. "I figured if I was doing my own thing I could seize my destiny. Crap like that. I guess you seized it for me."

"I made sure you still had one. You regret not becoming an active part of the family dynasty?" Shay scanned the restaurant while listening to Peyton. It was habit as well as a practical function. Size up each person, determine their ability to fight back, consider their most likely moves.

"Leaving them? Becoming an information broker? Not becoming some wind-up doll for my father?" He ticked each one off on his fingers.

"Yeah, all of those." Shay looked over Peyton's shoulder. Mother with two small children and nice set of muscles on her. She'd be willing to kill if she had to, no problem. Group of teenage boys scarfing down pizza. They'd run at the first sign of trouble. Same with the overly-muscled man picking up a pie. Show muscles but not meant for anything practical except lifting a car.

"To be honest, I don't know." Peyton ran a hand through his hair, looking even younger than his 24 years. Shay swung her attention back just long enough to look him in the eyes, make him feel heard. Best way ever invented to draw someone in, get them to put down their guard.

Peyton looked down at his pizza and Shay went back to scanning the room, while still listening to his story.

"I think if I stayed in that environment, I would have died a different way. Even if my brother and sister aren't behind what happened, it's not like we got along, and the less time we spent together, the happier they all were."

"Not gonna say I had a stunning relationship with my parents," Shay said. "I can relate, a little. Not to the growing up wealthy and all that crap..." She shrugged, watching the middle aged man approach the counter, doing the same scan of the room. Short hair, straight back, not even trying to hide that he's checking out the room. *Off duty cop.* "Look, I had to do the same thing, seize my destiny if that's what you want to call it."

"By..." Peyton glanced around. "By going into *that* profession?"

Shay snickered, glancing up at the man as he curtly thanked the cashier and picked up the pizza box. If anyone overheard Peyton's coded conversation, they'd assume an attractive woman like her had become a call girl, not a brutal professional killer.

"That profession saved your ass. There was some other shit going on, but yeah, that was my destiny, for a while. When I started making my own money, I took control. I made my own decisions. I could live the life I wanted without having to rely on anyone."

Shay's face tightened as dark memories filtered into her mind. *Don't press further.* That was about as deep as she wanted to go into her past.

Peyton picked up his glass of Mountain Dew. "Here's a toast then. To all of us who got fucked over by our families, may we control our destinies from here on out."

Shay picked up her orange Fanta. "Hear, hear."

They clinked their glasses together.

9

The next morning, Shay sat at her oak desk in the office in her condo. She frowned as she scrolled through her financial records on the computer.

"Shit, shit, shit. Really? Shit."

She let out a pained groan.

Shay should have been ecstatic. The recovery of the diamonds had further confirmed her skills, and she'd taken a step closer to moving Peyton from a spoiled rich boy playing at being a criminal to a useful potential team member, but the financial review sucked out her happiness.

Her new business was still barely profitable.

She rubbed her temples, still wondering if she'd done the right thing saving Man-Boy. She knew she would need the kind of backup Peyton could provide if she wanted to succeed in her new career. But she'd spent her previous career working alone – killing people made office help nervous — and even the thought of depending on another person made her stomach tighten. A man like Peyton was potentially unreliable, an unwarranted risk she would have never taken in the old days. He liked to play around in dangerous waters but ignored the sharks around him like they weren't a big deal.

That wasn't confidence. That was arrogant stupidity or naivete. Neither one was good on a resume for what she needed.

Fuck me. I'll chase after a hitman because I'm curious, and I'll swim under falling logs, but force me to trust someone for a few minutes, and suddenly I'm ready to throw up.

Then again, I've had friends try to kill me on more than one occasion.

Shay looked at the financial records on her computer screen. *This is the larger problem right now.* The tomb raider business wasn't building like she wanted.

When she'd come up with the idea, she was convinced it'd make her a pile of money that would leave her hit contracts looking like the pay of a shitty job that involved wearing your name on your shirt.

That wasn't how things were working out. She broke even on her first job and after expenses and the fence's cut for the diamonds, only made a small profit on the lake raid.

If only I'd got my hands on that damned pin.

Maintaining five different warehouses and all her equipment wasn't cheap. The various casual bribes she had to throw around for everything from keeping her warehouses secure from local scum to ensuring certain powerful people didn't look her way, even accidentally were eating into the profits, too.

Life was expensive when you were already supposed to be dead. Funny how that worked.

Running out of money wasn't an immediate concern, but that didn't mean Shay could continue to ignore the issue either. For now, her previous career had left her with a generous savings. Some of it was hidden in various accounts throughout the world, while enough to start all over again was in a vault in the most secure warehouse. The way the world was unwinding, though, left her wondering how much of it could really be secure anywhere.

Huh... Maybe I should look into some of that Trollcoin after all.

Shay wasn't overly fond of her finances being dependent on technologies or governments she didn't have personal control over. But the balance between safety and accessibility was a constant magic trick of its own kind.

In the end, if it wasn't her own vault, the tomb raider preferred a bank she could enter, even if it might be in a different country. A physical bank meant there would be a physical banker, and she could always threaten to kill him for better service. It was a lot harder to intimidate an algorithm or blockchain.

Shay narrowed her eyes, leaning toward the screen as she clicked around on her spreadsheet, reviewing the expenses and revenue from the most recent job one more time. The sale of the diamonds covered the costs of her lake raid, but her profit margin was pathetic. She wasn't supposed to be depending on savings at all. "There is nothing lucrative about this if I don't change things up."

Her great list of seven items could turn out to be artifacts she didn't recover for decades into the future, if at all. The more she considered them, the less she believed they would be a reliable method for building her reputation.

"Fuck, fuck, fuck."

Shay sighed and leaned back in her chair, thinking about her last conversation with Natalie. Retirement for a 27-year-old woman technically on the run wasn't a possibility. She still had her whole life ahead of her and at this rate would run out of money eventually. Sooner if she kept buying equipment. She lacked contacts to back her up in the event of trouble. "No couch surfing for me." Peyton was the closest thing she had to an actual friend in Los Angeles. "That is pathetic."

Shay shot to her feet and started pacing, trying to get out her nervous energy.

More than the money, Shay's modest success grated on her ego. She had no delusions about that and felt no shame over the realization. She didn't just want to be a tomb raider; she wanted to be *the* tomb raider, the one spoken of in quiet, hushed voices when people thought about asking for artifact recovery help. Can't get Shay, settle for sloppy seconds.

Shay had been at the top of her game as a professional killer. People who weren't the best didn't last very long in a vocation where death was the desired outcome for someone. But in her new career, she had only a few modest successes under her belt and no reputation, yet.

Not only was she not the best, but she was barely better than a novice, no matter what she told Peyton. Field archaeologist or tomb raider, it didn't matter what she called herself if she couldn't bring home the artifacts.

The ex-killer gritted her teeth.

Fuck. I'm stumbling as a tomb raider. What am I missing? Is there some way to make this business better? I need to clear my head.

It took an hour for Shay to drive the Spider to Warehouse Four, her personal favorite. She chuckled to herself as she ran her hands along the spines of the books filling one of the many bookshelves lining the twenty-foot walls of the warehouse. Peyton would probably be shocked that her personal library rated more concern than her weapons and specialty equipment. Only Warehouse Five, where she stored extremely high-value goods, her personal money vault, and the occasional magical artifact was more important.

Wall-to-wall floor-to-ceiling bookcases filled the main warehouse space, along with several rolling library ladders. The collection ran into the thousands of volumes and represented a multi-million-dollar investment.

The vast majority of the books concerned history and the occult, with a smaller number focused on related subjects such as archaeology, anthropology, and even a few newer books on extra-dimensional engineering, the fancy university term for magic.

Scientists kept trying to make it catch on with the public, but almost everyone preferred to use the simpler and more familiar term.

There were even two books on magic bionics – a frowned upon topic even in the dark underworld.

A tech nerd like Peyton would have questioned why

Shay maintained such a laughably old-fashioned library in an age of ebooks and the internet. The answer was simple.

Shay preferred the heft of a book in her hands and a physical book wasn't something that could be hacked or disrupted with an EMP. They didn't leave a trail of what she was studying, either. As a hired killer, she'd succeeded on more than a few assignments because some idiot was relying on some enhanced gun with too many electronics.

It wasn't that Shay didn't mind the use of technology, magic, or whatever tool would help her the get the job done. Simplicity wasn't her focus, success was. But, when it came to owning knowledge, she made sure no EMP or lightning spell could wipe everything out.

Some of the books were so rare that she owned the last existing copy. Many had never been digitized.

Her finger stopped on a slim monograph detailing a Polish graduate student's thesis on the magical beliefs of the aristocracy in ancient Japan. It was written over a hundred years ago and was the only copy.

But anyone looking into the past couldn't be sure if they were reading about someone's misinterpretation of nature or an actual eyewitness report of something magical.

Shay's glance ticked up a few rows to the translated, *Annals of the Joseon Dynasty*, records from medieval Korea. Most of the records concerned the most banal of government functions, but there were hints of more mysterious events and potential contact with magic or Oriceran beings, including a report from September 1609 that spoke of a strange flying "washbasin" that made a thunderous sound despite appearing in cloudless skies and flying as "swiftly as an arrow" before "disappearing into sparks."

Before everyone learned about Oriceran, many people thought the incident was proof of aliens from beyond the stars visiting ancient Korea. That might still turn out to be true, too. Shay had learned to stop guessing at what came next a long time ago.

How often can some asshole from Oriceran come over here to troll the local humans?

Shay let out a relaxed sigh and smiled warmly at the collection in front of her. Even before the hitman decided to become a tomb raider, she'd had an interest in history and had started collecting the books through rare dealers, even if she didn't always take the time to read many of them. *I'll have the time in the future. If there is one.*

Almost got my ass iced in my own house. Nice.

Maybe in another life Shay would have become a history professor instead of a killer. She amused herself with the thought far too often.

I like history, but I can't change the past. Can only change the future.

Shay glanced to a side door with a black steel frame and glass inserts, connected to the main room of Warehouse Four. Although she kept the humidity and temperature in the main warehouse constant, the other room was for some of her centuries-old books that needed an even more controlled environment, including air filters to ensure a nearly dust-free room.

The tomb raider's rare book library was superior to what was in many universities. Good thing no one but her knew of its existence.

I've got the skills. I've got the instincts. I've got the books and the resources. So why can't I get this business going the way I want?

Shay let out a long sigh. "Maybe I should listen to Peyton's ideas after all. If they are crap, I'll just ignore him and threaten to kill him until he shuts up."

Shay collapsed to her knees, sweat soaking her body. Her shorts and tank top stuck to her body.

She looked back at the tall wall marking the end of her obstacle course. Her heart thundered, and she couldn't even move for a moment as she took in deep gulps of air in a desperate attempt to pull some precious oxygen into her strained lungs.

Shay had lost count of how many times she'd shoved herself through her Warehouse One obstacle course that evening, but her aching muscles made it clear she had pushed well past her normal limits.

"I need… to do… this shit… more often."

In a world where magic was real, being the best human wasn't always enough anymore. Every small advantage could mean the difference between life and death, or worse.

Her body might be screaming at her, but the cleansing pain pushed all the lingering doubts from her mind, and she let out a quiet laugh.

Shay saved Peyton for a reason. He was doing her no good locked up in the warehouse waiting around for her to figure out a use for him. She could pretend to be the experienced tomb raider all she wanted, but that didn't change the fact that she needed advice and help. If he could provide it, even if just a different perspective, then she would be an idiot not to take advantage of that.

Only problem was, she was rusty at taking advice... from anyone.

Shay took a deep breath and slowly let it out. "Okay, I can do this shit. If I can kill a room full of men or dive into some dangerous lake looking for magic Nazi shit, I can ask for help. No big deal. No big deal at all. It's just Peyton."

She almost believed that.

10

"Okay, hot shot," Shay said the next day as she hopped out of her car, ready for the morning. "You get your chance." She was taking large steps across the warehouse floor, her heels clicking on the hard cement, excited to get started.

Peyton stuck his head out of the office door. "What? Huh?" He was holding a grande cappuccino in his hand and some of the froth was still on his upper lip.

"You've mentioned several times you have some better way to improve my business model or some shit." Shay shrugged. "Not saying I believe you do, but nothing wrong with doing even better and if you can help with that, well… I'm at least willing to hear your plan." She held up her hand. "Not saying I'll follow it, though. Just to make that clear." *Okay, this is a kind of trust, right?*

A smile lit up Peyton's face. Man-Boy wasn't the right name for him. Man-Puppy was more appropriate.

"It seems to me," he began slowly, testing the waters, "that you're interested in your rep."

Shay nodded slowly. "Bigger rep means bigger connections. I have an alias I'm using online right now for jobs."

"And how do you go looking for jobs?"

"Different sources… a couple of dark web forums out there for tomb raiders. A lot of people swapping information out there."

"People give information away for free? You can't trust those sources."

Shay sat on the comfortable leather couch set up in the office. "Not for free. You have to give a little to get a little."

Peyton rubbed his chin. "Okay, consider looking less at the end result and more at who might be interested. You know, reverse the process basically. Not the object but at the future owner. Hell, I could do it and cross-reference with a bunch of other stuff to really narrow down some good job candidates from people already highly interested. That way you could focus your efforts."

"It's worth trying." Shay crossed her long legs and sat back against the couch. "Tell me you got more than one of those." She nodded at the cup in his hands with the familiar green logo.

Peyton swallowed hard as he raised his eyebrows. "Next time? Hard to know when you're gonna make an appearance."

"Time to invest in one of those machines."

"Office perk. I can swing with that. Used to have one back in my old apartment."

"Of course you did."

Peyton gave a nervous smile. "If I'm going to be effective for you I'll need access to the forum."

Shay stared at Peyton for a long moment. Giving him

forum access meant she'd be giving up her first major secret. He could easily fuck her over if he screwed up.

Take a fucking contrary action. You can do it. Shay took in and slowly let out a deep breath. "Okay, I'll show you the forum."

Trust. It was more foreign to her than most of the strange Oriceran creatures she'd heard about.

Congrats, Tech Magician. I guess you're the first official member of my inner circle.

Shay went out and got a high-end coffee maker that involved a lot of moving parts and could make more than she needed. Peyton was thrilled when she got back and immediately set it up.

Shay tucked herself into a comfortable overstuffed chair in a corner of the warehouse set up with a goose-neck brass lamp. She kicked off her heels and tucked her feet underneath her, settling in to read. She slowly worked her way through a German news article on her phone detailing the recent public assassination of one Hans Mayer in Munich. The picture revealed Hans was the old man from the café.

Shay arched an eyebrow as she read Herr Mayer. *A fellow hitman. Well, both of us are in the past tense. You a little more.*

He had in fact carried out hits for numerous organized crime groups throughout Europe, Africa, and South America. The Munich police and Interpol had no leads on the death.

Apparently, unlike old soldiers, old killers don't fade away. They just die in the cheapest places possible, kitchens and alleys.

"I've got a good possibility," Peyton shouted from the office.

"That didn't take him long. Good sign." Shay pocketed her phone and slipped her feet back into her shoes, loping across the floor to the small office. She went and stood behind Peyton, peering down at the computer screen.

"More fucking gold?"

Peyton shrugged. "Yeah, I know, I know… artifacts are your main business model, but if you mix in some normal stuff, it'll still let you build a rep and pay your bills." He looked up at Shay like he wanted to say something but closed his mouth and looked back at the screen. "Besides, I think there's some magic involved, and dealing with that will definitely be good for your rep." He tapped the screen. "In Arizona, in the middle of the 19th century, the Peralta family of northern Mexico found a gold mine in the Superstition Mountains. They worked the mine and shipped the gold down south until they got taken out by some angry Apaches who ambushed one of their gold caravans."

"Can't spend gold if you're dead."

"Clever how you've managed to redefine *dead*."

Shay thumped him hard on his shoulder, but a smile was spreading across her face. "We are a couple of pretty fresh zombies."

Peyton held still, not sure what to do next, his hands lightly resting on the computer.

"Go on, already. If you're going to be afraid of me at every turn, we're done here."

"Noted... Let me know if there's a policy change in the company."

Shay let out a loud laugh and patted him on the back. "We are going to get along just fine, Man-Puppy."

"I'm going to need a new nickname. Something like Tech God. When I get close, computers just start working."

"That's going to need a tweak or two. Later... First, tell me about my next job."

"Right... first things first. Most predictable thing about you. Okay, back to our story." He flexed his hands, cracking his knuckles and pointed at the screen as he looked back at Shay. "Later, a German immigrant claimed he found the mine again. He went by the nickname *the Dutchman*, so they took to calling it the Dutchman's Mine. Even though he allegedly told another person about it, no one's ever been able to find that mine or any of the gold that was shipped out. These days it's known more as the *Lost* Dutchman's Mine."

Shay frowned. "Lots of lost mines legends out there. Why is this one any different?"

"There's a treasure hunter who already went after it, Adolf Ruth, who was mysteriously murdered in the desert, his skull blasted half-away by a shotgun, after he allegedly found a map to the mine."

"That doesn't sound like magic to me. That sounds like good old-fashioned American greed."

"A lot of drone and imaging surveys of the area haven't turned up much, but if it's concealed by magic, they might not be able to. No evidence of anyone suddenly striking it rich after Ruth's murder either. So even if they found the map, they didn't find the mine."

Shay was about to write off Peyton's first attempt when the map comment sparked something in the back of her mind. Some of the details seemed familiar somehow, even though she couldn't remember ever reading about the Lost Dutchman's Mine.

Shay furrowed her brow. "That's not a huge amount to go on, and if I do modify my business model, I definitely don't want to start spending a lot of time and money chasing down old rumors."

Peyton grinned. "What if you're not spending your money?"

"Listening…"

"I've got a client lined up who is willing to pay for you to find either the mine or the gold, including a deposit or a retainer or whatever the hell you want to call it."

Shay held up her hand for a high-five from Peyton. "I guess it couldn't hurt to talk to the guy. You get to live another day. These are the jokes, Tech-Wizard." She let out a laugh as she saw a shudder pass through Peyton.

***

The next afternoon, Shay found herself sitting at a table in A.J.'s Kitchen, a local diner that she hit up on occasion. Although they didn't serve pizza, they did serve grits, an old favorite from childhood.

Most places, especially places on the west coast, couldn't get them right, but A.J.'s always did. Not too runny, not too thick with the right amount of salt and butter.

Shay eyed a man sitting two tables down digging into

his grits with a spoon. She resisted the urge to throw a fork at him and yell, *always use a fork, idiot.*

Instead, she picked up her fork to scoop up a bite of her grits. After swallowing, she took a sip of her coffee and glanced down at her phone. The client would be arriving any minute.

Shay glanced around the room and resisted a sharp laugh. She was sitting in the corner, her back to a window-less wall. Without even planning it, she'd practiced defensive seating. *Instincts are ingrained in me.*

The comforting weight of her 9mm resting in her shoulder holster under her jacket and the knife in her boot were less of a surprise. There were just certain accessories a prepared and fashionable woman didn't leave home without.

A man in a slick gray suit and salt-and-pepper hair entered. He was pushing his mid-fifties and attractive in a rumpled sort of way. More importantly, he matched the description of the client.

Shay eyed him for a moment, glancing toward the window to make sure she didn't see any other suspicious movement. She waved to him, and he made his way toward her.

The man looked her up and down for a moment, blinking in obvious surprise, as his pupils widened.

"Greg Abbot?" Shay asked.

The man nodded. "And you're the retrieval specialist?"

"Field archaeologist, tomb raider, whatever you want to call me. For now, just call me Shay."

Greg stared at her for a moment before taking a seat.

"Problem, Greg?" Shay said.

"I... uh... I guess I didn't expect such a beautiful woman."

"Not on the list of requirements to get the job done."

"No... of course." His face reddened as he sat down.

Good sign... Shay paused as a waitress came to take Greg's order. He only asked for some coffee. Shay waited patiently while the waitress came back and poured the man's drink.

"The coffee is good here," she said. "Not from a drip maker."

Greg took a sip and nodded, steadily becoming calmer and more focused. "I don't really know the protocol for this sort of thing. Honestly, this is the first time I've really looked for your specific kind of help on this issue."

Shay looked him up and down. "First things, first. I guess I want to know a little about you."

"Does that matter?"

"Yeah. Because if you're, for example, a piece of shit, that means you'll have piece of shit enemies, and they may ambush me with mercenaries. It's good to know ahead of time who I might have to shoot."

Greg blinked and nervously chuckled. "You're very blunt, Shay."

"Delicacy is required on the job, not before. The best way to have this turn out as a success for all of us is to have all the risks on the table."

"I don't have any of those sorts of enemies. Mine are very white collar and boring." Greg took a deep breath. "I'm a distant but direct descendant of the Peraltas, the original family that owned the so-called Dutchman's Mine."

"Did you bring proof?"

Greg looked surprised but reached inside his jacket for a folded piece of paper and laid it flat on the table, turning it so Shay could read it. It was a family tree that showed the line weaving down to Greg Abbot. Not exactly direct, Shay noted.

"I suppose treasure seeking runs in my genes. I made a fortune in finance, taking chances just like my ancestors. I just got smarter and did it with other people's money."

Shay nodded. "Not as dangerous as smuggling gold."

"You'd be surprised. The point is, I have through strenuous effort recovered some legal documentation that proves my ownership of the mine and the gold, but I need to find the mine or the gold first, for it to mean anything. My research has turned up a particular miner's. mark pressed into the gold that left the mine. I can use it to prove ownership if it hasn't been melted down."

Shay took a bite of her grits and swallowed, giving her time to think before responding. "Sounds like you've gathered a lot of good information. Why so much trouble finding the mine?"

"Hard one to explain, exactly. I've tried to fund expeditions of more conventional treasure hunters, and they've run into failure, sometimes before they even started. Several men have already died."

"Really?" The question came out sounding more filled with curiosity than fear. Shay assumed the dead men just weren't good at what they did.

"Yes, I half-wonder if the mine or gold aren't cursed somehow." Greg's face pinched in displeasure. "With those... Oricerans influencing our world, who knows what sort of strange magic might be mixed in to all of it? Maybe the mine was cursed from the beginning."

"And that's why you're looking for a tomb raider rather than a normal treasure hunter?"

"That indeed, Shay." Greg leaned forward, intensity in his eyes. "I'm willing to put down twenty-five thousand, upfront."

Shay resisted a snort, but she didn't resist a comment. "That's not a lot of money to me, to be honest."

Greg gave a small nod, letting out a sigh. "I can imagine, given your profession. If you can find the gold or the mine, I'm willing to pay you two hundred and fifty thousand dollars more. I'm sure that would be adequate compensation."

Shay grinned. "That's more in line with my usual fee, Greg."

His gaze momentarily roamed away from her face, and she resisted a frown. "See something you like?"

Greg pressed his lips together and looked away. "I'm only interested in the money, even if you do have a smoking hot body. You're a bit young for me."

"Now that's a new one. You'll find I don't mix business with much of anything else."

"Good to hear. I'm only interested in your tomb raiding skills and I need this to work."

"Okay then, mine or gold, you said? How much gold to trigger a payout?"

"Even four bars would be worth more than enough to make this worthwhile. Today's rates would mean two million dollars. If you recover more, I'm sure we could negotiate some sort of bonus."

"Okay. How about 250,000 plus five percent of the value of any recovered gold? If I find the actual mine, I don't want a percentage. I'm not greedy, but I do want a million dollars in that case."

Greg's eyes widened. "Are you serious?"

Shay gently scratched her forehead with a well-manicured nail. The key to any negotiation was knowing just when to push and when to pull back. All her instincts told her to push hard.

"I just found a pile of diamonds lost for almost one hundred years on my last job. If you want some loser budget treasure hunter who will waste your time by dying on the job, then go ahead and hire one. I'm sure they'll do just as well as last time. But if you want a field archaeologist with actual experience dealing with magical artifacts and threats, then don't cheap out on me."

Shay locked gazes with Greg and he returned the look, evaluating his options.

The man let out a long sigh as his forehead wrinkled. "A twenty-five thousand retainer?"

"Correct. That will act as your proof that you're serious about this before I waste any of *my* time."

"I... am willing to pay, but I must admit, I'm not all that comfortable with this."

Shay shrugged. "You have to spend money to make money. You, of all people, should understand that."

"It's not that."

"What is it then?"

Greg frowned. "It's like I told you. There may be a curse involved. Danger. And... well, you're a young woman."

Shay snorted. "Trust me. Compared to a lot of what I've

done, your little penny ante curse barely qualifies as danger. Spare me your chivalry."

"You're sure, then?"

Shay picked her fork back up to shovel down some more grits. "Trust me, as long as your gold's not under a lake, I'm not worried."

11

S hay rubbed her forehead as Peyton paced back and forth in front of her in Warehouse Two. She was sitting in the new office chair she'd bought Peyton, waiting for him to calm down.

A mixture of annoyance and confusion risked giving her a headache. If she got one, she was going to pop the Tech-God in the head so he would have one, too.

"It was your fucking idea," she said. "Why are you freaking out about it now?"

"Yeah, I know, I know, and I've been talking about trying to help you, but I'm not as sure now. The more I've looked into the legend, the more I think you were right to begin with. It's just all rumors and legends. It's a waste of your time." Peyton shrugged.

"So what? I can afford to waste my time. Abbot's giving me 25 K upfront. That'll take the sting from me spending time on this over the next few weeks. If it turns out to be nothing, then it's just a lot of money he paid me to do research."

"I think it's a lost cause, Shay. And I'm worried that failing will leave a bad mark for you under your new alias. Then I'll have fucked you over. Maybe I was wrong about all of this. I…"

Shay rolled her eyes. This was the problem with people who played at independence but grew up wanting for nothing. Peyton wanted assurances and no risk. She didn't live in that kind of world. Never had. And now neither did he, and it was time he accepted that.

"Calm down, Man-Puppy," she said, "before you wet yourself."

Peyton stopped pacing. "Man-Puppy now?"

"Would you prefer Man-Boy?"

"Huh. I think I'd like a third option. Tech Genius…"

"Not today. Earn it." Shay gave him a dead serious glare. "Look, I'm the one who decides on what jobs I'm gonna take in the end. Non-negotiable. If this gold hunt ends up being a big fucking waste of time, that's on me, not you. Adjust your panties so they aren't in a bunch already."

Peyton sighed, putting his face in his hands for a moment. "You're doing the deal either way."

"Yeah. You know why?"

"What?"

Shay ran a hand over her stomach. "I've got a good feeling in my gut."

Peyton groaned. "The last time you said that you were almost buried alive underwater."

"Almost dead counts in my world. It means not dead. You know what else counts? The treasure was there, and I escaped with diamonds. My gut was right."

Peyton inhaled and crossed his arms. "What about the

whole building a rep for your alias? What if it ends up being a big bust and this Abbot guy spreads shit about you?"

"Hey, it's an alias. If this goes south in a bad way, then you can use your fancy IT skills and knowledge to make a new alias for me." Shay marched up to the man and leaned in close till they were nose to nose. "I'm doing this. Stop whining and get on board. It's my time and my life to risk. Understood?"

Peyton winced, taken aback by the tomb raider's intensity. He held up his hands in surrender, still staring into her eyes. "Okay, okay, message received. Man-Puppy is on board. Tell me your plan. Are you going after the gold or the mine?"

Shay took a step back from Peyton and let a smile appear on her face again. "The gold. Fuck the mine. That *is* a waste of time. It might be actually lost or filled with motherfucking zombies or some other mysterious shit. The gold I can locate and pile into a truck and drive it right out of there. I'd rather take the easier road this time."

"Okay, that sounds good in theory, but do you even have any idea where the gold is?"

Shay gave him a sly grin. "Your little Mexican legend, show and tell the other day kept pricking something in the back of my memory. I knew I'd heard some of those details before. Eventually I remembered that I'd already heard of the Peralta family."

"You have?"

"Yeah, I have some old books from Mexico that mentioned them, along with the ambush where the main members were killed and gives additional details that I think I can use to narrow down the search coordinates. Details that don't seem to be readily available to others. I just need to review those books." She pointed at Peyton. "This time you're gonna help me with data filtering after I do the initial research. I didn't save you to be an *idea man*. I saved you for your technical skills."

"Sounds good, boss."

Shay winced. "Don't call me that. Just call me Shay. It's either that or *Your Most Illustrious and Alluring Imperatrix of the Galaxy*."

Peyton chuckled. "I'll stick with Shay."

"Glad we're in agreement."

"Do you have it narrowed down at all, yet? The possible location of the gold?"

"Yeah, from what I remember, it should be in Baja California Sur."

The man paled, and he swallowed. "Baja California Sur?"

Shay laughed. "What's wrong? Get a bad sunburn on spring break there once or something?"

"I've never been there."

"Then why so freaked out?"

"That's Nuevo Gulf Cartel territory."

Shay shrugged "Well aware, I've crossed paths with several of them. All dead now. So what?"

"So what?" Peyton shook his head. "They want you dead, Shay. They are the reason you had to fake your own death and ended up in L.A. instead of New York. I kind of think that's a big deal."

Shay wagged a finger. "Correction, they *wanted* me dead and now, they *think* I'm dead. It's not like there are gonna be wanted posters of me in every bar in Mexico or something. If I run into anyone who looks like they recognize me, I'll just kill them. See? Big problem with an easy solution." She picked a small piece of lint off the sleeve of her pale pink silk blouse.

Peyton scoffed. "That simple?"

"Yep. That simple, especially since I'm not exactly planning to hang out in the city." Shay smirked, crossing her arms over her chest. "That's half your problem, Peyton. You're a rich city boy, who thinks of everything only in rich city boy terms. Hell, I bet your Boy Scout troop had catered meals."

"Not all the time," he grumbled.

"Just saying that I'm *a tomb raider*. My job description often involves me hitting out-there places. This will be no different."

"The gold's not under some Walmart or split-level three bedroom?"

"That would be handy, but pretty sure it's not." Shay winked, swiveling the chair around to check her phone. No updates on the area where Shay felt certain she'd find the gold. She had set up an alert system using the satellites over the area to let her know if there was unusual activity.

Peyton sighed. "Let's get this straight. You're gonna go to, I'm guessing, the middle of the desert in Mexico, passing through territory controlled by the cartel who wanted you dead to begin with, to find some gold that even your client thinks might be cursed, and that's assuming you can even find this gold."

Shay nodded. "That's the long and short of it. Sounds easy and a little fun." She pursed her lips together for a moment. "I guess I really do like that spice of violence." She sucked in a breath and chuckled.

"Have I told you today that you're insane?"

Shay pulled her Spider in front of the gray cement blocks lining the front of Warehouse Four. Unlike Warehouse One and Two, there was no easy direct vehicle access. The cement barriers might not be enough to stop a car bomb, but they could at least cut down on mass damage.

She pulled forward and parked the car under an overhang before walking around the corner toward a recessed back door covered by multiple dome security cameras.

A person of her background might correctly intuit from the excessive security the importance of the building's contents. Shay didn't mind. There were enough alarms and alerts that she would know right away if anyone tried to break in. For their sake, she could only hope that any future intruders were long gone by the time she arrived because they wouldn't leave the warehouse alive.

Before even trying the door, Shay pulled her phone out of her pocket and brought up her custom security app. She tapped the lengthy code to disable the alarms and motion sensors only for the front doors.

With that accomplished, Shay pulled out her key to get past the first door. Another door with a keypad and retinal scanner blocked further progress. She tapped in the code and placed her eye against the scanner. The huge internal bolts locking the door retracted with a loud thunk, and she pulled the door open to step into a dimly lit metal antechamber.

Hrmm. Never realized how much this looks like the kind of room they stick you in before they start torturing you.

A huge reinforced steel door blocked her progress again. It was a bitch to install since she couldn't let the workers actually know where they would be working. Instead, she arranged for them to be blindfolded and driven to the site by Shay, after sweeping them to make sure no one had any tracking devices. The workers had all been taken inside before their blindfolds were removed so they couldn't use environmental cues to begin to try and figure out where they were.

It was amazing what people would agree to when you splashed a little extra cash around. The premium price was painful, but she took comfort in knowing that the workers had no clue where Warehouse Four was located. Of course, the not-so-veiled threat that she'd murder them in their sleep if they ever asked around about the job helped.

Too much? If they came here, I'd have to kill them anyway, so don't know if that's better than murdering them in their sleep. At least I warned them.

Shay placed one of her fingers on the door's DNA reader. A burning sensation followed, and she shook out her hand, waiting for the scanner to confirm it was her. The door bellowed out a loud echoing click, and she pulled the heavy door open.

A few steps into the library brought a smile to the woman's face. Her history books and records would help her find Abbot's gold. She didn't even care about the lack of magical artifacts. Not this time, anyway.

Shay licked her lips, her heart kicking up. Something excited her about this particular chase. Maybe because it was one of the first times her knowledge was helping lead her to the treasure rather than technological tricks or throwing around money.

She also didn't mind the idea of pulling off a job right under the noses of the Nuevo Gulf Cartel.

Fun, fun. Too bad you assholes didn't actually finish me off.

Shay took several more steps closer to the books where she inhaled and enjoyed the musty smell of the old books. The collected knowledge represented by the books managed to humble her every time.

Shay had equipped Warehouse Five with traps, but she'd elected not to do that with Warehouse Four, fearing a stray bullet or explosion might set the place on fire and destroy all the accumulated wisdom resting in the pages.

Losing all the books would hurt her more than anything she could imagine. She could easily say it was worth more than a few lives.

I guess I'm just the ruthless pizza and history girl. Too late now to do the history professor gig. Doesn't mean I can't have fun on this job.

Shay smiled to herself. It was time to do some more research.

"Welcome to beautiful Mexico," Shay said with an easy laugh. If she didn't know Cabo San Lucas was in the same state as the mountainous desert wasteland she currently traversed, she would have questioned why anyone ever came to Baja California Sur.

The Land Rover rumbled over the dried, cracked ground, the bumpy terrain worsening by the minute, and the mountains looming over her like some angry Oriceran giant. The clear blue skies stretched off into the horizon, and she could imagine the night sky would be a beautiful tapestry so far away from light pollution. Too bad she didn't plan to stick around that long.

Her vehicle closed on the coordinates her research had indicated, a triumph of her old-school book collection over her advanced technology. She never imagined that her history books she'd purchased would prove so useful in a future job.

Guess I picked the right hobby.

Her experience in Austria had impressed the importance of having the proper equipment to recover all possible treasure. Her alerts were still quiet. No one around to bother her.

"This should be easy," Shay muttered to herself. "I have a whole damned vehicle I can shove gold into. This isn't some sad old-school donkey. Or maybe I should start using donkeys. Probably some Oriceran donkeys that have magic and wings." She frowned. "Donkeys that could fucking fly."

Shay shook her head. Spending too many hours alone in her own head could do strange things, but trust for the most part still remained foreign. Bringing Peyton into the operation didn't mean she was ready to run around with a partner in the field *yet*.

Trusting someone to have her back in a fight was something she'd yet to experience. Few people she met were as good as she was when it came to killing. At least when it came to normal human methods and not strange magic, and she wasn't sure how much she could trust someone who relied on magic. The few marks from her old job that almost took her down were almost all people with access to magic. Despite her job, the actual use of magic *still* left her uneasy.

Shoving a piece of lead at supersonic speeds into someone's head is a kind of magic, though. I guess it's all a matter of perspective.

Shay let out an uneasy grunt and tried to focus on the current job.

Her plan was to locate the cache, then use a small cargo drone to transport all the gold, bar by bar, back to the Land Rover. After a simple drive back to town, she could unload the gold into the private plane she'd chartered and get the hell out of Mexico before any cartel assholes had a clue anyone had ever been in the area. Much less a dead woman.

How do you like that, you bastards? You tried to kill me, failed, and paid me for the privilege, and now I'm gonna grab a shitload of gold from underneath your noses.

A smile appeared on her face. She'd read the Nuevo Gulf Cartel was close to being pushed out of the area by another cartel.

Always a bigger group of assholes looking to take over territory. Enjoy the fear, fuckers.

Shay's only real concern was an odd reference she found in her research.

"*Todos aquellos que buscan el oro de la familia Peralta deben saber que la codicia ciega a un hombre a la verdad,*" Shay murmured.

All those who seek the gold of the Peralta family should know that greed blinds a man to the truth.

The phrase had been scrawled on an old map of the area. Shay had no idea if it was a simple moral observation or a riddle about the treasure meant to warn off seekers or help them find it. The truth, as much as anyone could know it, would present itself soon enough. She just hoped that the truth didn't involve another massive volcano.

Shay spared a quick glance in the mirror. She wasn't expecting to see anything other than shimmering Mexican desert air or mountains, which was why the two dust plumes made her do a double-take.

"Damn it. Of course. This is just my luck for the lack of Nazi zombies in Austria."

Shay let out an exasperated sigh just as the alert went off on her phone.

Thanks, I know... Nobody followed me from town, that much I'm sure of. Some assholes who just happened to be rolling around in the desert? Maybe cartel or just local jerks, militia or bandits. I could still take them, but that'll cause a problem.

Avoiding being linked to a single dead body was easy, almost trivial. Trying to avoid attention when you left dozens of bodies in your wake, not so much. Minimizing deaths would be to her benefit both in the short and long term. Now if she could just get everyone else to cooperate with her by not tempting their fate.

Just don't follow me, assholes, and I won't have to fucking kill you. I'm here to take some gold. Nothing more.

Shay scanned the area in front of her. Crags, overhangs, and outcroppings increasingly dotted the land, plenty of places for good cover if she wanted to hide. But any good hunter didn't give up on the hunt just because they lost sight of the prey for a few seconds. She would need to both conceal herself *and* give her pursuers another rabbit to chase.

A magic invisibility ring would be handy about now.

A grin broke out on her face, deepening the dimples in her cheeks. She had just the idea.

Another ten minutes passed, and the dust plumes in her rearview mirror grew closer, the faintest hint of darker shapes as they became more visible. Shay found a nice overhang to provide cover for the Land Rover. She parked and calmly but quickly exited the vehicle.

Out of the cool air conditioning the choking heat smacked Shay in the face.

"Fuck, I bet even the cactuses are thirsty in this heat."

The tomb raider hurried to the back of the Land Rover to yank out a large desert camouflage tarp and draped it over the vehicle. Unless her enemies already had eyes on her exact location, they were going to have a hard time picking the covered Land Rover out from a distance. A brown, dusty object in the middle of hundreds of miles of brown, dusty landscape.

Shay grabbed her loaded backpack from the vehicle. After retrieving binoculars from the bag, she peered into the distance at the dust plumes.

Two white Escalades barreled toward her general direction. They both abruptly halted after about fifteen seconds.

"Lost me, huh? Just following my dust, assholes? Amateurs."

Shay could barely make it out as someone rolled down their window, and a man in a brown cowboy hat leaned out. At the distance, she couldn't pick out much other than the hat. A brief conversation followed, and one of the other Escalades peeled off, pulling hard to the left. Mr. Cowboy Hat's vehicle continued forward.

Shay grinned and hurried back to her Land Rover. She moved under the tarp to pull out a small emergency drone that came with the rental car. These days, with magic everywhere, just a car to rent wasn't enough for people. They wanted toys, too.

"I am no different. The app is all ready to go. Let's play."

Shay stepped out from under the tarp, placed the drone on the ground, and flipped three switches on the machine. She yanked her phone out of her pocket to bring up the control program and surveyed the options. Her eyes stopped on *Direct Control.*

She moved the control forward and watched the drone lift into the sky under the careful control of her fingers. She kept it low and near the ground, moving off at nearly a right angle from her original driving direction. The buzzing whir of the drone's propellers filled the air high above the desert, as if the world's largest and angriest mosquito had decided to invade the desert.

Her pursuers gradually grew closer as her shit-eating grin grew and she kept her attention focused on the drone's camera feed. A rock-strewn canyon appeared.

"Perfect."

Shay brought the drone to a halt, hovering as she pushed the control forward and the small drone lifted in a straight line from where it was. Three hundred feet would work for her plan. She only hoped somebody in the approaching Escalade was paying attention.

Her gaze cut to a large red button on the bottom right of the app display. She tapped the screen. "Let's do this."

A bright red flare dropped from the drone and ignited, burning in the distance. Shay waited a few more seconds and dropped the other flare. She disabled the drone's engine and chuckled as the ground rushed up to the drone in the camera feed.

FEED LOST.

Shay winced, suddenly realizing she was technically renting the drone. "Guess I'll have to pay for that. Next time I'll get a backup. Still working the bugs out of the system."

She brought up her binoculars and watched the Escalade. The vehicle remained still.

"Come on, asshole. Take the fucking bait. Just assume I'm some stupid gringo who got lost and come over to save me or kill me or whatever you have planned. I don't have time for twenty questions or a gun fight."

Shay licked her lips. The dry air surrounding her continued to draw all the moisture out of her body.

The Escalade swerved to the right and peeled off toward the drone's location.

Shay quietly golf clapped. "And the Oscar goes to Shay Carson for best use of a drone in a chase scene."

Shay drove on through the desert, this time without a tail and parked her Land Rover a hundred miles further west. She hadn't spotted anyone else following her for a while and a quick check with binoculars only confirmed that. She didn't want to risk sending a drone up into the sky for a larger survey. There were few things that screamed "I AM HERE, ASSHOLES" more than a drone suddenly flying around the middle of nowhere. After all, she'd depended on that logic to bait her pursuers.

The terrain had become impassable even for her four-wheel-drive vehicle, meaning the last leg of her journey involved a combination of climbing and hiking.

"This is why I train on the course," Shay muttered.

No convenient mountain path presented itself as she closed in on the coordinates. Now that she was farther up the mountains, the cacti had given way to sparse shrubs and bushes. She wasn't seeing much life of any kind, other than the occasional lizard scuttling away from her or a buzzard circling in the distance.

"I'm not dead yet, motherfuckers," Shay said, after seeing her fourth buzzard. She flipped off the bird. "You don't get an early meal."

Her sunglasses and safari hat spared her eyes most of the sun, but even her light clothing could only do so much to protect her from the heat. The cold waters of the alpine lake were looking rather nice in comparison.

Sweating as she gave thanks one more time for those hard workouts in Warehouse One, Shay finally reached a sheer cliff leading to a deep canyon. A small ledge protruded from the cliff wall about one hundred feet down. She looked up at the rock face easily picking out small handholds and picturing the direction she would need to take.

"You've got this, tomb raider."

13

Shay let out a quiet cheer as her feet landed on the ledge. A frown quickly followed as she glanced over her shoulder into the distance where the setting sun painted the sky an intense orange-red.

Temperature's about to do a radical drop on me. Fair enough, I saw this coming. I won't be getting back to town before dark.

Shay may have become a tomb raider, but the part of her that was used to being a calculating killer still assessed every situation, looking for the flaws. There was a constant checklist running in her head when she was on a job.

She wasn't standing in front of an obvious opening to a cave. That would have been too much to expect. That was the hard lesson Shay was learning on the job.

A shimmering field covered the narrow entrance, fading from opaque to translucent. She picked up a pebble and tossed it at the field. Nothing happened.

Just don't start an earthquake, please.

She reached out with a gloved hand to touch it. Again, nothing happened.

"Huh… promising..."

Shay took a deep breath and held it as she stepped through the field. No burning pain or piercing noises. She didn't get turned into a harpy or flung into the cavern. As far as she could tell, nothing happened.

Okay, that's... not what I expected, but not going to complain about not getting zapped with magic.

She reached into her pocket to pull out her phone. *Fuck me. The phone is off.* Several attempts to turn it on failed. She'd charged it in the car and used low-power mode on her hike to ensure she would have plenty of power remaining.

Furrowing her brow, Shay reached down to a belt pouch and grabbed a small electric flashlight. She flipped it on, but no beam came out.

"Okay, perfect. Some sort of electrical dampening field or some shit. Found the magic." She considered her options calmly. Her AR goggles would be useless, and if she moved too far away from the cave mouth, she'd lose the remaining light.

With few options, Shay walked farther into the narrow cave. The sound of something scratching the wall echoed from deeper in the cave.

Son of a bitch... What the fuck was that?

Shay pulled out her gun in one swift, smooth motion.

At least this baby doesn't require any electricity.

The scratching grew in volume as she lifted her weapon. Her eyes widened, despite her training as a writhing black mass rushed right toward her. She squeezed off several rounds, only to be greeted by a choir of inhuman shrieks. The mass closed in on her.

At least I'm not dying in my fucking kitchen.

Her heart thundering, she dropped down, hoping to avoid the attack. Shrieks echoed over the narrow cave. As it poured over her the sound broke up into a pattern of high pitched squeaks along with another noise... the flutter of wings. Shay lay on her back, watching as a continuous stream of hundreds of bats rushed overhead and out of the cave in the waning light.

"Beautiful..." she whispered.

The horde of bats exited the cave as Shay sat up and rose to her feet, her core muscles taut as she whispered, "thank you" that so many animals flew over her without one of them crapping on her. *It's the small things.*

It was getting difficult for Shay to see her hand in front of her face. She fished out a thin, flashlight that easily fit in a small pocket carried for just this kind of occasion. It ran on stored energy that wasn't affected by the dampeners but provided a dimmer light. Better than nothing. It provided just enough push back against the inky darkness swallowing the deeper parts of the cave.

Shay pushed, spelunking further into the hillside, rubbing her chilly shoulders through her jacket as she rounded a corner in the cave. The heat of the desert was a distant memory as the dipping sun combined with the cool air of the underground cave surrounded her.

Her travels brought her to a wider underground chamber. Several long, vertical, tight narrow cracks led farther into the cave, but no human, not even a child, could fit into them. She suspected the bats were making good use of them.

Shay moved the flashlight back and forth to illuminate

different parts of the chamber. The strong beam of light revealed four rotting wooden chests. Her heart beat faster with excitement even as her training kicked in and she took in the data, assessing the situation.

She marched over to the nearest chest and set down her backpack, pulling out a pair of lined gloves. No electrical shocks this time. She tapped on the lid as the wood crumbled into small, jagged pieces. A stronger push moved the entire lid off the chest.

"That's what I like to see."

The bars of gold inside gleamed in the light of her flashlight.

Shay took a deep breath and slowly let it out.

Preparation and persistence meets opportunity.

Shay grinned as she moved the light around to get a better look. "Found you, you bastards." Not so fast. "Now what sort of whacked-out magic is protecting you?"

She slowly reached down, gritting her teeth and waiting for the pain. No guarantee the gloves would protect her from anything.

Nothing zapped her. No earthquakes shook the area. No portals opened to another world. She picked up a single gold bar, enjoying the heft of the valuable metal.

Shay flipped it over, looking for the miner's mark Abbot had sent in an email. A circle containing a stylized P set in a bull over the shining sun sat embedded in the back of the bar.

"Congratulations, Greg," Shay whispered. "You're about to get a lot fucking richer."

Quick removal of the other chest lids revealed more gold, and near the fourth chest, Shay's breath caught as she

spotted words clumsily carved into the rock wall above
and behind the chest.

The Spanish was a little old-fashioned, but she could
still get the gist of the story. The survivors believed the
massacre of the Peralta family was a sign from God. A
curse on the gold and the Apache that hunted them down
were his instrument. The survivors hid the gold to protect
people from the curse and used a spell to hide the entrance.

"Somebody in that family was a Witch." Shay rested
back on her heels. A connection to Oriceran and magic.

"*Greed blinds a man to the truth*. Well played. Have to
appreciate a good riddle."

She burst out laughing, the sound echoing around the
cave chamber. "I did it... I fucking did it." Money *and* a
reputation. Not a bad day's work.

Shay knew from her old line of work. Sometimes a
massacre was just a bad fucking day.

"Of course, if this gold is cursed, Greg Abbot will find
out soon enough. But trust me, I'm not dying from any
ancient fucking curse."

Shay stood and stretched her arms out to the sides. The
cargo drone would do most of the work on the longer trip
from the cave to the car, but she still had to move all the
gold past the dampening field and out in the open.

"Time for me to get in an extra workout and grab some
gold. Ancient Witch, I thank you for the spell that kept this
hidden till I could get here..."

Exhausted from her long day, Shay slept in the Land Rover

overnight after loading the gold into the back, figuring the tarp would be enough protection from a prying drone or anyone using binoculars to survey the area. By the time she was on the last trip her arms were shaking from the effort, but nothing was going to stop her from getting every last bar. *Financial bullshit, officially over.*

Arrangements for a private plane were made before she left Los Angeles, setting up the last stage of the job to be easy compared to lifting hundreds of pounds of gold. Last stage of the journey was to get to the airport, load up the gold, and fly back to L.A. Straight forward as firing a gun, assuming she didn't run into more random assholes in Escalades with their own firepower.

The rising sun woke her up early and she set out for town, chewing on a Lara bar as she drove, grateful for a trip free of any Escalades.

But, the minute she hit the edge of town, she spotted a shiny black Cadillac tagging along behind her.

Little late to the party.

Shay frowned into her rearview mirror, checking their distance and scanning the roadside for anyone looking in her direction. She needed to know if there was a general plan in motion or one random car following her.

A troublesome concern of magic filtered into Shay's mind. There were rumors all over the dark web of the cartels hiring necromancers, especially the cartels with members who worshipped Santa Muerte.

Shay could kill a man or woman with ease. She didn't know if she could take down a *zombie.*

"Motherfucking zombies."

Back in the states, the bounty hunters kept the worst

excesses of magic threats in check. Large cities in Mexico were also safe enough, but the rural cartel-controlled zones were their own empire where the rules were known to change and often involved dark magic.

Stay cool, Shay. No zombies driving the Cadillac. They tend to walk in groups at their prey.

A shudder passed through Shay despite the hot desert air.

She drove on for a few more blocks, making a sudden hard turn into a narrow street in the opposite direction of the airport. Leading mercenaries straight to the plane wasn't going to happen. The money she paid the pilot didn't include staying grounded in the face of oncoming cartel enforcers.

The Cadillac turned onto the street after her. *Not even trying to hide what you're doing.* Shay was relieved. Their arrogance was going to be easier to deal with than a well thought out plan. She could still make the plane on time.

"Not the first morons to underestimate me. Let's play…"

Shay slowed the vehicle and turned into a small dirt lot, waiting. The Cadillac pulled into the lot and slowed to a stop. All four doors opened, and three very large Mexican men in dark suits and sun glasses, stepped out, along with one tall, hulking woman. All of them wore holsters on their belt and were carrying automatic weapons.

At least they aren't zombies.

Shay didn't kill her engine. She opened her door and hopped out of the car, offering the group a smile.

"Can I help you?" she asked in Spanish. "I noticed your car following me." Her tone was calm and measured. If they had known her better, they would have recognized the warning and gotten back in the car. It was nothing personal. Shay was reverting to her old instincts in her former business. Take it all in as data. *Look for the kill moment.*

"You're gonna give us your Land Rover, bitch," one of the men said, patting the side of his holster.

"Who are *you* and why should I give you anything?"

He sneered. "We're from the Nuevo Gulf Cartel. You're in our territory without our permission. That makes us think you're trying to steal from us."

"I haven't stolen anything from the cartel."

"We're not very good at taking someone's word for anything, bitch."

Shay's gaze darted between each of the men. They'd already made a fatal miscalculation by not shooting when she first got out of the car. The only question she had left was whether they recognized who she was. That would present serious problems if she let them live.

"I don't know what you're talking about," she said. Her voice was still an icy calm, her eyes narrowing in the bright morning sunlight. "I was just hiking in the mountains. I didn't steal anything from the Nuevo Gulf."

"Lying will make all of this worse." The man glared at her, glancing back at the others in the group. A man with a bushy moustache hanging down past his chin gave him a subtle nod.

The leader of the group. Interesting. He's letting this mouth-piece speak for him to throw me off. Clever. Shay noticed the family resemblance between the leader and the large, muscular woman next to him. *Family that fights together. I can respect that.*

"You think you can run drugs in our territory without us knowing? Without our fucking permission?"

The man's voice came out in a low growl. "Turn over the truck and maybe you can leave this town alive." His finger moved toward the trigger as the others spread out, moving to her sides.

Now or never.

Killing four cartel members wasn't exactly on the checklist for keeping a low profile, but they were leaving her no choice. Well, *almost* no choice.

"Have it your way," Shay shouted in Spanish. Her hand had been resting on her belt, easily covering a sonic grenade that fit in the palm of her hand. She pulled it off her belt, dislodging the pin and threw it into the center of the group. The distance was just far enough that the blast knocked her back without taking her out.

It was all the time she needed.

The leader was down on the ground but already rolling over, his gun raised as Shay put a bullet in the side of his head, just above his ear. *One down.*

The woman let out an angry battle cry and pointed her gun. Shay picked her off as the next man's eyes widened in recognition. *Too bad. I was still on the fence about the last two. Not anymore.*

Shay kept her gun moving, taking a kill shot, no negotiations left. "Sorry, guys. I can't let the wrong people find out I'm still alive." She smashed their phones with the butt of her gun and removed the SD cards, ensuring the destruction of any surveillance photos. She carefully picked up any shell casings and the remains of the grenade leaving no evidence that might somehow tie back to her.

At the last moment she fired a bullet into the GPS in the Cadillac, making it harder for anyone to find the bodies any time soon.

Shay walked away satisfied, turning to give a wave to the crumpled figures as she headed back to her vehicle. "And I have a flight to catch." She left the bodies for the vultures and the beetles common to the desert to devour. By the time the cartel discovered whatever was left, Shay would be long gone

Not a bad day's work for a dead woman.

14

Shay got the gold transported back to the States and safely delivered without another hitch. She gave the pilot a bonus and went home to sleep, leaving Peyton a text that the mission was a success.

She turned the ringer off on her phone even as she saw the texts back from him asking for more details. *That will have to wait.*

She flipped her phone face down and passed out on her bed, grateful to be in air conditioning under a comforter on her specially-made mattress. Her reward for sleeping in a rental car.

It wasn't till the next morning before she got up and made herself go to Warehouse One and work out, running the circuit. It was tempting to cut it short but that's how tomb raiders ended up dead. She had seen how her training paid off in the desert.

After a shower and a feta and bacon omelet, she drove back to her condo and fired up the laptop as she waited for the news that the money was transferred.

Time to look for new digs. It was a promise she made to herself as soon as the bank account warranted the move. The condo was never meant to be a permanent location and wasn't secure enough to suit her. Too much foot traffic that could expose others to danger and made it easy for someone to notice too much just by walking by on the street.

She needed a place where she could shut the door and let down her guard at night. This wasn't it.

Her phone buzzed with an alert. The money was transferred. *I like this work. Will have to grab Peyton for pizza and finally answer all his questions.*

She looked back at her computer screen, scrolling through pictures of the same two-story brownstone she had found on Redfin before, checking to see if it was still available. It was on a quiet street abutting a commercial district that emptied out after business hours. It could be perfect.

Her phone rang on her end table and she snatched it up, answering on the first ring.

"Hello, Greg."

"I've transferred the money to your account, both the full fee and the bonus. We're both a lot richer today."

"Glad to hear it." Shay understood the need to doublecheck that she knew the project was completed to her satisfaction. "It's been a pleasure doing business with you."

"Before you go, there's something I wanted to talk to you about."

Shay looked away from the pictures of the renovated

kitchen and focused. She could smell a new opportunity a mile away.

"I'm listening."

Greg hesitated for moment before speaking. "From what I can tell, you're new at this business."

Shay felt a thin thread of anger pass through her chest. *Is this fucker about to complain?*

"I delivered your gold, didn't I?"

"Yes, you did, which means you not only have skills that a lot of other people only claim to have but you're a natural. Even gifted. I think we should meet to discuss some other opportunities."

"Why?"

"You're going to make a name for yourself, whether I'm involved or not. That's obvious. The projects you get will only get bigger from here. The whales will come looking for you at some point. I can help you get there faster in exchange for the occasional smaller job. I might not be as wealthy, but I've established a lot of connections in the search for my family's gold. Look, I'm more of a barracuda in this story. I'm the guy you come to for a six-figure payout. Nice for some, but you already scoffed at my initial twenty-five thousand dollar offer."

Shay let out a laugh. "Don't be offended. I took the job once we worked out the back end."

"No, I'm not offended. Part of doing well in life is having no illusions and playing in your lane. If you want the real payouts and the big jobs sooner rather than later, you'll need an introduction to the higher-end connections. People like Father O'Banion."

"Father O'Banion... A priest? Church types don't

normally like me. I'm pretty sure I would burst into flames if I stepped into a church."

Greg laughed hard. "The only church he belongs to is a church of his own making in the nearest bar. The title of *father* is just a nickname someone gave him a long time ago. He becomes Father O'Banion with a few drinks in him, and he becomes preachy. He can be a bit much to take sometimes. Actually, he's Doctor F.J. Smite-Williams. He has a day job as a professor of historical extra-dimensional engineering, and a rather sizeable side-business hiring people like you." The man cleared his throat. "He's the real deal and almost exclusively deals in high-end magical items. He's always on the lookout for skilled tomb raiders who can deal with *special circumstances.*"

Magical artifacts. That does carry a hefty payout. "You've piqued my interest. I'd be willing to meet this guy."

"I figure we can all meet and talk about it. I think I can get you a meeting if I pull a few strings."

Shay tucked a long strand of blonde hair behind her ear. "Send me the details of where and when. Keep in mind, I don't take orders from anyone. I decide what projects I'll take and work out the details myself."

"I'll keep that in mind as I pass things along."

"Good. Get me in touch with this Smite-Williams, and I'm sure I can find some sort of finder's fee to give to you after my first job assuming he's legit and you're not blowing smoke up my ass. I don't tend to take that very well, just so you know." Her tone took on an icy edge. She didn't know Greg Abbot well enough yet to be sure there wasn't some angle he was playing.

"I don't know if I should be concerned or amused by your bluntness."

Shay looked back at the pictures of the brownstone, already picturing herself living there. A smile came across her face. "Depends on your agenda."

Greg laughed. "Okay, then amused."

"That works. Set up the meeting and let me know." Shay hung up and took a deep breath as she called the number on the listing.

"Hello, I'm calling about the brownstone on Mercer Street. Is it still available?"

Can a former paid killer have her own piece of happily ever after?

Shay shook her head and patted her cheeks. The past didn't mean shit. Stay in the present moment. *Only thing I can control.* "Yes, that's the one. I'll take it at list price, all cash if you can close in a week." She was moving up in the world. If this Smite-Williams was half of what Greg claimed, then she was about to make her reputation in cement as the most badass tomb raider on the planet. At least her alias was...

Bet the guy asks me to find the fucking Nazi pin first. Shay snorted at the idea. *At least I know where it is.*

Shay unleashed a series of vicious jabs into the face of her opponent, a man who had a good forty pounds on her. She took a detour to Steel Gloves, a boxing gym she sometimes hit up when she wanted an opponent not filled with sawdust. She had sent Peyton enough details to satisfy his immediate curiosity. The rest could wait a little longer.

She needed to work off some of the adrenaline. Too much good news could rattle her cage. There was something that came with training with a live opponent that steadied her nerves.

Her target grunted and stumbled back. He let out a little growl and brought up his gloves.

"Warned you I hit hard," Shay said, barely intelligible from the blue mouth guard in the way. "Also mentioned you would regret sparring with me." She was wearing tight black Lycra shorts and a black sports bra with her long brown hair pulled back in a mound of hair. Her muscles outlined along her legs and down her back as she bounced lightly back and forth in front of him, her skin covered in a sheen of sweat.

The man spit out a trickle of blood. "I've been holding back because you're a chick, but you're starting to piss me off."

"Don't hold back then. You know what they say. Practice like you play."

The man narrowed his eyes. "You asked for it. You better not bitch when I hit you in your pretty face."

"Beauty's a weapon, just like anything else." Shay winked. "Not my fault you're so vulnerable to it."

"You should learn that a few lucky hits and some trash talking ain't the same thing as being good at boxing."

"Are you gonna just keep blathering at me until I fall asleep? Is that your strategy?"

The man grunted and threw a right jab, quickly followed by a left uppercut. Shay ducked just in time to miss the last punch as it grazed the top of her head. She always appreciated a close call. Made the work out worth it. She put up her gloves just in time to block a jab and stepped back to regroup.

"Maybe you should wear some glasses when you fight," she said. "Because I don't know who the fuck you're trying to hit."

Her opponent let out a laugh despite the determined look on his face and centered himself as he shook it off.

He narrowed his eyes and took a step forward.

There's the tell. Shay watched for the flicker of muscle and saw it coming as he unleashed a series of moves, barely missing her as she stayed just out of reach, like a well-choreographed dance.

"Little lady is running you all over the ring." An old man leaned on the bottom rope on the sideline, smiling at them. A few of his front teeth were missing and his left ear was in the shape of a piece of cauliflower.

Shay laughed and hunched her shoulders, throwing a hook with her lead hand, pulling back at the last moment and connecting with a cross from her left. Her opponent recovered quickly and landed a blow to her midsection, knocking the wind out of her even as she took in small sips of air to stay alert and on her feet. That just made the fight more interesting for her.

Shay feinted to the side, and the man brought up his gloves, prepared to take the expected blow. Instead, she slammed two quick punches into the side of his head, leaving the man stumbling backward, his gloves raised, covering his face.

She followed up with a solid blow to his midsection, returning the favor.

He fell back hard, landing with a thud on his tailbone as the old man standing outside of the ring let out a whoop and rang the bell.

"Leave some for the next guy, little lady." He smiled, his tongue darting between the space in his teeth, licking his lips.

Shay offered a hand to the fallen boxer and helped him to a standing position.

"Good fight," she said, knocking gloves with him when he regained his feet.

"You've got some talent. Gotta give you your props. Look for me next time you're in here. I'll be ready for you."

"Deal."

"Haven't seen you around in a couple weeks, girl," said a familiar woman's voice from the side of the ring. "I see you're still kicking ass and taking names."

Shay turned around to find Bella standing on the floor just behind the ropes, still dressed in her street clothes. A tight suit that managed to look conservative while still hugging her curves. *She's got to be with the government.* Shay had sparred with the blonde woman a few times, impressed by her skills.

Their first bout, Shay was taken off-guard making the same mistake her last opponent made about her. She thought the attractive woman was just in the gym to play at fighting, but she quickly found out Bella could land a solid punch and was there to win. The blonde might lack the murderous intensity of Shay, but it wasn't like she needed to kill people from time to time.

Fuck. I'm lying about just being an archaeology professor. Maybe that office she keeps referring to is the CIA.

"Hey, Bella. I've been busy with work. Hasn't been much time to swing by this place."

"Busy with work?"

"Yeah. The pots won't dig themselves out of the ground, and no one's invented a good archaeology drone yet. Only as good as your last big find at the university."

Bella laughed softly. "Can't work all the time, girl. You should go slap your department head around to get him to give you more time off. Don't you have a union or something?"

"Not so far." Shay picked up her towel from her starting corner of the ring and wiped her forehead, smiling. "I like my job. Makes it hard to know when it's time to take a break."

"Still doesn't mean you don't need to decompress every now and then and have some fun." Bella picked up her gym bag and held the top rope for Shay. "That's why you come to places like this, right?"

Shay stepped through the ropes and dropped to the floor. "Maybe this is my idea of fun."

"This is work. Fun but still work. You'll know it's fun when you're not there to get anything else out of it." Bella gently bit her bottom lip. "You have any plans tonight? A few friends of mine are going out dancing."

"Can't say that I... dance much."

Bella held up a hand. "Those of us with men aren't bringing them. It's just gonna be a chill girl's night. We all dance in a sloppy mash up. You'll love it, I promise."

Shay furrowed her brow. "I don't know."

"Come on. Dancing is a lot like boxing, just with less punching." Bella smiled. "Think of it as an extra workout if that gets you there."

"The punching's the fun part." Shay grinned as she slipped off the gloves and unwound the cotton around her hands.

Bella laughed. "Will you still come? Just give it a chance. If you don't like it, I'll never ask again."

Shay stared at the other woman, pursing her lips while considering her options. Bella had managed to surprise her again.

Hanging out with her made perfect sense and would give her another chance to practice her cover story. The last time had too many hiccups. Hell, just going out was taking as much preparation as the Mexico job.

Time to stop being such a chickenshit about the regular life crap. You said you wanted your own crowd to run around town with. Suck it up and do something normal-ish.

"Okay, Bella. I'm in."

15

Shay had made her next stop Warehouse Two, pizza in hand to fill in Peyton who was calmer than she had expected and was busy looking for the next job.

He turned the tables on her and told her, "Leave the pizza. I'll eat it while I work."

She smiled in admiration even as he bent down from where he was standing to look at the multiple screens he had set up in the office.

"Hey, are those new?" Shay looked at the equipment, turning around in the room.

"Yeah, another alias ordered it all and paid with a new credit card. Don't worry, none of it can be traced back to this location and I figured you would pay it off before the month was out." He looked back at her as he opened the box and smiled as the warm smell of pizza wafted up to him. "All necessary, trust me."

Shit, I actually do. "You really don't want to know more about what happened in Mexico?"

Peyton talked through a mouthful of pizza, grease dribbling down his chin. "You found the gold, killed off a few more cartel members. That was a bonus favor to society. Got the whole load back to the states and delivered it safe and sound to our client who paid us handsomely. I'm using the royal *us*, of course."

"Of course." Shay smiled and looked at her only office help. *Okay, crazy clothes but still... there's some street smarts in there somewhere. I can work with this.*

"What are you still doing here? Didn't you say you had somewhere else to be?"

Shay let out a laugh and threw up her hands. "Okay then... I'll leave you to it. Enjoy your pizza."

Shay stood back, moving in front of the mirror in her bedroom as she pulled a simple black dress from her closet. *This will have to do.*

Burning down her house and faking her own death took a large bite out of her wardrobe. All that was left was what fit in a compact go bag. There wasn't much left to choose from for a girl's night at a club.

"Need to go on a shopping spree soon," she muttered to herself. "Could even ask Bella to come along. Make a day of it." She held the dress up in front of her with one hand, holding her hair up with the other.

Shay was far too practical to mourn the loss of a wardrobe, even if every stitch was high end. Didn't hurt that having a versatile, good quality wardrobe made it that much easier in her old line of work.

Getting close to a target was often necessary, and a good killer could infiltrate any sort of environment with the proper clothes, especially when a *killer* body like hers met up with the right clothes.

Wonder if I can write those clothes off on my taxes.

Shay pulled out her only other choice. A low-cut red strapless number. She held both up in front of her body.

"Hmmm… Going with the black. Save the red for when there's a man involved." She hung the red dress back up and slipped into the black number, reaching back to pull up the wide zipper.

Her shoe collection had suffered the same fate as the rest of her clothes, but she had taken that more personally and didn't waste any time when she hit Los Angeles. There were already a few selections of heels from shops in Beverly Hills that neatly lined up alongside her dozen pairs of workout shoes.

"These will do." She pulled out a pale violet pair of Tamara Mellon suede pumps with an ankle strap and slipped them on, turning in the mirror to get a better look.

She glanced over at the bedside clock.

"Loose curls will have to do." She ran her fingers through her hair and leaned closer to the mirror as she picked up a lipstick, checking the color before she pressed it against her lips.

Her phone buzzed from the bed, and she hurried, setting the dress and shoes next to it.

Peyton had texted her.

I've got a line on a good job that I think will be right up your alley.

Shay picked up the phone to text back.

I'm in the middle of some shit tonight. Is the job time sensitive?

Right, your night with normies. Nope, it can wait. This one's been sitting around for a while. A long while.

I'll stop by tomorrow, and we'll chat.

Okay. See you then. Pack a toothbrush, just in case.

Peyton ended the text message with a flamingo emoji. Even his emojis had a flashback yuppy flare.

Alright, then. I have a girl's night to get to.

Shay stared down at the phone. *Dancing with friends. Fuck... It's so normal.* The last time she went dancing it ended with three dead men and a cake blown up by a grenade. She felt worse about the cake.

So, this is change, huh? Okay, bring it.

Shay grew more excited as the Spider got closer to the club. She had the windows down, the wind blowing through the car. Her nerves kicked in as she turned onto the boulevard where the club was located.

I'm nervous about a night out dancing. That is a little fucked up.

Unlike hanging with Terry and Lisa, Shay actually gave a shit about keeping Bella as a friend. She liked the woman and saw her in one of her favorite haunts. The boxing gym. If the night ended up a disaster, it would complicate things and damage one of the few friendships she had made on the west coast.

"You can keep your shit together for one night." She turned the radio up louder, singing along.

The light in front of her car turned red, and she rolled to a stop, drumming her fingers along the wheel.

Happiness was something Shay couldn't say she'd ever experienced for any lengthy amount of time. Satisfaction at a job well executed, sure, but not much that looked like middle-class happiness. Go to a job where gossip or a layoff was the biggest danger. Go home, make dinner, watch Netflix.

Normal was as foreign a lifestyle as Oriceran magic to her.

Shay had escaped her old life on the East coast and embarked on a new career, one that was actually gaining traction. *Maybe this will be my version of happy.* She sang the chorus louder, ignoring the packed minivan next to her with kids in the back, their noses pressed against the window, smiling and pointing at her.

Shay gunned the engine as the light turned green, pressing her foot down on the accelerator as the kids cheered. She laughed as she looked in the rear-view mirror.

We all have our skeletons in our closets. I have an entire vault filled with them. Maybe a few zombies and vampires in there, too. Yeah, my version of happy may not look like anyone else's.

The club appeared, its bright neon façade almost blinding. Shay turned off the street and pulled into the parking lot and carefully maneuvered down the rows to an open spot.

She killed the engine and hopped out of her Spider and headed toward the club. She spotted Bella and two other women standing near the edge of the parking lot, a pale brunette and a woman with warm, dark skin and short hair styled into a curl along each high cheekbone. Both were stunners, model beautiful really, just like Bella, or for that matter, Shay.

She hurried toward the trio, waving. "Sorry if I'm late."

Bella smiled. "You're fine." She motioned to her friends. "Shay, this is Kara and Janelle."

Shay stuck her hand out to shake Kara's hand. "Nice to meet you."

"You're a hot one, aren't you?" Kara said, laughing. "Stay away from any boyfriends I snag until I've had my fun."

Shay held her clutch in front of her. She could feel the small outline of a switchblade. She never went anywhere completely unprepared. "We can divvy them up. Divide and conquer."

Janelle put out her hand to shake. "I can be the wingman tonight. My Darius is too fine to even be flirting with some other dude."

Kara and Bella laughed as Shay felt a wave of relief come over her. So far, so good.

Janelle looked Shay up and down. "Love your shoes! Bella tells me you're an archaeologist. That's cool. I've never met someone who can dress like that and go dig in the dirt."

"Yeah, all it takes is the right equipment." Shay put her hands on her hips as Janelle gave her a thumbs up.

"I like your attitude," said Kara.

"It's just a j-o-b."

"Girl, you're finding out the truth of our past." Janelle batted the air in front of her. "All the magic nonsense out there, I bet you're learning all sorts of things that would keep me staring at the ceiling at night. Finding all sorts of things, too."

"I can... work on the edge of things at times."

Janelle nodded and clucked a noise of approval. "You just keep doing what you're doing, and we'll help you find a good man to chat up tonight." Janelle put her hands over her head and swayed her hips to music only she could hear.

Shay grinned. She already liked them. She had her cover story ready. All of the details already worked out. One background for her life in the warehouses, another out in the world. This could work.

Bella nodded toward the club. "Let's head inside and have some fun."

The four turned as a unit and strolled to the club, ready to dance their asses off.

The heavy bass was sending a steady hum through Shay's cheeks. The roar of the techno music rendered any attempts at conversation futile. Lights changed directions overhead, their colors shifting in kaleidoscopic madness. Everything about the place defined too busy, too loud, and too crowded.

Shay *loved* every fucking second of it.

Their tight little pack of women were jumping up and down to the beat of the music, their hands in the air. Men danced closer to them, gyrating with the beat of the music and moving away just as quickly.

Bella, Kara, and Janelle bounced and moved in time with the beat. Shay hadn't lied to Bella. She'd been dancing before, but it'd been a long time since it was just for fun and not part of a scheme to get closer to a mark. Dancing with abandon, without worrying about the night ending in her strangling someone, or shooting them, or drowning a target in a toilet was giving her the feeling of a glorious release.

Fuck. How many guys have I drowned in toilets? She put her hands on the shoulders of a man who came right to her eye-level, putting her head back and closing her eyes as she danced with abandon. She let go and opened her eyes, grabbing Bella's hand and twirling in a circle under the flashing lights.

Friends. These women could be her friends for this part of her life. They could never know the truth of the other half of her life. No matter.

Most people's idea of relaxation involved not talking about work. Shay could have a normal little crew to chat about normal little things like Tamara Mellon shoes or where to find the best pizza, and not cartels or cursed gold.

Of course, if they ever did need to know the best kind of sniper rifle to use in a windy environment or the best angle to hold a head in the toilet with minimal splashing, Shay had it covered.

Shay burst out laughing, the sound swallowed in the wall of music.

The other women grabbed the hand closest to them, making sure to include Shay, forming their own circle, still moving in time with the music.

I could almost forget there is another life... Almost. Fuck... I love it all. So, shoot me.

16

The next morning Shay stepped out of her car inside Warehouse Two, leaning over to get a better look in her side mirror. Dancing and cutting loose had put her in the mood for a change. She had stopped by an all-night CVS and picked up a box of L'Oreal 4G Dark Golden Brown. The second she hit the door of her condo, she was heading up the stairs to take a long hot shower, washing sweat from the dance floor and brown hair dye down the drain.

"Bye bye, Blondie." The light from the windows above was playing nicely on the new color on her head. "I think I might like being different people all at once."

Shay took in a deep, contented breath and suddenly stood up straight, her hair forgotten. A familiar but unexpected smell struck her nose. The heavy scent of bacon. A delicious coffee aroma hung in the air as well. That wasn't all that unusual, but it didn't smell like the coffee she purchased for Warehouse Two.

Shay took a few steps away from her Spider before she

realized different coffee and bacon aromas weren't the only differences. A small electric stove rested near the office, which was separated with the help of a few low cubicle walls. Several of the crates were also moved away from the office area into the corner.

A maze of the interconnecting walls were erected on either side. It looked like the office had sprung to life and was spreading out tentacles like an invasive species.

"Someone's been busy."

Paintings hung on the walls in the cubicle area, mostly graphic art from local artists. A drawing of a Betty Boop character with an arrow through her heart and safety pins in her lip got a smile out of Shay. Art with a sense of humor. Another was a pen and ink with a large arm rising out of the ground, resting on the roof of a rundown wooden church. Next to it was a fiery painting with men wielding swords. Shay recognized it as Oriceran's version of their own history.

Peyton emerged from the office, a cup of coffee in hand and piece of bacon hanging out of his mouth. He was wearing lime green pants and a white soft collar shirt with matching green piping along the edges with white sneakers. "Hey, Shay," he mumbled around the bacon. "Nice morning, isn't it?"

"You've been… busy this last couple of days. None of this was here yesterday."

He chewed the last of the bacon, working it into his mouth, and swallowed. "It was here, still stuffed in boxes. Figure if I'm going to have to live here for a while, I might as well make it more comfortable. Gave it a little West Coast flavor."

Shay surveyed the rest of the room, looking for more changes, but most of it was confined to the area near the office. "And you had all this stuff delivered nearby?"

"Well, some. I went to get some of it." He tapped his foot, giving away his nerves at spilling the story. "Probably should invest in my own car. I rented a van to haul the cubicle walls."

"And did you stop by a dealer to buy some marijuana and Oriceran dust before that?"

"Very funny. I don't do drugs, Earth plants or Oriceran." A defiant look passed over his face.

Shay stared at him, silently glad he was showing some backbone. "Well, if you're not high, then are you fucking insane?"

Peyton snorted. "I'm not your hamster, Shay. I go out."

"This is more than *going out*. You're supposed to be keeping a low profile. Going on a shopping spree dressed like a traffic signal isn't keeping a low profile."

"Oh, yeah, because so many hitmen hang out at office supply stores and local art studios." Peyton rolled his eyes and took a sip of his coffee.

Shay narrowed her eyes, studying him. "You never know."

"You took me out for pizza just the other day. So, what, I can go out if it's for pizza, but not for cubicle walls?"

"I was with you. If you're with me, I guarantee that I'm taking precautions even if I'm not telling you. I made sure not to drive directly to or from the pizza place to throw off anyone. Did you take similar tactics?"

Peyton blinked. "Is that why you did that? I kind of just thought you were lost, but I didn't want to piss you off by asking." He held up a hand. "I'm not a total dumbass. It's not like I called a Lyft over here to the warehouse. I hiked at least a mile away from this place in a zigzag pattern, and went old school, flagging down a cab to take me to a rental place. Paid with your new alias' credit card."

"That card has to be warm to the touch."

Peyton rolled his eyes and wandered back to his desk and the plate of bacon resting there. He picked up a piece, chewing and talking all at once. "I've made tons of fake identities for both of us, so nothing to link back here, and I'm using cryptocurrencies to fund prepaid cards, and using those to make payments. There's no way to trace things. It's like a ghost went on a shopping spree."

"Did you drive the same way back that you came?"

"No." His face flushed red.

"What are you not telling me?"

"I didn't drive the same way back that I started out because I kept getting lost."

"You were holding a phone."

Peyton shrugged. "Too caught up in the adventure."

"Your inconsistent attention to detail is a little disturbing." She blew out a breath and crossed her arms.

"Is this the part where you threaten to kill me or something?" Peyton asked.

"Not yet." Shay pointed at him, picking up a new separate hard drive and looking at the new curved key board. "Keep your outside trips to a minimum. If you need a bunch of shit, just tell me, and I can get it. All it takes is one mistake, and you're dead, but this time no take backs." She shook her head. "Seriously, if you like breathing, you need to keep your playtime to when I'm with you. I know how to case places ahead of time. Choose the ones where there won't be trouble."

Peyton tipped his cup and drained the last of the coffee. He shrugged, not looking at Shay, as he poured more into his cup, pouring a cup for Shay, too. The gesture didn't go unnoticed.

"So, teach me," he said, handing her the cup. "This is looking more and more like a long-term relationship. Not my norm, by the way. Teach me what I need to know to stay above ground."

"That can be arranged but it'll take time." Shay gestured around the large open area behind the office. "Besides, you shouldn't mess with perfection."

"A bunch of crates and shelves is perfection?" He narrowed his eyes and took a step closer to Shay. "Wait. Weren't you blonde? So much for not messing with perfection."

"Thank you, *and* I've been a lot of things." Shay reached up and ran a hand through her chestnut brown hair. She dyed it as a way to celebrate starting a new chapter of life with her friends. Closer to her natural color, anyway.

Shay spotted a couple of folding chairs in a cubicle room around a small table and an eighteen-inch TV on top of a mini-fridge. "What's this, your make-shift break room?"

"It's my living room." Peyton grinned, sweeping his arm to the side in a fair imitation of Vanna White.

She slipped into one of the chairs. "These chairs suck ass. Pick out some nicer ones, and I'll get them here."

Peyton's face brightened. "Thank you," he said, hugging

her tight, even as Shay peeled him off of her. "When you sit as much as I do, a quality chair is a must."

Shay raised an eyebrow, aware her schedule was slipping away. "I can imagine. Tell me about the new job."

Peyton's face fell. "The client suddenly wrote and said he was no longer interested. No explanation."

"Huh… Don't get too worked up. That shit used to happen to me all the time when I was a hired killer."

"People got cold feet about paying to have someone murdered? Big surprise."

Shay shrugged, sipping the coffee. "Damn, that's good. Greg Abbot may hook me up with some power players, so things will work out. They always do."

Peyton cleared his throat and looked away from Shay. "About your business… I have something else that might be handy."

"Go ahead and tell me. If it's useful, I'll give it a spin."

Peyton forced himself to look at Shay, staring at her forehead, avoiding eye contact. "I haven't been completely honest with you."

Shay snickered. "Then you're not a total fucking idiot. But go on."

"I've just been thinking that if you're going to start getting more into magical artifacts, that I could maybe help with that. And, you know, that seems to kind of be the business model you've been bragging about."

"Don't drag it out. I've shot people just to get them to cut that out. How can you help me?" Shay narrowed her eyes. "You can do magic?"

Peyton shook his head. "I wish, but no, not without an artifact at least, but I've studied a lot of magic. Folklore and legends, along with more modern extra-dimensional engineering stuff." He went and sat down behind his desk, typing away on the new keyboard, pulling up different images on the screens. "It's like you and history. I find it fascinating." He pointed at the screen. "Magic is like any other system. Instead of hacking a computer, people are hacking reality."

Shay stared at him for a moment, taking in the rapid-fire images he was showing her of different experiments people were posting online. *Useful. That's what he wants to be*. His face screamed it.

"That's all interesting. Why do I care? You know me, Peyton. I'm all about the practical. If you can do something for me, I'm happy to hear it."

Peyton rubbed the back of his neck. "You have to understand that when I was growing up, I was drowning in all that privilege. It's not like I wasn't aware I was suffering. It's why I tried to carve out my own path."

"Not a bad thing."

"Yeah, if you come from a family willing to smother you in your sleep, better figure out how to go it alone."

"You do believe the hit came from your family…"

"Not important," he said, waving it away, his voice barely above a whisper. He lifted his old money, square chin and shook it off. "That's where I think I can help you *and* myself."

Shay furrowed her brow but didn't say anything. Let him finish, it's his moment.

"I'm not a specialist on general history, but I am a specialist on magical history. I can help you find the good artifacts. Sort through the cooked history books and not just by doing some data filtering. I can help you see how magic makes the pieces all fit together. How you can even use magic on your assignments."

"The research help I can use. As for the magic... we'll see. I've gotten this far without any magic broomsticks, despite the rumors back East that I used one." Shay sat on the edge of the desk. "I can get you more involved. Lend you a few select books from my library warehouse."

"You have a library warehouse?"

"Warehouse Four. Pretty damned secure and the address will remain that way."

"You didn't take me there because you wanted a fallback?"

"Fallbacks. There's more warehouses. And those books are pretty valuable."

"More valuable than my life? Ouch."

Shay winked. "Really valuable."

"I think this could be the start of building my own legacy. Even if dear old dad comes out of his coma and can do more than drool, I need something that's my own. Something untouchable by my family, so I can be set loose on the world again and not have to spend the rest of my life hiding."

"Who do you think is more likely to have paid for the hit? Your brother or your sister?"

"My vote's gonna go for Randy and not my sister, even if they both don't like me." His face twitched.

"And why do you say that?" Shay leaned forward, staring at Peyton.

He rubbed his hands together, pursing his lips. *He's hiding something. Shit.*

"Spill it, Tech-Still-Letting-You-Live-Man," snapped Shay. Concealing his knowledge of magical history was one thing, but she could sense something far more serious.

"Least favorite nickname so far, just saying. Don't shoot the tech guy but I've been... using some of my well-honed computer skills to stalk my family from afar. I've been tracing their activities." He wrinkled his forehead, clapping his hands together in resignation. "Randy's movements and activities are a lot shadier than my sister's. I found several suspicious payments the day after you iced me. I'll give him credit, they were in different accounts, different amounts, for different things, but all on the same day, and all just conveniently happened to add up to the amount you were paid for my death." He picked at a scratch on the top of the desk. "Makes it a *little* hard to refute."

Shay rubbed a hand over her face. *Having an inner circle is fucking hard. No wonder it's taken me this long.* "Talk about your lame ideas. You're *good*, Peyton, but you're *not* perfect. Whether it's your whole family or just your slick brother, they might still be looking for you. Don't you think that poking around them in hackerland could end up being a big-ass flare saying you're still alive?"

Peyton put up his hands. "I know, I know. But I needed to confirm things. Still family... What you said before, I didn't want to believe it without some proof, but now I can see that you're probably right. I'll be more careful in the future."

Shay leaned over and poked him in the chest, her voice dropping to an icy whisper more for show than anything else. She needed to get her point across and have it last. "Next time you tell me right away. If your ass gets fried, it puts my fine ass in the crosshairs." She punctuated her sentence with a glare, but she couldn't blame him for wanting to confirm the truth. Maybe now that he saw the evidence for himself it'd help him adjust better to his new life.

Peyton stumbled over his words. "I'm sorry. I really am."

"Just don't let it happen again. I'd hate to dispose of a useful asset."

The man's eyes widened, and his skin grew pale as he held very still.

Don't worry, Peyton Coolidge. I'm not gonna kill you if I have any other choice. Your job is to keep giving me choices.

"We should go get tacos."

"I'm still afraid to move."

Shay smiled, turning her head away for a moment. It was too much. "Peyton, relax. I don't kill where I live, if I can avoid it."

She got up to walk toward her car with Peyton right behind her, jabbing his finger in the air.

"See, it's those loopholes you leave yourself that make the tiny hairs on my neck stand up. You either have a great poker face, Shay Carson, or I'm one foot away from a spring-loaded trap that I'm not seeing."

Shay opened her door and slid down into the leather seat. "Stick around long enough. You're bound to figure it out."

Peyton opened the passenger side door. "That's humor, right?" He shook his head. "I guess I'm sticking around long enough to see which way this goes. Clearly, I have issues with knowing when to leave."

Later that evening, long after Shay had driven out of Warehouse Two, Peyton eyed the various equipment lying on the table in front of him, jammers mostly. The more he could prove himself to Shay, the more she would let him into her business. The more he would learn how to roam the streets without giving himself away.

Her look from earlier in the day still made his stomach tighten.

That woman has killed more people than most Navy SEALs. I can't tell if she's fucking with me half the time, or if she'll put me down without even blinking. "Hell, she was friends with her own dead stand-in."

Peyton groaned as he ran his hand through his hair, turning around, slowly figuring out where to start. He thought he understood what it meant to deal with dangerous people when he traded information in the underworld, but Shay was a whole new level of fearsome. A vicious killer in a pretty package who could crack a joke and eat junk food.

Hard to get a take on her.

On some days she passed for normal, even fun, but on others he felt like if he said the wrong thing she might slit his throat and crack a joke about him needing a cough drop.

He snapped his fingers and ran to the keyboard. Anything to do with technology got his mind working. "I can check my research spiders."

Doing background checks on potential clients was one of the easier ways he could help Shay. But running their names through a few forums or websites wasn't thorough enough. A mild dose of hacking some of their systems could help prove they were who they said they were and help keep down the surprises for Shay on the job.

Peyton pulled his chair closer to him with his foot, still typing as fast as he could as he fell backward into the seat. He stifled a yawn as he watched the information flow across the screens. An alert window popped up with a sharp *beep*. His eyes widened in surprise.

"Fuck, fuck, fuck." His hands flew over the keyboard.

The problem with looking for someone is sometimes they look back. Someone was *counterhacking* and had already traced back through half of his proxy servers.

He had used an automated code he designed that crawled like spiders through both the crowded webs, light and dark. They were programmed to search for potential doors and holes that he could exploit. One of them had caught hostile attention.

Just killing his spiders wasn't good enough at this point. The hacker was tracing their path too effectively. He needed to lay down a false trail.

"Please don't let this end with a bunch of guys blowing in through the door with machine guns." Spit flew as he did his best to focus.

Sweat formed on his forehead as he typed faster, alerts beeping on his computer as the trace pushed through even more of his proxy servers.

"Come on, come on. I can do this shit. Shay may be a badass killer and tomb raider, but I'm a badass hacker."

With only two proxy servers left, mere inches in hacker worlds, Peyton laid down a false trail leading to the computer system of the Eastern Kalama Church of New Eden. It was a cult that sprung up after the truth of Oriceran's existence and spent their time yelling from street corners that everyone was going to hell. Magic was proof of it.

"Who knows? Maybe they'll get a visit from an angry Wizard, proving their point. Everybody wins."

Peyton took in and let out several deep breaths. He slapped the top of his head.

"That was *too* close. Shay will waste my ass if she finds out I almost led someone right to one of her warehouses. Fuck, I need to get out of here for an hour and relax. I've been alone so long I'm talking to myself and my only companion is a retired killer."

Peyton pushed out of his chair. After what he'd just gone through, grabbing a quick bite to eat didn't seem that dangerous. He patted his belly. "Food, you are my only comfort."

Peyton sat on the leather-topped metal stool, slowly chewing, wondering if cardboard was one of the ingredients. The place was mostly empty except for a couple of drunk bros, taking turns eating, going back over the details of their night and punching each other in the arm.

Peyton looked back down at the paper plate in front of him.

How the fuck does someone screw up pizza?

He swallowed the disappointing bite and felt his tongue. *I think it's going numb.*

Maybe the name itself should have been a clue. Pasadena's Best's Pizza, neatly tucked into downtown Los Angeles.

I've had crap out of vending machines better than this. "Excuse me." He stopped a tired waitress slowly cleaning the counter. "Do you have a vending machine here? You do?"

"It's usually empty."

Peyton blinked, staring back at her bored face. He rose and followed the direction she was pointing in, finding the machine back by the bathroom. Nothing but lifesavers. "Who still eats lifesavers," he muttered. He leaned his head against the glass and felt it slip down. The front was covered in a film of old grease.

His stomach lurched as he grabbed at small, folded white napkins, partially used from a nearby table and rubbed them hard against this skin.

"Try the Hawaiian. Tastes the most like food." An old man with long, stringy hair was standing behind Peyton with his hand out.

"You want me to pay you for your help?"

"No, I want money. Seemed kind of obvious to me."

He smelled like old sweat and grease and his thin body was in oversized jeans and a faded flannel shirt. Peyton dug out a five-dollar bill and gave it to him.

"The Hawaiian, you won't regret it... well, as much." He picked something out of his teeth, flicking it onto the ground.

"Really? Was that necessary?"

The old man shrugged and turned to go, lifting a hand

to wave. Peyton shook his head, waving back. "My first friend outside of the warehouse. Forgot to get his name."

He watched the old man walk out to the parking lot and turn toward the What-A-Burger. "Well played, old dude. Well played."

He walked back to the waitress and slapped another five-dollar bill on the counter. "I'm feeling lucky tonight. Something has to go right. I'll take a slice of that Hawaiian on my friend's recommendation."

The bored teenager standing behind the cash register gave him a quick nod. "I already closed the cash register. Can't take any more cash tonight."

"Seriously, how are you still open?" Peyton swiped his phone over the pay panel, grateful to one of his many, many aliases for paying for the food.

The teen pulled two limp slices out of the warmer and placed them on a single plate. She shoved the plate toward him and delivered the restaurant's catch phrase in a complete monotone, "Please enjoy another slice of the best pizza in Pasadena."

"Usually I love irony."

The teenager gave Peyton a blank look and turned to get a key on a long wooden stick with the word, Men's written in black magic marker. She handed it to Peyton and went and sat down, pulling out his phone.

"Is this some kind of friendly warning?" The kid didn't even look up as Peyton returned to his table carrying the stick and the slice of pizza.

Come on. I can find a slice of pizza to eat. It can't be that hard.
Peyton munched down and let out a sharp laugh.

"Tastes like food!" He waved to the teenager who looked up, rolling his eyes. An actual flavor... He swallowed, biting off another large bite. As he got to the last bite, his stomach rumbled, and he felt a gurgle in his throat.

"Truth in advertising. Respect." He pressed on his belly with his hand and grabbed the key, getting up to head to the bathroom. The waitress looked up and smiled at him.

"Finding good pizza is more of a secret skill than I realized."

"Tell me about it. I bring my dinner with me. Hot Pocket." She leaned against the counter and tilted her head, watching Peyton make a beeline past the vending machine.

17

S hay pushed the glass door, stepping into A.J.'s Kitchen. Greg Abbot had sent a text requesting a meeting, and this place was far enough away from any critical locations and still served decent food. That mattered to Shay.

She spotted Greg in a corner booth and walked over to him, taking quick looks from left to right looking for immediate threats. It was L.A., so of course there were a few people who looked shady, but no one who looked like professional trouble.

Shay slid into a seat across from Greg. "Hey, did I keep you waiting."

"Good afternoon, Shay. No, I got here early. Gives me the lay of the land. Nervous habit. Appreciate you coming so quickly at the last minute."

Shay grinned, placing her hands on the table. "The promise of money can get me moving pretty damned quickly."

"There's a potential client for you. He's big money. A million is on the table for delivery."

"That sounds very good to me."

"You'll have to really want this one."

Shay drummed her pale pink fingernails on the white Formica top. "As opposed to what? I'm a tomb raider. I take jobs. Why would I have to *want* it? I take jobs to find shit. I find the shit. I get paid. Pretty simple. I like simple." She rolled her eyes. "I'm not an LA actor. I'm not finding lost objects, so I can write a book about it."

"You don't understand." Greg leaned across the table. "There are some complications that make this a lot more difficult than the Dutchman gold."

"Complications? Worse than gold being stuck in the middle of cartel country?"

The older man nodded. "Those criminals didn't know about the gold. There are some rough characters interested in the same job. They're working for a rival client and they are closing in. If you take the job, you're going to have to deal with them. It's not a question of *if*..."

Shay tapped her foot under the table, doing her best to contain the sliver of anger. "It's nice that you care but I can take care of myself. You're not going to bring me jobs with caveats all the time, are you? That'll get old. No, wait... got old."

Greg glanced up at the waitress as she put down two glasses of water. He took a sip and chewed on a piece of ice.

Shay did a short count. One Mississippi, two Mississippi, three Mississippi. People skills when you wanted someone to live still weren't her strong suit. She took a deep breath and let it out, narrowing her eyes. "I'll start again. No one becomes a tomb raider if danger bothers them. I've already almost died a few different ways."

She smiled and waited for him to say something. *He doesn't know your resume. Let it go.*

"You're sure?" Greg said, uncertainty lingering on his face.

The waitress stopped at the table to take their orders. Shay ordered jalapeno cheese grits, and Greg ordered a grilled cheese and bacon sandwich. "Hold the tomato, and can you put mayo on one side?"

"You have to be from the South."

"Hard to hide sometimes," said Greg, smiling more easily. "What about you? Cheese grits..."

"Picked it up on a trip. I've lived all over, never for very long."

"Holler if you need anything else." The waitress stepped back, her pad resting on her hip as she turned and went to the next table clearing dishes.

"I want the job. More importantly I want the million dollars," Shay said in a low voice. "The job's kind of a requirement for that."

Greg took a deep breath and reached into his pants pocket. He pulled out a small piece of paper and slid it across the table to Shay.

"That's the client's contact info. Since you're going to take the job, I'll try and do what I can on my end to encourage him to hire you."

"Thanks, Greg. This one's on me. After all, I'm about to get a lot richer."

"That's not a lot of details so far," Peyton said over the phone.

Shay glanced in her side and rearview mirrors to make sure she wasn't being followed before purposefully taking a wrong turn. Going back to the warehouse from a meeting required extra security protocols.

"The million dollars is the detail I care about."

"Even though Abbot is trying to warn you off?"

"He led me to it. I'll go in prepared. That tends to make things less dangerous. I'm not worried about that kind of danger."

Shay narrowed her eyes as she passed a pizza place she didn't recognize.

How the hell did I miss that? Or are they just new?

"Okay, what's the play now?" Peyton asked.

"I've got the client's contact information, but I want you to set up a way to contact him online and exchange information that can't be traced back to me."

Peyton whistled. "A guy's going to throw a million dollars around, but doesn't care about meeting you? I don't think even my dad's that kind of rich."

"Greg's got enough clout that he can vouch for me, but run it through an online alias. Make sure there's a secure distance from me and tie it to my new tomb raider rep."

"How about Pizza Girl?"

"As an alias?"

"Yeah."

"Are you shitting me right now?"

"It fits you."

Shay snorted. "It makes it sound like I'm a delivery girl."

"Technically, you kind of are. You go find something, then you deliver to the client."

"But I don't deliver fucking pizza."

"Okay, okay." Peyton muttered something under his breath Shay couldn't make out over the phone.

"How about *Aletheia*?"

"Aletheia? As in the Greek Goddess of Truth?"

"The one and only. Unless you want to go Roman?"

"Nope, the name sounds good." Shay smiled, slowing down at a light. Goddess of Truth. She liked that. Goddess of Truth and Asskicking, but no Greek goddess covered both of those.

"See, I'm not just a well-dressed techie."

"Things are really going to break out from here. When I finish this job, I can finally land a meeting with Smite-Williams."

"What if you can't finish the job?"

Shay scoffed. "I don't fail to finish."

"You never failed in your old job?"

"Came close a few times, but I don't walk away. Half measures add up to nothing. I do what I'm paid to do. Set up a boiler plate contract. We can't wait on this one. Need to get there before whatever douchebag patrol gets there first."

The next morning when Shay arrived at Warehouse Two she noted the presence of yet another cubicle room. The invasive species was growing.

"Good morning," Peyton called from the office, a bright smile on his face. "I can't believe that guy hired you so quickly. Does my cool nickname have anything to do with it?"

"Or Greg vouching for me." Shay shook her head. "This one reeks of magic, though. That's promising for my rep."

"Oh? Tell me the details, woman."

Shay gave him a cold stare.

"Okay, uh, tell me, *please?*"

Shay moved to Peyton's cubicle living room and took a seat. "Here's the short version. There's an island off the coast of Nova Scotia called Oak Island. I'm already liking the location."

Peyton joined her, sitting in a chair across from her. "Why the warm and fuzzy over the locale?"

"Fewer murderous cartels running around in Canada, let alone Nova Scotia."

"If you leave out the eighteen-million-dollar maple syrup mafia. Some pretty murderous Mrs. Butterworths."

"I'll make a note to steer clear of pancakes while I'm there."

"I've confirmed there is another group on the move, and they've brought along some nasty help. A bunch of thugs calling themselves *mercs*."

"A little hired help doesn't bother me. If I kill someone like that, at least I'm not gonna end up with half a country on my ass."

Peyton snorted, sitting cross legged in a chair. "What's so special about Oak Island?"

"Back in 1795, a teenage boy claimed he saw some mysterious lights coming from the island. That was the great era of piracy. Treasure was being squirreled away all over the map. This kid heads over and finds a circular hole cut into a rock wall, big enough for say, a thin man with a peg leg to crawl into it. He comes back with his crew, figuring it might be pirate treasure and they go to town on it. They find evidence that the original hole was manmade but jack shit for all their work."

"Not exactly a stunning example of treasure hunting."

"There's more. A legend grew about the place."

"Rumors run amok."

"Pretty much. Other people came to try their luck and, eventually years later, 90 feet down from that original hole, some treasure seekers found a stone with mysterious symbols on it. No one could decode them, but that didn't stop the people who found it from keeping it from the public. People spent a lot of time digging in what came to be known as the Money Pit, convinced they would find some pirate booty. People dug so many holes and shafts to find treasure and to drain out water from looking for treasure that the original site's long since lost."

"But you think you have a good idea where it is?"

Peyton flipped his hand back and forth in the air. "Our client provided some survey data that gives me a good idea, yeah."

"My plan is to investigate, secure the site and excavate if necessary."

Peyton scratched the day-old growth on his chin. "This seems pretty straightforward, except the whole mercenary and weaponry thing. But no one's found anything in over two-hundred years?"

"Lots of people have searched, a few have even died, but no

one really found anything important. Occasionally someone claimed they found a gold coin or some shit like that, but not much was really confirmed other than coconuts and that stone. Hell, even Teddy Roosevelt took a swing at the place."

"Coconuts? Aren't those on islands anyway?"

"Not Canadian islands."

"Good point." A confused look spread over Peyton's face. "Another gold hunt, then? Pirate treasure. Arrrrgh... Someone had to do it."

Shay grinned. "I'm not after the gold this time. The important thing here is that mysterious stone."

"What about it?"

"The symbols aren't so mysterious."

Peyton leaned forward, his forehead wrinkling. "They aren't?"

"Our client came into possession of the original stone some years back. They have a large collection of curiosities. He's learned a few things about them."

"Anything we can use?" Peyton rested his chin in his hand.

"The reason no one could translate them or figure out what they mean is because they belong to a language that never existed on this planet. They're from a lost Oriceran language."

Peyton lifted off his seat in excitement. "The mysterious lights?"

"I'm guessing someone from Oriceran was opening a portal, which means there's a good chance there's still an Oriceran artifact there. The client's information said there should be another matching stone."

Peyton looked away for a moment, lost in thought. "I wonder what it does."

"Don't know. Don't care. Only care about the million and the boost to my rep."

"You honestly don't care about a magical artifact? Untold powers?"

Shay gave a hard shake to her head. "Look, my policy is to only use tools I understand. An artifact with instructions in a language I don't understand doesn't strike me as something I want to mess around with. When the day comes, and I find a magic trinket that's worth more to me as a tool than a payday, then I'll worry about it." She stood and raised her arms over her head, stretching her back. "For now, I need to do more background checks to make sure this shit isn't a trap."

Peyton grinned, looking too damn smug for a man in his position. "Already did. This is clean. It's a good job."

Shay looked down at him and shook her head. "I'm glad you did, but it's still not good enough."

"You still don't trust me. Be nice to know what that might look like."

"Trust is a moving target. You're earning your points, but no, I'm not ready to risk my life on you yet. Keep this up, though and that day will come."

"Look at you. Offering me a little ray of hope."

"It took so little."

"Still counts, sister."

"Always brushing against the line." Shay winked. "I'll tell you this, Peyton. Going after the client first like you suggested is making this a lot easier. Next on the agenda is figuring out what to bring. How many guns, if I need any special protection from magic."

"You need more than one gun?"

"This time, I know I'm gonna have a few dance partners, and I don't want to have to stop to reload." Shay got up to grab her phone. "Might bring my rocket launcher."

"It's one small rock. Don't want to blow up the profits," Peyton called after her.

1 8

S hay crept through the forest, her AR goggles set to night-vision mode. The old Money Pit tourist site wasn't far away, but the owners of the island had stopped allowing visitors ten years back, after a tourist died falling down the exposed pit.

Maybe that's just a cover story. Hope that doesn't mean those assholes already found the stone.

Shay winced as she caught sight of a bright light. She squeezed her eyes shut and flipped her goggles up. She took a few deep breaths and slowly opened her eyes.

Darkness had cloaked the island, but someone turned on massive floodlights around the main pit area.

"Damn, already here and set up," Shay whispered. "Good thing I moved quickly on this one."

Her background check found that the Alpha Explorers Treasure Hunting Company was on the island, along with some hired mercenary muscles. Alpha Explorers were rich-boy wannabes more than real tomb raiders, but they had a *professional* level of ruthlessness.

More than a few treasure hunters and tomb raiders had ended up dead when sniffing around Alpha Explorers sites, but the members possessed enough influence and savvy to avoid any prosecution so far.

Shay didn't give two shits about the treasure hunters. Her focus was on their muscle, six mercenaries, many of them veteran special forces operators out of South Africa. An online rumor was circulating that an elderly Witch was working with them, as well. That was a lot of muscle for an old Oriceran stone.

Shay darted from tree to tree, keeping her movements low and precise. There were no drones visible in the air, but that didn't mean they weren't floating in the darkness. Once she closed on the site, she could easily deploy jammers, but that required her to first get close enough and avoid getting shot. The minute the jammers went on, the competition would know she was there. Need to be ready for that moment. It's all about the planning.

Maybe having someone watching my back wouldn't be so bad.

Not like either one of them had a lot of choices. Tech-Genius wouldn't last five seconds in the field, and she couldn't take out a help wanted ad for an evil genius who's easy to get along with, won't steal her stuff and can keep a secret.

Not a lot of people out there like that. Peyton came with the added bonus of having no where else to go.

A nearby bush rustled, and Shay silently whipped out her 9mm from one of her shoulder holsters. Yellow eyes gleamed back at her, and a fox padded out from the bush, running off into the night.

"That's right. I have the gun and the opposable thumbs. You better run. What do you have? Teeth and rabies?" Shay winced. "Okay, that's actually a good weapon."

Shay continued moving toward the flood lights in a low crouch, listening for any chatter. She caught murmurs on the wind as she covered the acres still separating her from the flood lights, but still couldn't make anything out.

She came to the edge of the trees and the lights to a main area surrounding the Money Pit. Several large buildings in various states of disrepair stood near the perimeter. Weed-infested gravel and dirt fields stretched out beyond the buildings, leading to a fenced area where the actual pit lay.

Formerly fenced area was a better description. Only about a fourth of the fencing remained standing, the rest of it was bent over or completely collapsed.

Shay could make out two men in camouflage with tactical harnesses and assault rifles patrolling the perimeter of the semi-fenced area. One other man in a khaki jacket stood within the fence line, standing near a small covered area. Three other mercenaries were spread out on the other side. Shay didn't see anyone resembling a Witch and wondered if the intel was bogus.

The covered area was over the current main entrance to the pit. Over the centuries different holes were dug and filled in, and for most people, it was hard to pinpoint the probable source of the treasure.

Shay's intel was on point locating the site. Her major problem was going to be securing the site.

A rumbling, grinding noise bellowed from the pit area, and Shay's heart rate kicked up.

I swear if you guys woke up some sort of ancient demon, I hope it eats you all, balls first.

After a few seconds, Shay realized she wasn't hearing a yowling demon, but some sort of drill. She grinned, resting back on her heels.

Okay, you want to dig it up for me. That works, too.

The only question was knowing if Alpha Explorers knew where to find the stone. If they did, a little snatch and grab didn't bother Shay. The bastards didn't get permission to dig on the island any more than she had.

Shay flipped her AR goggles back down and turned on normal binocular mode. Her magnified vision revealed the Alpha Explorers didn't appear to be digging in the existing pit hole, but instead had started their own sloping tunnel nearby. The hole was massive, easily ten feet in diameter, and the large cable running down the tunnel suggested they brought serious equipment with them.

The cables connected to a massive array of batteries sitting in the back of a large military-style flatbed truck. After thirty seconds, the awful grinding yowl halted, lingering in the forest echoes.

They must have a good reason to do that. Like they know exactly where to look.

A buzz sounded above Shay. They have drones.

The six mercenaries suddenly were gesticulating wildly, pointing in her general direction. The two treasure hunters fled into the hole without looking back.

That ends the major stealth portion of tonight's program. Knew I should have used the jammer sooner.

Shay gave a hard tap to a silver bracelet on her wrist, turning on the jammer. The buzzing stopped as two drones fell from the sky and crashed to the ground and the lights were doused. She whipped out her 9mm and darted toward one of the nearby buildings.

Shouts filled the night air, along with heavy footfalls on the gravel. Several shots rang out and bullets whizzed into the forest near her position.

Shoot first and search pockets later, huh? If that's the way you want to play it, let's do this, bitches.

Shay pressed her back up against a wall, her gun ready. Six opponents, well-trained and well-armed, but even if they did spot her with their drones, they didn't know what kind of backup she brought with her.

An important fact of human battlefield psychology Shay learned from her time as a hitman was that most people make the obvious mistake of assuming their tactics, strategies, and beliefs will be reflected by their enemies. Commanders in battle situations tended to assume their enemies have similar sized forces, if not more. After all, it only makes sense for someone to attack six men using six men.

It was old school training, tried and true and easy to exploit.

It would make the mercenaries cautious, and as she finished them off, she could all but depend on them to panic and overestimate the level of opposition.

This was progressing nicely.

Shay yanked out two frag grenades and tossed them in opposite directions, away from the path of charging mercenaries.

A chorus of shouts erupted. "Grenades!"

A smile was on her lips as the loud explosions cut through the night.

More heavy footfalls followed, as the men broke into two groups, just as Shay expected. She jerked around the corner and fired off several rounds. An unfortunate mercenary needed to work on his point-to-point movement. Two of Shay's bullets caught him, and he went down with a yelp.

Shay tossed one of her two remaining frag grenades toward the man. Her two smoke grenades would be saved for when they could be more useful. Another scream signaled she had wounded another man. *Four left.*

Shay ducked low and ran in the opposite direction, standing upright and firing as she cleared the wall. Two surprised mercenaries fell back, blood blossoming over their chests. Shay hit the ground and rolled, quickly springing back on her feet. A third mercenary made the mistake of charging, spraying his gun on full auto, hoping suppression would save him.

Shay downed him with a single shot between the eyes. *One left.*

She swapped a new magazine into her pistol.

"Need to hire better quality mercenaries," she murmured. The thugs had gotten lazy with unarmed treasure hunters. They weren't making the ex-killer break a sweat.

Shay jogged to the side of the building, listening for footsteps or gunshots, but not hearing anything. A crack of a branch sounded from behind her. She spun around and put three quick rounds into the final mercenary as he turned a corner. He fell to the ground, his eyes wide in surprise.

"Sorry, pal. Just business. You were trying to kill me and I got the job done first. Better luck in the next lifetime."

Shay kept close to the wall. Just because she'd only spotted six men didn't mean more weren't out there. A quick sprint to the end of the wall and a dash between the last two buildings left her convinced she'd killed all the defenders.

The Alpha Explorers didn't have to die, provided they didn't get clever. She kept her gun raised and jogged toward their new hole. Movement near the edge of the large metal pipe leading to the older pit caught her attention, and she pivoted.

A single pale hand gripped the edge of the pit. Another hand followed.

Shay groaned. "And here comes the damned Japanese ghost. Fuck."

No Japanese ghost presented itself. Instead a beautiful long-haired platinum blonde woman with crystal blue eyes crested the pit. She wore a white leather jacket, white jeans, and white boots. The anti-Shay.

Something familiar about the outfit tugged at the edge of Shay's memory, but she couldn't quite place it.

"Got no beef with you, sister," Shay shouted, her gun up. "Just put your hands on your head, lie down, and I'll zip tie you. I'll go on my way, and you get to live."

"You killed all those men," the woman said, her voice soft and tinged with a noticeable Russian accent. The accent combined with the outfit only poked at Shay's mind more.

Should I recognize this woman?

"To be fair, they tried to kill me first."

"It's impressive, I must admit, for anyone to take on six men."

Shay shrugged. "Just a normal Wednesday. On the ground *now*, before my finger gets twitchy."

The woman shot a faint smile at Shay as she noticed the blue crystal wand in her right hand and the six tiny blue stones orbiting the woman's legs.

"Oh fuck," Shay groaned.

"You know who I am, yes?"

Shay took a step back. "Yulia Solokova. Sometimes you go by Snegurka or the Snow Maiden."

"Those are my names, but do you know *what* I am?"

"A tarted-up Ice Witch."

Yulia let out a soft laugh. "You are very well informed. You've come, I assume, to steal my clients' treasure?"

"I've come to recover an artifact, which doesn't belong to your clients. You can walk away. I'm not here to kill people. Old job."

The Witch clucked her tongue. "Nor am I, but here we are, yes? I will give this one chance, a professional courtesy to walk away..." She frowned. "You know me, but I don't know you. What is your name?"

"I don't do names. Too messy if both of us live. Someone might track me down to kill me later. Sorry."

Shay kept her finger hovering over the trigger but did everything she could to keep her face neutral. She'd heard of the mercenary Witch. Even though Snegurka wasn't paid to kill, more than a few men and women had perished at the end of her wand.

For the first time in a long time, Shay didn't know if she was in a fight she could win.

The two women stared at each other in silence, the seconds passing, neither daring to even blink.

Shay pulled the trigger three times in rapid succession. The three bullets dropped to the ground in front of the Witch, all encased in ice.

Yulia whipped up her wand and shouted something in Russian. The blue stones whipped in front of the wand and an encircled blue hexagonal pattern of light appeared out of nowhere. Seven long, thin ice spears shot toward Shay.

Shay jerked to the side and returned fire, but ice shard after pointed ice shard kept firing her way. Only her long experience in evasive training allowed her the erratic movement to escape behind a nearby shack without any of the ice spears landing on their target. Her ass.

Shay whipped around the corner to fire off several more shots. All ended up as useless ice cubes in front of Yulia. An ice spear whizzed toward her, ripping through her jacket and piercing her arm.

"Fuck that hurts." Shay sucked in a breath, ignoring the pain. "That was one of my favorite jackets, ice bitch!" she yelled.

Yulia laughed softly. "You cannot win. You must realize that now. My defensive spells are too powerful for your pathetic toy."

"Knew I should have brought the rocket launcher or the damned bomb drone from the boat," Shay muttered. Her left hand dropped to her final grenade. At least, her final fragmentation grenade. She reached down and grabbed the two smoke grenades, grinning through clenched teeth at a last-ditch idea.

The pins came out.

Shay spun around the corner, hurling the grenades in opposite directions. Both nearby but not directly at the witch. Yulia jerked back, her wand up.

Oh. So, your shield isn't fool-proof, ice bitch?

Thick smoke shot from the grenades, and Shay snapped up her gun sending round after round toward the Witch's last known location. Right before she ran out of rounds, she sent her final fragmentation hurling toward the center of the smoke.

The grenade exploded. No scream sounded, instead there was the sound of a splash.

"Did I get her?"

Shay pulled out a knife and rushed through the smoke. She suppressed a cough, her eyes burning, and found no sign of the Witch or her body. The pit caught her attention.

She came crawling out of that shit like a ghost. Why the fuck was she even in there? Do I even want to know?

A cough refocused Shay. She sheathed her knife, reloaded her gun, and rushed to the pit. A rusted metal ladder led down into the darkness. She couldn't see anything, even as she pointed straight down and emptied her clip. After reloading for good measure, she emptied another clip into the pit.

Shay glanced around looking for something to seal the hole. A six-inch thick metal lid lay flat on the ground. She holstered her gun and ran to the lid, lifting it end over end. Training in the Warehouse was paying off again. The pain in her arm pulsed with every exertion. No time to bitch out now. With a mighty grunt, she picked up the lid and managed to slam it over the top of the pit.

"Damn is that thing heavy."

A turning metal rod was on the top of the lid, forming a lock between the lid and the pipe. She pushed in the rod, shoving with her weight as metal ground against metal. Wonder later why anyone would need to secure the pit from the outside.

Shay rummaged in her backpack, locating a small vibration sensor and placed it on the lid. She pulled out her phone and synced it to the sensor. If the Witch survived and escaped, Shay's phone would let her know.

Okay. Doing good. Six mercs and one Witch down. On to the artifact.

Shay patiently waited for two full minutes, timing it by her watch, her heart pounding, to see if Yulia would do her best snow ghost impression. Wouldn't pay to turn her back on the Witch and her wand.

The lid didn't move, and her phone didn't chirp. She let out a breath, her shoulders relaxing as she thought about how she could brag to Peyton over pizza about taking down the Ice Witch.

Shay wrapped a piece of cloth around her arm to stem the blood flow, tying it off, holding one end in her teeth. She jogged to the larger tunnel dug by the industrial equipment the Alpha Explorers brought with them onto the small island.

She swung her backpack around and reached into it, pulling out a wrist lamp and a headlamp on a band. She put both on, reloaded her gun, and plunged into the gradually sloping tunnel.

Shay jogged down into the hole, listening for any hint of the Alpha Explorers.

Shay followed the beam of light, the thrill of the chase making her smile. "Just need a sign that says, *abandon all hope, all ye who enter here.* Damn, I love this job."

19

No bullets or ice spears greeted Shay as she hurried down the tunnel. The deeper she delved, the more her quiet footsteps turned to splashes. The Alpha Explorers didn't care about water infiltration. That told Shay they knew exactly where they were digging and thought they could evacuate the tunnel quickly in case of trouble.

The water only grew deeper with every step. If things kept up, she might have to go back to her boat and bring her diving gear. She slowed, hoping the Alpha Explorers wouldn't hear her coming.

Shay's lights caught sight of a smaller tunnel that ran off to the side ten feet before the back of the drill. Thinner cables ran into the smaller tunnel as well. The other treasure hunters had used a similar drill. She approached the sub-tunnel, her gun raised, wondering when she was going to run into the men.

This far underground they would not have been able to

get decent radio reception. The Alpha Explorers might not know yet that Shay finished off their guards.

The tomb raider stepped into the narrow sub-tunnel, her light revealing only more mud, water, and rocks. No treasure hunters.

What the fuck? It's not like there's a lot of room to hide down here.

Shay continued forward movement. Some splashing was unavoidable in the calf-deep water. The sound of running water was reaching her ears and coming from the distance. She jerked her gun up as metal blinked in the beam from her light. Closer examination revealed it was an inactive tracked multi-armed drilling platform the size of a large person, rather than a two-legged enemy. She knelt down and felt under the water, finding the submerged cables supplying its power.

As Shay approached the equipment it became obvious why they'd stopped drilling in the smaller tunnel. The Alpha Explorers' efforts uncovered an older large vertical shaft, complete with a set of rusted metal handholds. They had moved on to the bigger prize.

A look above her revealed a mass of dirt and rock. It remained unclear why the obstruction didn't continue farther down until she spotted the rough outline of a metal platform that was providing a nucleus for the blockage. The handholds descended further into the darkness. Entrances to other narrow tunnels dotted the path down in the darkness, with irregular spacing. It looked like hobbled-together giant ants had pushed their way into the Money Pit.

Water poured from the Explorers' shaft, accounting for

some of the noise she heard, mixing with water from several other tunnels connecting to the shaft.

Shay furrowed her brow, considering the implications. Whatever the Alpha Explorers had done, it must have punched a hole to a tunnel leading to the ocean surrounding the island, or tremors had shifted the soil, allowing the same result.

"That has to be the case." Shay's voice echoed in the narrow passageway.

Otherwise, the entire tunnel system would have already been filled with water. Playing around in an underground tunnel system filling with water wasn't on Shay's list of fun evening activities.

Need to find this shit and get out of here.

Shay killed her lights and lowered her AR goggles over her eyes. She activated infrared mode and desperately hoped the Alpha Explorers didn't toss a flare in her face. She stuck her head farther into the shaft and peered down. No thermal traces on the handholds or walls, but thick enough gloves might account for their absence.

Shay zipped her phone into an inside pocket. She didn't want to risk losing her phone down a moldy old shaft. She reached up to tap a button on the side of the goggles, changing over to night-vision mode. "Voila."

The goggles only magnified existing light. In true absolute darkness, she could only see pitch black but, in night vision mode she could make out the handholds glowing in a faint, eerie green. A patch of light emerging from an opening twenty feet down was the likely location of the Alpha Explorers.

Shay holstered her pistol and pulled gloves from her

backpack, slipping them on as she made a descent on the grime and rust-encrusted old metal handholds.

These are still here. Damned good craftsmanship. Congrats, you magnificent Canadian bastards.

The tomb raider approached the source of the light and paused just above it. She deactivated her goggles, turning her headlamp back on and pulling out her gun. Even though she couldn't hear the men, she suspected they were laying right inside the lip of the tunnel.

Okay. One... two... three...

Shay leapt into the tunnel, almost banging her head, still ready to shoot anyone stupid enough to have a gun fight 100 feet underground. Except the Alpha Explorers weren't there. A faint greenish glow suffused a mound of dirt at the end of the tunnel.

A few cautious steps brought Shay forward, and she frowned, glancing down at the pile and back over at the entrance to the tunnel. She shined her light on the edges of the entrance and spotted the rotted remains of a wooden door.

Did the Alpha Explorers pick the wrong tunnel? Are they above me? Below me?

Shay gritted her teeth, her arm began to ache again. The whole environment was perfect for ambushes. She didn't hear any hint of the Alpha Explorers, though the water draining from the tunnels into the bottom of the main shaft might have been covering up their voices.

None of that changed the fact that a suspicious pile of glowing dirt sat right in front of her. Shay unzipped her pocket and pulled out her phone to check the coordinates but couldn't get any bars, which meant no way to calibrate the GPS.

Fucking great. I should have seen that one coming. Singleness of purpose. Go get the glowing weird artifact in this pit.

Shay knelt in the dirt and reached out her hand, jerking it back. No one found a powerful artifact sitting in a side tunnel all these years. That suggested some sort of trap or magical protection.

She stood there in the tunnel, staring down at the glowing dirt, trying to decide the best course of action. The sound of the steady trickle of water convinced her she had one choice. Trust her gut and take a chance.

Shay pulled a small trowel off a loop connected to her backpack and started digging.

Several layers down she uncovered a small stone adorned with Oriceran symbols. The stone was a matte silver sitting in a glowing dome of light that prevented any dirt from touching it.

"Well, fuck," Shay muttered, biting her lower lip. "Come this far." She took several deep breaths and pressed her injured arm to her side, darting her good arm into the field and snatching the stone from the field. Nothing happened. "Really? A little luck for a change." She blew out the breath in her lungs.

The stone felt warm to the touch, but not impressively alien or magical otherwise. She pulled out a soft cotton cloth from her backpack, wrapped the stone, and tucked it in a mesh pocket inside the backpack.

"Time to get the *hell* out of here."

Her trip back to the Alpha Explorers' sub-tunnel went swiftly, and she was just about to enter the main tunnel when she heard the splash of footsteps up ahead. She slowed her pace, the echoes of the running water cloaking her steps.

"That bitch is probably already dead," murmured a man's voice. "There had to be some sort of trap. She must have set it off. *We* can go get the artifact now."

"We should have just jumped her when we had the chance," said another man. "We should go in there, knock her ass out, and blow the tunnels like we planned. Glad I brought the charges. Who the hell knew someone would attack our dig?"

"Maybe it's karma." The man chuckled.

Shay took shallow, quiet breaths as she approached the main tunnel. From the sound of their voices, they were closer to the main drill rather than further up the tunnel. She readied her gun, counted silently to three, and made a half turn into the opening.

Two very surprised Alpha Explorers turned her way.

"Oh, fuck," said one of the men.

"Guess shit didn't work out for you," Shay said with a grin. "I'll be leaving now. I *won't* kill you if you toss your guns my way. I'm feeling generous."

"We don't have guns."

Shay didn't believe them, but as long as the men didn't go for a weapon, they didn't need to die. She could secure them and their weapons.

"You didn't bring guns on a dangerous expedition?" She kept her gun steadily pointed at them.

"That's why the fucking mercenaries and Witch were hired. How the hell did you beat Yulia?"

Shay snorted. "Don't bring a wand to a gunfight. Now…

let's keep this simple. Get down on your knees, hands behind your back and I'll zip tie you. Too bad for you, turns out there was no trap on the artifact."

"What the fuck? There had to be." The bigger man gave a quick glance at his duffel bag.

"Uh uh uh…" Shay waved a finger at them, stepping close enough to pull the duffel bag to the side. She could tell by the heft she had found their weapons.

"I told you, Jim," said his shorter but just as bulky compatriot. "It wasn't about the trap at all. It was about that translated inscription. *Only when the time is right will it present itself again.* The magic needed to seep into Earth from Oriceran for the artifact to reappear."

"Luke, that's not necessarily…" Jim groaned and nodded at Shay. "It doesn't matter now."

Shay gestured with her gun at the ground. "He's right. Doesn't matter *now*. I'd feel bad about this, but none of you have the nicest rep. Be happy I'm not blowing your brains out just to be careful."

Luke shook his head. "Come on. We can cut a deal. We'll split the profits with you." He smiled. "We dug the tunnel."

"And why the fuck would I split the profits? I have the artifact, and you have nothing but a bunch of dead mercenaries."

"I don't recognize you, which means you're new to the game. We could be useful contacts, get you jobs. Hell, you're pretty damned impressive, maybe you should join our company." His smile was strained.

"Thanks, but no thanks. I have my own contacts. Now

get on the damned floor. I'm losing patience." Shay glared at the men.

Luke locked eyes with her, hatred and defiance in them. "Jim, you thinking what I'm thinking?"

"Just like Alexandria all over again." A smile appeared on his face.

Shay narrowed her eyes. "I'm tired of playing fucking gam—"

Both men jumped backward and to either side of the tunnel. Shay clipped Luke in the shoulder, but the large drill took the tomb raider's next several rounds meant for Jim. The intact treasure hunter clumsily unzipped his coat and yanked out a gun.

Luke groaned on the ground, blood staining his shoulder. "Fuck it then." He reached into his pocket and laughed.

Shay looked between the two men, spinning around and climbing toward the surface. As she neared the surface an explosion rocked the tunnel behind her. Another shattered the earth in front of her, knocking her off her feet and coating her with a shower of mud and rock.

Her ears were ringing as she pushed herself up and continued stumbling forward. Water was pouring freely from the lower blast, filling the tunnel. Shay didn't look back as she rushed toward the surface.

"Help me, please!" Jim's voice was an echo from deep inside the tunnel. "I'm pinned. Blowing this shit up wasn't my idea."

Shay kept running as she yelled over her shoulder. "Yeah, but shooting me was, fucker." A loud groan echoed in the chamber as the side walls collapsed into the lower tunnel.

The tomb raider emerged back at the surface, enjoying the caress of the night wind. She moved away from the cave entrance and made it another thirty yards when an odd cracking sound caught her attention. She turned around. Her phone chimed several times, but she ignored it.

A sink hole had formed around the new tunnel and the entrance was rapidly filling with mud, rocks, and dirt.

There is definitely something interesting to dig up now.

Shay grabbed her phone to look at the alerts. All were the same timestamped message.

VIBRATION WARNING FROM SENSOR ALPHA ONE.

Shay glanced over the other pit entrance. The lid still remained firmly in place. No Witch, just the nearby tremors.

"Things change. Time to get the fuck *out of here.*"

Shay's Edorado Marine speedboat hugged the shoreline as she sped away from Oak Island toward Nova Scotia.

"I really need to stop nearly getting buried by shit."

Her phone chimed, and she pulled it out her pocket.

VIBRATION WARNING FROM SENSOR ALPHA ONE.

It didn't take long before another alert chimed.

SIGNAL LOST FROM SENSOR ALPHA ONE.

Probably another sink hole. There's no way the Witch survived. She would have come up for air earlier.

Shay chuckled to herself and shook her head, a fine mist of ocean spray in her face.

Then again, I'm supposed to be dead. Guess it's only fair to have a dead Witch chasing a dead hitwoman. Glad I never gave her my name.

20

Shay wouldn't normally bring an artifact back to Warehouse Two, but until she was ready to bring Peyton to Warehouse Five she had no choice.

Part of expanding her business required her to take advantage of available resources and if Peyton wasn't blowing smoke up her ass about his interest in magical history, then he was going to be very useful evaluating the true worth of potential artifacts. First things first, she needed to know what the hell she'd found on Oak Island.

Peyton was waiting by the rolling door with a mug of coffee as Shay stepped out of the Spider, wrapped stone in hand.

"It's your time to shine, Peyton." Shay unwrapped the stone, holding it out for him to inspect. "I want to know what this is before I sell it off to the client. I need to know if it's too dangerous to be sending out into the world."

Researching her clients would give her more assurance she didn't end up providing a deadly cartel or terrorist group with a new weapon. Still left a lot of gray area. Work

MARTHA CARR & MICHAEL ANDERLE

would always come from some pretty awful people at times but handing over something like a magical nuclear weapon strained even her mercenary tendencies.

Peyton's eyes grew wide as he looked down at the stone. "Do you know what you have there? I couldn't tell from the drawings of the first stone and it never occurred to me this is what you were after." He turned in a circle, waving his arms.

Shay rolled her eyes. "No, I don't know what I have, but you're the expert in magical history, so fucking deliver already."

He bent closer to the stone, his hands hovering just above it. "I can't read it, but that's an ancient Gnomic script. I've heard of these stones. A small number have been found in other locations. Something about celebrating the last time Earth and Oriceran were directly connected, tens of thousands of years ago."

"This stone has been here for a while."

Peyton bounced up and down. "I think those stones have been in Canada for over twenty-thousand years. They are priceless historical artifacts."

Shay nodded slowly. "And, they do what exactly? Open magic portals? Act as magic batteries? Create bionic animals?"

Peyton shook his head, his face scrunching up in confusion. "No, they're like little time capsules, really. I mean, they obviously have some magic to survive undamaged throughout the years, but they don't do anything other than, you know... hold words. You seriously need to donate this to a museum. The few others that have been found are all in private hands."

A fucking time capsule with an Oriceran High School Class of 24,000 B.C. Gnome Club Was Here, message? You've got to be fucking kidding me.

Shay shook her head. "It's not going to a museum."

"But, Shay, do you realize the historical implications? It'd be like finding a Chinese artifact in the New World that proves their fleet did reach California in the 15th century. You have to—"

Peyton fell silent at Shay's raised hand.

"What do you see when you look at me?" Shay asked, a faint smile on her face.

"Um, a dark-haired attractive woman?" He winced and took a step back as if he expected her to slap him over the comment.

"Relax, already. Well, I am that, but you know what I'm not?"

"What?"

"A fucking volunteer." Shay rolled her eyes. "We have a client, and he's going to pay for it. Just because I lie to a few people about being a UCLA archaeologist doesn't mean I act like one." She pointed to her chest. "I do this for the money. Got it?"

Peyton shrugged, properly abashed. "Sorry, knee-jerk response. I'm still used to hanging out with the *we'll donate anything if you put our name on the side of the building crowd.* It's like a reptile brain response. I regurgitate that bullshit before I know what I said."

Shay eyed him, her arms crossed. She suspected the real bullshit was his explanation.

She didn't care. Peyton's belief wasn't necessary, only his compliance.

Shay put off the delivery till the next afternoon. She was cruising down a side street, glancing at the cargo drone camera feed on her phone.

"How is it looking?" Peyton said over the speakerphone in the rental Honda sedan Shay was driving.

She was making the delivery in a warehouse district far from any of her holdings. She was close enough in the rental car to hit the scene if necessary, but not so close to draw undue attention. As much as it pained her to leave the Spider, she figured a flashy red sports car might be too memorable.

"The drone's almost there." Shay glanced over again at the feed, looking up in time to slow down with the traffic. "I'm placing a lot of faith in you."

Peyton checked the numbers he had fed into it. "It's shielded. It'll save it from low-level EMP, and if it gets any frequency interruptions, it's programmed to fly back to the safe point I programmed into it. An easy hand-off. If someone does try to take the cargo, you'll sweep in and take them out, right?"

"Yes, but the whole fucking point is that it's not traceable to me. Otherwise I would have delivered it directly."

"You're being extra-cautious on this one," Peyton said. "Why?"

"Let's just say the occasional extra bit of caution leads to fewer blowbacks."

Shay left out a mention of the possible survival of Snegurka. She wasn't sure he'd handle the news well, but she couldn't ignore that a powerful and very angry Ice

Witch might be interested in tracking her ass down and freezing her in a solid block of ice. Whatever she could do to shield herself directly from exposure on this particular job was prudent.

Shay pulled into a parking lot, pointing her car away from traffic and left the engine running.

"Okay Peyton, there's the contact. Maneuver the drone in."

A suited man in glasses was visible on the camera feed. He was patiently waiting as the cargo drone lowered itself to the ground. The man reached out, and the drone's cargo clamps released the small box it carried into his hands.

He gave a polite nod to the drone and turned to leave. He pulled out his phone and tapped something into it.

Shay blew out a breath. "Okay. Here's the moment of truth."

"What will you do if the client stiffs you?" Peyton asked.

Shay gave a dark chuckle. "I'll track him down and make him understand that's a *lethal* mistake." An alert popped up on her phone, and she grinned. "Not gonna be an issue. I'm now a million dollars richer."

"Do I get some sort of bonus pay?"

Shay laughed. "I'm not paying you *anything* right now."

"Yeah, I think that's called slavery. Not cool, Shay."

"We should talk salary. Everybody deserves to get paid. How about I take you out for pizza and we talk about it? My treat. We need to celebrate anyway."

"Fine. Just whatever we do, please don't take me to Pasadena's Best Pizza!"

Shay made a gagging sound. "I'm trying to celebrate, not torture you."

The Spider pulled up outside of a place Shay liked but hadn't been to in a while. Olio Pizzeria in Beverly Grove.

Peyton glanced around the area. "Hmmm…"

"What? This place has great pizza." She poked him in the arm. "If you've been messing around with shit like Pasadena's that proves you don't know crap about picking good pizza."

"No, it's not that. I was wondering if this was near another one of our warehouses? I'm guessing you hit places close to your warehouses."

Shay threw open her door. "Stop guessing, it's safer for you that way. Get out and let's go eat pizza."

Peyton followed her inside the pizzeria. No customers sat in the dining room, and no waitress or waiter waited at the front to seat them.

"This is never good" Shay's instincts kicked in and she looked for clues, motioning to the bar. She felt her muscles tense. "We'll wait there."

Peyton looked around, more interesting in finding a seat. "The wine any good here?"

"Yeah, it's all right." She looked out at the parking lot. Two more cars. *Something is off.*

They headed to the bar and took a seat.

Shay tapped her fingers impatiently against the counter. "Never seen this place so dead. There's no way their quality went to shit that quickly…"

Someone cried out in pain in the back.

Shay narrowed her eyes. "Stay here. I'm gonna go check

that out." She slid off the barstool and moved toward the kitchen door.

On the other side, the owner was slumped over and holding his stomach over his stained red apron. Three gang members stood over him, their green bandanas and t-shirts and the skull tattoos on their faces identified them as part of the Demon Generals, a local Mexican street gang. *Big ass bold for the middle of the day.* From what she heard they weren't that big of a threat in the neighborhood. Things keep changing all the time.

"Call the police..." The owner groaned, rolling onto his elbow.

The gang members turned and looked menacingly at Shay.

The largest of them gave her a feral grin. "Leave now, *bitch*, unless you want trouble."

"Always with the bitch." Shay sighed. "You see normally, other's people shit isn't my problem."

"Good, we have no problem then. Get the fuck out of here."

"That's *normally.*"

"What the fuck are you saying?"

Shay shrugged, putting her hands on her hips. "It's just I'm hungry and this place has good pizza, and you know, it's *hard* to find good pizza. If you guys kill the owner, it's gonna be an inconvenience for me. I'm asking you all nicely to go out the back door there and never come the fuck back." She gave them her best bright smile even as her voice took on an icy edge.

The gang member laughed and waved his arm at her. "Get a load of this crazy *perra.*" His smile disappeared. "You

MARTHA CARR & MICHAEL ANDERLE

think we won't fuck you up, bitch? Just because you're a chick?"

Shay cracked her knuckles. "I've got good news and bad news. The good news is my punch card is almost filled for a free slice and I don't want anything getting in the way. I'm not gonna kill you. More good news, you're leaving soon. Bad news is I'm willing to break a few bones to make my point."

A thug rushed her swinging his fist, his fingers covered in heavy rings. Shay ducked to the side, jabbing the man in the base of his throat. She sent him flying back with a roundhouse kick while he was still gasping for air and holding his throat. He crashed into a stack of pizza trays.

His friends charged, but Shay danced around the men, easily avoiding their attempts to grab her. She leapt up, smashing her knee into the face of one man, swinging from an overhead pipe. Blood spurted from his nose and he stumbled back, groaning loudly.

Shay used the man's falling body as a springboard to launch herself toward the other man. She slammed into him, wrapping her legs around his neck and taking him down on the hard tile floor. The gang member landed with a grunt, gasping for breath as the air was knocked out of him.

Shay bounced to her feet, hurrying over to the downed man and jerking his arm up before bending it back and dropping down hard on her knee. The cracking humerus echoed in the room as the gang member howled in pain.

A gang member stumbled to his feet, swaying and unsteady. His hand dropped behind his back, but Shay had her gun out and pointed before he could even touch his weapon.

"Don't." Her expression was cold. "Like I said, I don't need trouble from the cops, but if you're aching to fucking die, there's a lot of people in this neighborhood who won't cry if I blew your fucking brains out right here. Take your friends and never come back here." Shay cocked the gun ready to go either way.

"This is me holding back. If I hear that you're even sniffing in this direction, I'm gonna show up in the middle of the night at your crib, and I'm gonna cut your balls off and stuff them down your throat before I put a bullet in your brain. Understand, asshole?"

The man put his hands in front of him. "I get it. I get it. We're out." He hurried over to help one of his groaning friends, who was cradling his broken arm, rise to his feet and limp out the back door, terror on their faces.

Shay let out a breath and looked back at the dining room. No sign of Peyton. "*Maybe* a little over the top there."

The owner rushed over and shook her hand as she holstered her gun. "Thank you. Thank you. Those *ganado* have been leaning on me for protection money for months. They keep increasing the price. I thought I was going to go out of business. Is there anything I can do to repay you?"

Shay flexed her hands and straightened her jacket. "Some pizza, maybe?"

"You can have all the pizza you want *for life*. This place is your home away from home, as far as I'm concerned. What do you want? Margherita pizza?"

"Thin-crust pepperoni and sausage to start."

The owner looked around the kitchen, anxiously

wringing his hands. "Just let me, uh, mop up some of the blood, and I'll get that going."

Shay smiled. "Take your time." With a wave, she headed back out front, pushing the swinging door.

Peyton sat at a table, checking his phone. "Should I be calling the police? Uh, or the coroner? Heard the commotion but I've learned to wait for your reappearance."

"I was making some new friends. Eat all you want. It's on the house."

21

Shay whistled to herself as she relaxed in a chair in the cubicle living room, skimming through a tomb raiding forum. Rumors about the two missing treasure hunters from Alpha Explorers was filling up a lot of the forums in recent days. The rest of the Alpha company was attempting to quash the stories, claiming that the men had quit because they couldn't handle the lifestyle.

"If by *the lifestyle*, you mean still breathing, that's technically true."

"You say something?" Peyton shuffled into the living room and fell backward into one of the lounge chairs Shay had recently purchased. The warehouse was looking more like a home than an office. Chalk one up for Peyton.

He was in a dark mood and doing his best to stay calm.

Shay looked up from her phone. "What's wrong?"

"My dad's no longer in his coma."

Shay sat forward. "That's a good thing, isn't it?"

"No. He's moved from coma to dead."

"I see... Sorry to hear it, Peyton. I know... you wanted to clear things up with him before the end."

Peyton shook his head. "I wanted the chance to clear the air, say a few things..."

Shay looked away, unsure what to say. Comforting people wasn't in her wheelhouse.

"I need to go," Peyton said.

"Sure. I can take you out somewhere. To a pizza place or a movie or something to get your mind off things."

Peyton shook his head. "No, you don't understand. I need to go back to Connecticut to his funeral."

"Not going to happen..." Shay took a deep breath and slowly let it out. "That's not a good idea. That's too much danger just to get a little closure."

"It's not about closure. It's more about my mother. She needs me."

"I'm gonna say this once, so listen up. You can't go to that funeral. You're *dead*. If anything, you showing up is just gonna make things worse for your mom. Tell me your explanation for letting her think you're dead."

Peyton stood and rubbed a hand over his face. "I can at least watch from a distance."

"No, you can't. It's too risky." Shay shook her head. "Let me give you a little advice from an ex-killer. If I wasn't sure someone was dead, there are three good places to catch them sneaking around." She held up one finger. "At the birth of their kid." She held up a second finger. "At their kid's wedding." She held up a third finger. "And at funerals."

"That's just theory."

"Bullshit. I've found and killed marks at more than one funeral."

"Those marks weren't already supposed to be dead."

Shay stood, locking gazes with Peyton. "You can't go. You will die if you go, and I didn't go through all the trouble of saving your life so you can throw it away in some pointless sentimental gesture that won't accomplish a fucking thing."

"How would you know it won't accomplish anything?"

Shay rolled her eyes. "Because your father's dead. You can sound off at him just as easily here. Hovering around his funeral does nothing for your mother and if your brother gets wind of things… Even if you don't get popped there, he'll know to start hunting you again, and then it's only a matter of time."

"My choice."

"What? To fucking die?"

"It's my life."

Shay groaned. "Don't be a fucking idiot for once."

"Giving a shit about your family isn't being an idiot," Peyton thundered.

"You belong to the Adams Family. They really are a screa-um. I guarantee you," Shay began, keeping her voice calm, "your siblings still have people on the lookout for you. If anything, with your dad dying, they'll be on hyper alert to make sure you don't pop up out of nowhere to peel away part of the fortune."

"I can take care of myself, especially around my family."

Shay scoffed. "Remember how you got here."

Peyton threw up his hands. "Just because you're good at

killing doesn't mean you're the queen of *all* badasses, Shay. Sure, I had a hit on me, but I have a few technical skills."

"Telling yourself bullshit doesn't make it any less bullshit. You were a rich boy ignoring the game you were playing with a dangerous crowd. The only reason you're not dead is because I saved your life, and now you just want to throw it away."

Peyton snorted. "You don't give a shit about me. I'm just a tool to you. Why do you care if your hammer runs off and gets broken? Buy another hammer."

"Fuck you, Peyton." Shay wasn't ready to admit to herself that he was that rarest of commodities in her life… a friend.

"I'm leaving, and you can't stop me unless you kill me."

Shay narrowed her eyes and took a step toward him. "I'm not a one trick pony. Locking you up for a while works just as well."

Peyton stood his ground, glaring at her.

Shay's voice was filled with venom. "If you leave, this place will be empty an hour after you get on the plane, and I'll have a different phone number." She stomped over to the Spider. "Do what you want." She sounded calm despite the knot in her gut.

She threw open the Spider's door and slipped inside, already thinking about where she could move everything important from Warehouse Two and *finally* throwing out all his crap. Things could go back to the way they were, predictable.

"Fuck that," Shay muttered to herself, and started her car. "Maybe I should grab what I need and burn this entire damned place to the ground." *Thank God I never showed him any other Warehouses.*

———

Shay tapped boxing gloves with her opponent and moved backward in the ring, keeping her focus on him. She'd already forgotten his name. Trevor something. It didn't matter. He was just an unfortunate living punching bag for her today.

She'd driven straight to Steel Gloves, wanting the release that only punching someone could bring. Exercise on her obstacle course might be cleansing, but fiery rage cleansed her soul.

I saved that stupid kid's life, and now he's gonna go and get himself killed to pay his respects to a piece of trash father?

Her opponent stepped forward, throwing a few test jabs, which Shay easily blocked.

He gave her a cocky grin. It reminded her far too much of Peyton. She launched a series of quick jabs, forcing the man back. He finally found an opening and sent a powerful hook her way, but she ducked the punch at the last moment, and hit him with a series of body blows.

Focus on the task at hand. Stay in the moment. Her mind continued to drift. *If his mother knew all this shit was going on and looked the other way, she's just as bad as the rest of them.*

Shay's distraction let her opponent land a solid punch that sent her staggering back. She let out a growl and shook her head.

"You're good," her opponent said, bouncing side to side on his toes. "But I'm better."

Cocky little Peyton. I gave you a new life. A new purpose, and this is how you repay me? Fuck you. Stick with your training. Singleness of purpose.

Shay rushed the boxer, gliding between his blows like he was announcing them. She slammed a glove into his face and immediately followed up with another hit.

He stepped back, but her speed made his escape attempt futile. Blow after blow landed, each hit bringing out a grunt.

The angry tomb raider forced him into a corner where he finally collapsed, a trickle of blood coming from his nose.

Shay brought up her elbow to slam into his neck, blinking, pulling back at the last minute.

Fucking get it together, woman. This is just some douchebag in the gym, not a mercenary trying to kill you.

Shay took a deep breath, moving back several steps, shaking her head and trying to clear out the murderous bloodlust.

Her opponent pushed himself off the ground, sniffing as he dabbed at his nose. He worked at pulling his gloves off.

"Sorry, I got excited after I got some good hits in."

The man let out a low grunt, glancing at her as he looked at the blood on his fingers. "It's okay. Nothing to apologize for. I'm impressed with your skills, and I under-estimated you. Not many guys can beat my ass. Guess I shouldn't have taken a chick so lightly."

Shay let out an annoyed sigh and looked around at the small crowd who were already gathering to watch them.

Pick your battles. Fuck Peyton. It's his own damned fault if he gets killed.

She held out her hand to shake. He took her hand as she leveraged her body weight and flipped him onto his back, dropping to her knee and whispering to him, "We all make mistakes. Some live to try again." He looked at her nervously as she grinned and stood back up, holding out her hand. Everything changes. Always a permanent part of any plan these days. The return of magic was teaching her that much.

Shay blew a good hour driving in the Hollywood Hills, still clearing her head. She considered tracking down the Demon Generals to lay waste to the gang. She rested one hand on the top of the steering wheel as she cruised around a curve on Nichols Canyon Road.

Mapping out kill strategies always calmed her down. But she accepted that killing dozens of gang members was just as idiotic as Peyton going to the funeral. Only an idiot murdered a bunch of gang members and didn't expect blowback.

The Spider cruised down the road, heading in the general direction of Warehouse Two. She still had a while before she arrived, even with the light traffic, unusual for LA.

It was a good day to take her favorite route, winding through the canyon, lowering the risk of being tracked. That gave her more time to make a mental inventory of everything she'd need to move.

I'll need a van or a truck. Fuck, I'll need to stop off at Warehouse Three for explosives or thermite charges.

Shay turned sharply at a blind curve, almost clipping another driver. He honked, but she ignored it.

There's not going to be room for anyone getting that close to me in this lifetime. Stick with a virtual PA. Never has to know who I really am. I can get what I need and pay them, move on with my day.

Shay's stomach was still in a knot. She'd made a mistake with Peyton. Do that too often and she was as good as dead. Time to correct the mistake, starting with emptying the warehouse and removing any trace that she was ever there by blowing it out of existence. No more cubicle walls.

"Who knows?" she muttered. "Maybe this will be cathartic." *Fuck me. I miss the yuppy Peewee Herman.*

22

The fire in Shay faded into a dull pain by the time she made it back to Warehouse Two. She decided to wait on collecting her arson supplies. There'd be a delay, she figured, between Peyton being captured, tortured, killed, and traced back to her.

A soft sigh escaped Shay's lips as the loading bay door closed behind her car, and she turned off her engine. *A fucking waste.* That's what it was. He could have made something of himself with his tech skills and her training. He would have become a well-rounded badass who didn't have to run from his family.

If only Peyton Coolidge could have understood everything he wanted was within his reach, instead of letting his emotions get the better of him and pushing him into an act of suicidal stupidity.

Shay stepped out of her car and made her way to the cubicle jungle and the office. She halted, blinking, surprised at her relief.

Peyton was sitting in his lounge chair, the footrest up, a

comic book resting on his chest. He didn't acknowledge her or move. For a second her heart rate kicked up, and she wondered if someone had gotten to him when she was gone, but the shallow rise and fall of his chest proved he was still alive.

Shay got close enough to give a kick to the footrest, her arms crossed and stared down at him in silence, her face a careful, stony blank.

"Comic book seems a little on the nose."

Peyton looked down at the Green Lantern rare edition from twenty years ago. "Some things are a cliché for a good reason. It's the way I relax when I'm stressed out. You should try it."

"My way helps with population control." She smiled despite her best instincts telling her to kick him out. "Fuck me." She said it under her breath but Peyton still noticed and raised an eyebrow, staring up at her.

"I owe Player 4839 a ten spot. I bet him you didn't have a beating heart."

Shay easily lifted him onto his feet and dropped him to the ground. He landed on his side and rolled over, jumping to his feet. "I know this is your version of an office party. I missed you too."

Shay took a step toward Peyton as he leapt onto the desk and leap-frogged across the room, never landing on the floor. His comic book slid to the floor and he gave a worried look back but didn't go back to retrieve it.

Good instincts.

"That was stupid and impressive." Shay was doing her best not to prove him wrong or laugh. "You set up the room just in case you had to get away like this, didn't you?"

"My own jungle gym. Had to entertain myself somehow all those hours cooped up in here. Invest in cable. It's not fun to watch a seventy-year-old Hoda drink wine and cook cauliflower pizza." He stayed where he was, ready to jump again, if necessary.

Shay was tempted to take a run at him just to see him move through the rest of his hidden training circuit.

"Nice try, Shay. I can see the wheels turning. I told you, I managed to keep myself alive all these years and I proved I'm useful to you. Quit underestimating me."

"You made a gym out of office equipment."

"Have to use what's handy."

"It's entertaining but don't get ahead of yourself. Your skills were impressive when you were back East right up to the day you had a target on you. They're not enough anymore."

Peyton scoffed, jumping down even as he kept his distance. "I thought about what you said, all of it, and I realized you own my ass. I'm fucking dead, and you're right. If I headed back home, Randy would make sure I was full of Russian poison within a couple of hours. I'll make your day and admit you were right. I'm not ready to deal with him, otherwise I would have left."

Shay dropped into a lounge chair. "Speaking as someone who has been dead longer than you, it's not so bad once you get used to it. It's useful in its own way."

"Useful? How the hell is being dead useful?"

"Most people have to carry around their baggage with them forever, but once you're dead, you can let it all go, reinvent yourself, and do it the right way this time. Come up with a new version of yourself."

Peyton sat down in the other lounge chair, scooping up the comic book and brushing it off. "Is it really so easy? Just let it all go. I had a life, people I gave a crap about, at least one person. I…" He sighed. "Not to be a prick, but it wasn't like you were a social butterfly before you faked your own death."

"That's where you're wrong. I traveled all around the world and met all sorts of interesting people. Sure, I killed a lot of those same people, but I did meet them and often talked to them before I killed them."

"You have a strange definition for cocktail party conversation."

Shay shrugged and leaned her head back against the chair "People are less judgie when they're about to die."

"Word."

"You have to accept that your old life is over as if it never existed. You're never stepping back into that identity. If you're willing, I can help you figure out the new Peyton. Hell, I'm doing it myself."

"By becoming a tomb raider?"

"Among other things." Shay pointed to her hair. "Like going back to my natural color. I'm gonna move to a new place, too. Shit like that."

"I guess I can add a few more cubicle rooms."

"Make a maze if you want and put a minotaur in the center."

"All your shit would be safe then." He looked over at her. "I saw how happy you were to see me."

"You were asleep."

Peyton let out a contented sigh. "Clever techies are hard

to find. Especially the kind that will help you clean up after a kill."

The smile faded from Shay's face and she briefly shut her eyes, mapping out how to target Randy Coolidge.

"Are you meditating? A Zen master killer tomb raider."

"My own version."

"Good idea. Don't point a weapon at me but you're wound a little tight."

"I'm glad you stayed, Peyton."

"I know. Everybody needs a sidekick and these days a troll is hard to come by. Popular as fucking rock stars and I eat less."

"Marginally…"

They didn't speak about the funeral at all the following week even though it was the subtext behind every brief conversation.

Shay dedicated her week to training and poring over historical research as a welcome distraction, waiting for Peyton to find the next client. She wasn't used to waiting on anyone.

She was spending more time at Warehouse Two, if only to cut down on Peyton's cabin fever, even if some of his outfits were like staring at a moving 3D image. She suspected the wardrobe was part of the reason he was still alive. It would be hard to fire straight at him without looking away.

Peyton convinced Shay to replace the couch with something larger that he immediately nicknamed couch island.

Shay found it a nice place to recline as she scrolled through the news. "Ever wonder how warped things would be if they didn't have bounty hunters bringing in magical criminals? At least I had the decency to keep my killing in the shadows."

Peyton blinked and looked up from his laptop. "New definition for decency but I'll take it." Peyton was lounging at the other end of the large, L-shaped sofa. He looked up from his laptop. "We should start a new kind of urban dictionary for hitmen. Bet it would sell a million copies. Why are you making that face? I know that one. You make it when you feel a disturbance in the force."

"It's not important. I'm annoyed at myself. I want Greg to call with a meeting time with Smite-Williams." She looked at Peyton's four-leaf clover shirt. At least his skinny jeans were normal. "Is that your lucky shirt?"

He arched an eyebrow and went back to looking at his screen. "Good one. Keep your murderous day job. You need more bait to tempt the fish."

Shay shrugged and rested her head on her arms. "Maybe the guy's just busy. Fuck him. I'm in no hurry."

"That sounded totally believable. What if I told you that I have a job to distract you, complete with a fifty thousand euro down-payment, and a hundred and fifty thousand euro final payout?"

Shay bolted upright. "Give me details."

"That was like throwing chum in the water. Remember a while back when I thought I had a lead on a job and the guy backed out? He wanted to cheap out on me."

"I remember there wasn't much more than that."

Peyton gave Shay his best shit-eating grin. "He's back and he's ready to pay. Best part... The job is in Paris."

Shay tilted her head. She could combine a little mini-vacation with the job. "Already liking it so far."

"Forty years back, a businessman named Francois Martine had his mountain chalet robbed by a high-end cat burglar. A real expert. French police even suspected magic was involved because there were no clues other than a missing owl."

"I remember reading about that heist. A solid gold owl."

"That's the one! The thief took only the one item. Ignored all the other art, jewelry, computers. Just wanted the owl."

"The owner refused to say why it was so important. Everyone figured it was a solid gold artifact."

Peyton nodded, smiling. "Give the tomb raider a kewpie doll. My research says it's a magical artifact and has a lot more value than just being a big block of gold."

"And what did the client say?"

"The client is Martine's daughter, Elaine. She says the owl has been in her family for generations. There's a bonus if we don't press for details."

"That's a first. We'll need to do a thorough background check to make sure we aren't arming the devil." Shay rubbed the back of her neck. "I'm guessing you have some leads."

"Yeah, this is where it gets really weird."

"Magic gets there eventually."

Peyton shook his head. "No, that's *not* the weird part. Not that long after the theft, rumors popped up on the net. Someone claiming to be the thief said he had the owl and left eleven clues to its whereabouts with five in a cipher that no one's been able to figure out."

"An actual treasure hunt with clues."

"Initially, a lot of treasure hunters went after it, but a lot of them got cold feet when several turned up dead. The clues have always pointed to Paris."

"A very big city with just as many old catacombs underground. Can you narrow it down?" Shay put her phone down on the nearby wooden crate that was doubling as a side table. The warehouse was still a decorating work in progress to Peyton and getting crowded to Shay.

"Elaine has additional information she recently came into that might narrow it down more."

"And when is she going to share the rest of the information?"

"She already did after she sent the fifty-k non-refundable deposit."

Shay laughed. "You buried the lead. You managed to get a non-refundable deposit out of the woman? Not bad."

"It's our new company policy. Only way to do it. Makes the client have some skin in the game. That way, Elaine won't hire six different hunters to up her chances. *All or nothing* kind of deal."

It wasn't the first time Shay had looked at Peyton with a budding admiration. Still, there was a small piece of doubt that kept her on guard, ready for a sign of betrayal. It was all too common and ended in a permanent layoff. *Maybe not this time.* "What's got her motivated enough to part with that much money?"

"The key that will allow the ciphers to be broken. She's passed along the five clues in decoded form."

Shay blinked, her eyes wide. "Now, that's interesting. Wonder how she got her hands on that."

"Don't know. Didn't ask. She didn't tell. Look, from what I can tell this shit is straightforward. No one else is currently seeking the owl, so all we have to do is crunch through some clues."

"If she's willing to part with fifty thousand euros just to take a chance, there's more to this story. What about the guys who died trying to locate it? What exactly did them in?" *Don't say icicles.* Shay tried to hide the involuntary shudder that passed down her spine.

"Several died of unknown causes."

"How in this day and age could the cause be unknown?"

"When the pieces don't add up. They were hit by lightning on a clear, sunny day in the middle of an empty parking lot. In another attempt, a guy froze to death in the middle of a chapel in the middle of the summer."

Fuck me, he said ice.

"Uh…" Peyton winced.

"Spit it out."

Peyton shrugged. "One operative was reduced to a gooey puddle and the liquid was identified as human matter. They used DNA to figure out who he was. That has got to be painful."

Shay worked her jaw a little. "Sounds like magic."

"Do you still want the job?"

"My business model is all about retrieving magic artifacts. Can't back out because one of them belongs in a horror film."

Peyton smiled. "Did I mention I'll provide backup for this one from here?"

"That's one way to get you to stay put. Threaten you with flash freezing or melting." Peyton shook his head, his stomach lurching. "Seeing that could put me off pizza. Getting this back to the owner will solidify your rep as a reliable delivery system."

"I'm a tomb raider, *not* a delivery girl."

"Still, we're reliable as the post office. Neither wind or rain, or dark of night will keep you from your paid rounds. Has a sentimental ring to it."

Shay snorted. "They're not all that reliable anymore. Postal drones are the worst and the occasional rogue gargoyle isn't any better."

"You know what I mean." Peyton shrugged. "You're the one who had a rep for never failing as a hitman. A one hundred percent kill rate. You take a job, you get it done."

"If you're going to survive as an entrepreneur you make sure your word is trusted even by the untrustworthy, especially them." Shay narrowed her eyes. "You did good, Peyton, but next time check with me before you take someone's money." *Frozen to death. What is in Paris?*

Peyton grimaced and nodded quickly. He was fidgeting, all over the place. Shay marked it up to getting his hand slapped. *He has to learn I'm in charge.*

Despite Shay's harsh tone, she felt something approaching gratitude for Peyton's initiative. She liked the idea of having a clever assistant who could take some of the workload off her shoulders. It was a bonus that he saw the angles before they hit him in the face.

Shay hopped to her feet, already walking to the Spider. "I should go get some equipment ready, get a plan outlined. Send me the information on the clues that you've already gathered, along with the other client communications. I can study it all on the plane."

Peyton got up and followed her to the car. "You know, if you set me up with access to all your warehouses, I could have what you need set up ahead of time."

Shay stopped in her tracks and pivoted, placing her hands on his shoulders and squeezing enough to cause a little pain. "You don't have the skill set to know what is needed and you don't need to know those places yet. We're becoming friends and coworkers but don't forget *who* I am."

Peyton looked into her dark eyes and forced himself to smile as Shay gradually let go, dropping her arms.

"I understand."

"Company meeting over." Shay's voice was calm and slow. A warning. She turned to walk the rest of the way to her car.

Peyton tapped something into his phone and tossed it to her. Shay snatched it out of the air with a frown.

"What the hell is this?"

"Just look at it."

Shay pressed her lips together in a straight line as she looked at the image on screen. It was a satellite image of a warehouse with the address for Warehouse Three.

"Just tap the screen once," Peyton said.

Shay tapped, holding her finger steady despite the rush of anger. She saw an image of the warehouse from the street level, confirming it was Warehouse Three.

"See? That one's not secret anymore, so there's no reason to hide it from me, right?" Peyton smiled nervously, proud of his accomplishment. He was playing a dangerous game. "From the power usage, I'm guessing that one is an equipment warehouse, weapons storage."

Shay calmly tossed his phone back to him, her face a blank slate. Peyton caught it with both hands and almost dropped it. He saw the focused look on her face and froze. Somewhere behind him was the line and he had crossed way over it, even if he had done it on purpose.

Shay pulled her 9mm from her shoulder holster and neatly pointed it right at the center of his forehead, still calmly looking at him. "A few questions. Question one is easy. How?"

Peyton swallowed hard and set his phone down carefully on the armrest of the nearest chair. "Easy. I put a liquid tracker on you. Very hard to wash off, lasts for days."

"Question two is not going to be easy. Tell me why I shouldn't put a fucking bullet into your forehead and end my detection problem. You're good at what you do… clearly, but I have to wonder if you're an asset or a *liability*."

Peyton swallowed again, taking several slow deep breaths as he locked eyes with Shay. He could feel the seconds passing. "I've got a dead man's switch."

"A dead man's switch. You're *rigged*?"

"If I don't regularly check in online at a particular server that I control and enter a code, then information goes out across the web to some very particular locations. Multiple receivers. Among other things, it reveals you aren't dead. It'll also give the location of this warehouse and number three." Peyton licked his upper lip. His mouth felt dry.

Shay held the gun steady. Never break your own rules especially when they get you this far. *Fuck me, I broke it when I pulled him off the street.* Trust no one past an anonymous meeting place. "Question three. *Why?*"

"To make a point."

"What's your point? That I can't trust you because you'll try to fuck me the first chance you'll get?" She felt an ache and a grief in the center of her chest that she hadn't felt in a very long time. It hurt all the more to know that someone had gotten through her defenses, at last, and was just another cheap imitation of a human being.

Peyton shook his head. "That I never forgot who you are. It's always right here, first thought." He tapped his forehead. "I have leverage, too. Even as a walking dead man." He pointed at Shay, angry. "You don't think much of me. I know, we joke around a little more every day, you put me on your payroll, but you think I'm chickenshit. I tried to tell you, I can fight back, too." His voice was defiant. He was doing his best to stand up straighter.

"I can change the locations. I guarantee you that after this I'll be doing sweeps every time I'm done talking with you."

"You change locations, I'll find it again eventually. I'm an *information* guy. That's why you saved me, remember?" Peyton held up his hands. "I realized I have to show you I have claws, too. I knew I needed a way to make sure you wouldn't see me as fallout if something went south. More convenient to let me die if an enemy got too close. I mean, that's part of the risk, right? I needed to make it worth your while to not only teach me but protect me... even over an artifact."

"That's asking a lot." Her eyes were shining at the sting of the betrayal and the knowledge that she was the one who set it in motion. Her instincts to protect herself made Peyton look for a failsafe.

"I was sitting around here after you ordered me not to go to my own father's funeral like I was a second-rate bonded troll. Got under my skin. I'm not your fucking pet. Gave me time to think, though. I figure there must be eight or nine more warehouses like this one to find, so best to start now."

"This leaves us in an awkward place." Shay kept her breathing steady, her finger still brushing against the trigger.

"We've never really left that phase. You need to decide if you can work with someone you can respect instead of something you can control." His chest was rising and falling, and his heart was pounding. Peyton knew this was the critical mass. Either Shay would put away her gun and listen or pull the trigger. He calculated the odds when he went searching for the warehouse. Fifty-fifty. It could easily go either way, but a confrontation just like this was going to happen at some point.

Better to see it coming.

"There was a kill a few years ago that said something to me just before I shot him." Shay turned to the side, still pointing the gun at Peyton's head.

"That doesn't sound encouraging." Peyton wondered if his family would ever know he lived another month after his first death.

"He said, faith can't happen without a gap of information. You have to go first without knowing the outcome, *especially* when the information is lacking and the potential consequences are a bitch."

"Shit, is that what got him killed?" Peyton's voice cracked but he stayed where he was, refusing to run or look for a weapon. Both would be pointless if Shay made up her mind to shoot. Besides, first rule when faced with a skilled predator. Never run, it only gets them excited.

"No, choices he made years ago led to that bullet. By the time he and I met it was over, one way or the other. He knew it too."

Peyton pressed forward with the argument he worked out when he was searching for the warehouse. The words tumbled out of him. "The way I see it, if you really want a different life than being a hired killer till the day your consequences catch up with you..." Peyton dug his fingernails into the palm of his hand, determined not to let the fear show on his face. "Then you have to make a different choice today. You trust me not to fuck up and lead a mercenary back here or sell you out and I'll keep your secrets and help both of us get rich."

"There's another option."

"Yeah, I know. Not so fond of that one."

"I shoot you and start over."

"You know it won't play out like that." Peyton shrugged a shoulder. "Well, probably not... What's the likelihood you'll get someone else to help you after word gets out you killed the last information specialist? We tend to be a sensitive lot and bullets that penetrate our skull piss us off." Every muscle in his body ached from tension.

"You do have balls."

"Ever since birth." Peyton slowly sat down in the chair behind him, never taking his eyes off Shay. "Look, I've played my hand. Out in the open, somewhat at least. I mean, I told you what I knew. I didn't make you find out. I had to know you'd have some feelings about it. Time to choose. Killer *or* tomb raider. We work together and become fucking rich *or* you shoot me, blow this place up and start running."

Shay shifted her jaw side to side. "I underestimated you. That doesn't happen to me very often."

"Thank goodness it happened with a *somewhat* friendly."

"Tomb raider..." Shay blinked hard, sliding her gun back into the holster.

Peyton blew out a breath, puffing out his cheeks. "That was close. That was the worst job interview, *ever*. Only thing that could have made it worse was if I didn't get the job."

"You live for today. You're right, there are no guarantees. Might as well let that idea go and work with you till the day I can't."

"Yeah, this is going to stay awkward."

Shay picked up her purse and started walking away, shouting to Peyton without turning around. "Well, get up. You're coming with me to Warehouse Three. You can start familiarizing yourself with the equipment and layout."

"When do I get to see what's inside the other warehouses."

"When you find them, and if you remain in one non-congealed piece. You know there's a unique security system on each one, right?" She didn't bother to correct his count of warehouses. Let him find out for himself.

Shay turned and headed toward the Spider, trying to hide her relief. *End of my perfect record. First time I ignored my gut and didn't pull the trigger. I choose tomb raider.*

"Congealed? Are there *magical* traps on the warehouses?" Peyton scooped up his laptop gripping it hard to hide his shaking hands. He ran to the far side of the Spider and got inside, shutting the door. "New word for our hitman dictionary. *Job security*. Noun. A temporary and fleeting experience."

"How about *trust*? Noun. Intangible and necessary item that will get you killed one day and save your ass on another." Shay turned the key in the ignition, feeling the engine come to life as she pushed the button to lift the roll top door.

"Yeah, this book could be a real moneymaker. If I manage to live long enough to finish it."

"I suppose we'll find out eventually." *Never been wrong before and felt relieved at the same time. Unknown territory.* Peyton has real skills. If he could pull something like that on her, then eventually he might be ready to face down his brother and sister, even without her help.

Nice, Peyton.

23

A relaxed atmosphere hung over the Parisian café even though a few drones buzzed in the area. Shay found an outside table hugging the wall and sat back, watching the crowd from behind a pair of oversized Versace sunglasses.

No obvious hitman strolled by taking quick glances as they passed. No one sat down at any of the nearby tables with their backs to the wall, making a point of looking casual as they sipped coffee. That could mean that French killers were just better on the job than the man Shay followed in Munich, or it might be that for once, the universe was cutting her a break, and she could concentrate on her coffee and roll.

Strange things are happening all the time these days.

Shay scrutinized the other patrons at the outdoor café as she took a sip of her strong black coffee.

As far as anyone looking at her could tell, Shay was just another upscale tourist, dressed for the occasion. Her athletic body looked good in the vintage St. Laurent poppy print dress she'd purchased from a local shop.

She had studied the background extensively on the plane, occasionally distracted from replaying the confrontation with Peyton. She put it out of her mind as best she could and focused on the material. Her goal was to get it memorized, second nature by the time the plane landed.

It was her usual protocol, giving her time to sit peacefully and take in the locals, overhear interesting information that sometimes proved to be useful. At the very least, relax for an hour.

The first half of the decoded clues all pointed to the owl being in Paris. Another suggested a general part of town. The last of the ciphers the client had only recently found the key to translate them. The client didn't volunteer any information on how they had decoded the last ciphers, and Shay wasn't inclined to ask. Not necessary for the completion of the job.

Peyton had been right. Everything about the job was surprisingly straightforward. It was just this side of mundane. But given everything she went through on recent assignments, she wasn't about to complain about the lack of a gunfight, deadly logs, flying ice, or Nazi accessories. This job was about finding the owl quickly with the application of her brain rather than her trigger finger, so far.

The information in the decoded cipher clues led Shay on her little café jaunt. She went over the relevant clues in her mind, at least in their translated form. Her French was decent enough, but if there were some subtle hints encoded in the language usage itself, she was missing it.

Look from the old café, and you'll see the first point. It serves the heart's needs.

The second point is at the oldest that serves the body's needs.

The last point is at the oldest that serves the soul's needs.

The clues were hinting at some sort of triangle, with the target presumably in the middle, but without knowing the points, that left an entire city to search. Fancy scanners and gadgets would be useless without the locations of the outer points. All the technology, energy, and magic that was present would confound the operation further.

For all the combined experience and tools of her growing operation, Shay was forced to rely on a much more old-fashioned approach. Exploration on foot, no matter how frustrating it might be.

If I ever find the twisted asshole who stole the owl, I'm going to slap him around and make him go through my own set of clues. First one, 'The five knuckles form the painful thing soon coming at your face.'

Shay had been visiting cafes and looking out at the streets from tables for most of the day. She still had no idea what the café clue could mean.

"Oh, Harold, we have to visit the Louvre," said an elderly American woman sitting with her husband a few tables away from Shay. She was dressed in a pale blue suit, her hair neatly pinned back. She pointed in the distance, a heavy charm bracelet hanging from her wrist. "We can even see it from here."

Several nearby tourists in jeans and matching velour outfits with matching fanny packs were talking about the nearby art museum loud enough to be heard several tables away.

Just go already and leave me in peace.

Shay glanced over at the woman and just past her. She bit down a gasp as her eyes widened.

Son of a bitch.

Shay had been so focused on ancient clues and ideas that she'd forgotten that the owl wasn't stolen hundreds of years ago but only a few decades ago. Around the time the Louvre Pyramid was built.

Shay peered down the street, taking in the sight of the distant glass and metal pyramid making the Louvre.

Okay, thanks, old lady. Art serves the mind... and the heart. If that's the case, what serves the body?

The delivery of a bowl of soup to another customer almost made Shay cackle in glee. Inspiration flowed freely now.

Oldest café or restaurant?

Shay already happened to know that place, Café Procope. She'd always wanted to visit the restaurant but had never gotten around to it. Unfortunately, it was only a likely point in a triangle and not her final destination. She had no reason to check it out until after the job.

With two points figured out, she only needed to find the oldest place to serve the soul's needs in Paris.

Shay smirked.

Oldest brothel? Nah, that would the body if anything.

Shay picked up her phone to make the research easy on herself. She typed in *oldest church in Paris* into her search.

The Church of Saint-Germain-des-Prés? Okay, I have my three points, now just have to see what's at the center.

A helpful map application pinpointed an old mansion snuggled in a commercial district. That stood out enough that she didn't doubt she was on the right track.

Okay, I guess I know what I'm doing tonight. Just need to make a couple of calls first.

That night, boots, jeans, and a jacket and tactical harness over a sensible shirt replaced the beautiful dress and heels. A woman needed to dress for the function, and a tomb raid required a different fashion sensibility than a day tour of the City of Light.

Shay crept along in the darkness between the buildings, avoiding the street lights. As her backpack rustled, she wondered if, in the end, she preferred jobs that took place on remote islands or deserts in the middle of nowhere. Breaking into some old building in the center of one of the largest cities in Europe screamed complications.

Getting into a gun battle would bring her the kind of attention that would soon have the streets of Paris swarming with hitmen and cops.

Guess we'll see how much of a bitch it'll be to get into this place.

The last two decoded clues injected more tension into her body.

Burn the holy lamp and prove your faith with the holy fire. Only then will the prize be revealed.

Yeah, that could mean a lot of shit. Fires of hell, anyone?

Shay easily hopped a fence, approaching the target building from behind. The two-story building was once a nobleman's mansion centuries ago, and now served as a living museum during the day.

The drone survey didn't show any security guards and the cameras would be easy enough to loop and the alarms to disable once she was ready to enter. The only thing Shay still couldn't figure out was why the client had gone to the trouble of hiring a tomb raider at all. The job seemed like more of a simple snatch and grab, which meant there was information held back. Peyton searched for gossip on the dark web but there was nothing. Shay was going to have to learn on the fly.

The obvious explanation was the owl was a magic artifact, possibly dangerous. The background check confirmed the client was a legitimate businesswoman with a claim to a solid-gold owl. Shay was not turning over a weapon to a sociopath. More protocol.

The multiple dead bodies associated with the hunt for the owl might have been enough to spook the woman. The idea of a legitimate curse wriggled in the back of her thoughts.

Maybe she's throwing enough bodies at it until the curse is resolved. Fun, fun. I don't know if dying while looking for a golden owl is badass or lame.

Shay closed in on the rear of the building. She pulled out a small black rod and pulled it apart, extending three metal legs and a small antenna. She pressed a few buttons on the side and set it down, whistling to herself.

The simple device was insufficient to take down a serious security system, but Peyton reassured her that the mansion museum wasn't exactly an IT marvel in the heart of Paris.

The next job I'll probably end up in an ancient Atlantean city with some sort of magical super-computer making me answer riddles about Oriceran shit, and I'll miss being in Paris.

Shay waited for her phone to buzz. Peyton had consolidated most of her various alerts to the device. *I put a key detail for the mission in the hands of someone who went behind my back and created mutual destruction. Kind of clever.*

The alerts indicated the successful suppression of the security system. She approached a door and looked it up and down. All electronic locks.

Shay gave a satisfied smile. So many people thought complicated locks were more secure, but in most cases, they were easier for a person like her to defeat than something older with tumblers.

Shay pulled a small black disc from her pocket and placed it above the handle. She pressed a button on the side and counted. One Mississippi. Two Mississippi. A faint buzz filled the air, and the door opened.

She resisted the urge to clap. She half-wondered about recording the whole raid on a body cam to share with Peyton later. Not an entirely bad idea. Another time.

Okay, need to focus. Snegurka could be waiting for me in there.

No Russian Ice Witch ambushed her inside the building. The only enemy was the dust. She barely resisted a sneeze.

Shay sighed and pulled a small flashlight from her pocket. She'd brought her AR goggles in her backpack, but the job didn't require that level of hardware, yet.

She swept the room, looking for anything out of place. Nothing but a storage room filled with boxes and shelves. A quick inspection didn't net her a golden owl. The question remained if the owl was in the building, or if there was simply some other clue she needed to recover.

Deciding a systematic top-to-bottom search would be her best bet, Shay headed upstairs. Various bedrooms and closets contained interesting nineteenth century bric-a-brac, but nothing looking remotely like a golden owl. Her gloves kept her DNA and fingerprints off all the cabinets, boxes, chests, and drawers she opened.

Shay knew she could take her time.

She contacted Peyton after her café epiphany and he hacked into the place's systems and reviewed the security tapes. He verified no guards patrolled the building at night. Shay had hours to play around inside.

The lack of time pressure didn't ease any of her frustration at not finding any evidence pointing her toward the owl.

Is this one of those things where it's hidden in plain sight in something else?

Shay shook her head, trying to think of anything she'd seen that might hold the owl.

Maybe I'm in the wrong place.

Not likely. Peyton's additional background research discovered that the place had changed hands a few weeks prior to the theft of the golden owl. Coincidence wasn't something Shay believed existed. Magic yes, coincidence, not so much. If the damned artifact wasn't there, let there be some small scrap of evidence.

If necessary, she would track down the owner with

Peyton's help, but roughing up people for information wasn't smart. The more you threatened violence, the more she risked forcing the hand of the authorities.

Okay, nothing on the second floor. But still the rest of the place to check.

Room after room, hour after hour of careful searching, Shay summed up her situation standing in a baroque bedroom. "I'm fucked."

Her inspection of the first floor resulted in no more success than the second floor, other than the greater diversity of room types. The building didn't appear to be anything other than what they advertised, a living museum dedicated to old lame aristocratic living.

Inspections with her goggles didn't pick up anything more important than the fact the place was surprisingly well insulated.

Shay moved between the expansive dining room and the commercial kitchen a few times, looking for more clues, before heading down to her final hope, the large underground wine cellar that stretched under half the building.

What the hell am I missing?

Stacked barrels dominated one side of the room, and she didn't see any other exits. Shay sucked in a breath and lowered her AR goggles.

Come on. It's been a nice little trip to Paris, but I need that damned owl.

The tomb raider activated the goggles and shifted to thermal mode, looking around the darkened room. The back wall displayed large temperature differences from the rest of the room. It was several degrees colder than the rest of the room.

Huh. That's the only weird thing I've seen since getting here.

Shay made her way over and felt carefully along the wall. Her patience was rewarded, as her hand brushed over a small hidden button.

Shay let a stupid grin dominate her face as a secret passage slid open in the back of the wine cellar, the loud scrape of the shifting wall against the floor echoing against the concrete walls. A cold breeze passed over her, making goosebumps appear on her arms.

"Guess this really is gonna be the easiest money I've made in a while." Still, the hairs on the back of her neck were standing up, anticipating trouble. Shay didn't do well with *easy.*

Shay moved through the passage and down rough spiraling stone stairs that were connected to the hidden opening. She arrived in a narrow hallway with oddly textured walls. She lifted her flashlight to get a better look. Skulls stared back.

"What... the... fuck?"

Shay stumbled backward, going for her gun, her heart kicking into a measured gallop. Several seconds passed as she realized she wasn't being attacked by a horde of undead. Instead, skulls and femurs formed the walls.

"Ugh. The Catacombs? Of course. Fucking Paris. I think I prefer the stupid desert now."

Shay holstered her gun and looked back and forth. There were two paths, both curving away in opposite directions.

"Yeah, this isn't annoying or anything."

Thirty minutes into her exploration of the right tunnels, Shay decided she'd gone the wrong way, but that meant she'd lost a good hour by the time she'd returned and took the left tunnels instead.

Five minutes later, Shay threw her hands in the air and let out a loud groan.

"You have to be fucking kidding! It was right over here, and I took the wrong way? Why weren't there some damned clues about that? Assholes."

A high stone column decorated with a cross sat in the center of a chamber. A stone bowl sat atop the flat-topped column at about chest level. Thick lamp oil filled the bowl.

Shay recalled the final few clues.

Burn the holy lamp and prove your faith with the holy fire. Only then will the prize be revealed.

"I get the feeling I'm not going to like this."

Shay reached into her pocket and pulled out a lighter. She lowered the lighter to the oil and flicked it on. Blue-orange flame spread over the entire surface.

A huge curtain of flame burst into existence a few feet from the back wall and drifted toward the center of the room.

Shay leapt back, rolling to the ground, assuming she'd set off a trap, but the wall of flame didn't move past the center of the room.

She glanced to either side. The wall didn't extend out the doorways, and she couldn't see any obvious source. She assumed it was magical, but to her greater irritation, she also still didn't see a golden owl.

The intense heat from the flames radiated from the wall, making the room stuffy. Sweat beaded Shay's brow.

"Prove your faith with the holy fire? What's that even mean?"

Inspection with her AR goggles confirmed a very hot wall of fire now separated the room into two halves.

Shay flipped up her goggles and winced. "No." She turned to go out the way she entered. "I can come back with protective fire gear."

The wall suddenly thickened and extended. Flaming death now blocked both exits.

"Shit. That's inconvenient."

It was time to gear up for an escape. She was already wearing leather gloves that could protect her hands. She pulled off her coat to drape over her head and prepared to rush through one of the exits. The fire didn't seem to extend past the room she was in.

Shay took several deep breaths. She took one step, stopped and spun toward the back wall, aborting her run.

"No, no, no. That can't be it, can it?" Shay nodded. "Okay, okay, okay. I can do this. I can leap through a magical wall of flame to prove some damned point because some magical thief really liked his magical riddles. I wonder if the guy who froze to death tried to escape through a wall of snow." She paced back and forth, keeping up the argument. "Okay, it could be that I run through this wall and find a treasure, or it could be that I run through and end up horribly burned and behind even more fire than before. Yeah, fucking great." She shook her head, considering her options and odds of survival.

"Shit. *Whatever.* Still better than dying in my kitchen."

Shay charged through the wall of flame, her eyes closed. Something was off. She kept running, hesitating only a moment before she opened her eyes and looked around.

The flame hadn't burned her. Not only that, she couldn't even feel the heat from the flames behind her. She slowly turned around and looked. The fire had vanished, and a golden owl sat in the now empty stone bowl in the center of the room.

Prove your faith. The old mark's words echoed in her head. There has to be a gap of information and you go anyway, despite the consequences.

Shay slapped her cheeks a few times to make sure she was awake. She stepped toward the owl, reaching out her hands. Her still-pounding heart managed to beat even faster as she prepared to lift the owl from the bowl.

"Okay. One... two... three."

Shay snatched up the heavy artifact. The room didn't bathe her in flames or even frost. She filled her lungs just in case and turned to head toward the exit.

Why was the owl behind magical flames? Mystery for another day. The fact that different treasure seekers had ended up dead in different ways made her wonder if the coded clues had changed. Maybe even the location. That might explain why the owl wasn't found till now, and not just the convenient cipher decoding.

Shay pushed the thought out of her head. She had a client willing to drop a lot of euros for it. It wasn't her responsibility to solve the mystery of who stole it, only get the artifact back to the client.

Her heart beat returned to normal as Shay whistled, heading toward the stone stairs.

No logs, no water, no mercs. Just a magical wall of flame.

Shay snorted. It wasn't that long ago when killing mercs seemed like a much more normal day for her than running through magical walls.

Shay drove through the streets of Paris, the top down in her rented convertible. She was rocking sun glasses and a red maxi dress that clung to her toned body. Satisfaction emanated out of every pore in her body.

She grinned down at her passenger secured with a lap belt, swaddled in a cloth. A solid gold owl.

S hay stifled a yawn as she watched Peyton put one of
her wrist frequency jammers on the wrong shelf.
She was standing behind him, deciding if she
should go work out for a while and reset her system.

"Hey, not there. I like to keep the wearables separate
from the deployables. I already told you that." Shay shook
her head, trying to force out some of the cobwebs that
came from her jetlag. "Just putting everything together by
general type makes it hard to find later."

Another yawn bubbled up. She left Paris on the next
flight out even though she considered adding an extra day
or making arrangements for the delivery in the city. Better
to do a valuable handoff on her own playing field with her
own resources and safety precautions in place.

Peyton glanced down at the silver bracelet he was holding, and back at the shelf. "I don't understand your organi-
zation system at all. If I could set this up, it'd be totally
different. I bet you're losing all sorts of time to inefficiency.
Seconds add up…"

"When you get your own ultra-secret warehouse full of cool gear, you can organize it however you want, but as long as you're gonna party with me in my warehouses, we use my filing system." She wagged her finger. "And no weird cubicle apartments here. This place is just for business, not for you to… *Peytonize*."

He laughed and moved down the shelves, setting the equipment down. "I'm glad you're letting me in more and trusting me."

"We have an awkward understanding. Besides, my only real choices are to trust you or blow your brains out and moving a headless body by yourself sucks." Shay glanced up at him with a sly smile. "These are the jokes."

Peyton blinked and nodded slowly. "I recognize your flirting is kind of edgy… Takes dark humor to a different level. Good news… you'll get both your warehouses back soon and we can turn Warehouse Two back into a place decorating dreams go to die."

"Funny. Where are you going?" Shay sat up, her full attention suddenly drawn into the conversation.

"Stand down. I'm moving to an actual apartment soon instead of the warehouse. If we work together to pick a place and we *both* set it up, we can make sure it's secure. Then I won't feel so much like some twisted hermit."

"Hermits lived in the woods. Not in air-conditioned warehouses abusing Amazon Prime."

"Might as well be the woods far, far away from any fun."

"I can see that this is going to be a give and take relationship until death do us part."

"Look at you with the humor again."

Shay let out a laugh, even as she grew serious. "I know you're going to do it whether I help you or not."

Peyton slapped his hand over his heart. "You get me."

Shay did a slow roundhouse and kicked him hard enough with the top of her foot to jolt him forward. Peyton stumbled, catching himself. Shay lunged, bending one of his arms behind his back and squeezing him against the shelves.

"If this is foreplay, I'm not into MILFs." He squeezed out the words, his face pressed so tight, one eye was shut.

"*I'm* not a mother."

"You're a mother*fucker*...Argghh...you're squeezing my face!"

Shay let out a whoop of laughter and let him go, her blood finally flowing faster. *Almost as good as a workout.*

Peyton stepped back from the shelves, rubbing his face. "You're not getting a key to my place. Yes, I know you can break in faster than most people can turn a key. It's the principle of the thing."

"Just for fun, leave a few traps for me."

"I thought that was a given. Early warning, one of them will involve flames and not the magical kind. Ouch! Too soon? Go play with your buddies who like to get punched by you. Leave me to reorganizing this place." He looked at the smile on Shay's face. "If I didn't know better I'd say that the thought of mutual destruction was actually helping your mood. Little death on the table is your happy place."

"Doesn't hurt that we scored our little feathered friend."

Shay looked at the round metal side table sitting near the shelves. Normally, she used the table to fieldstrip weapons, but the golden owl sat on it now, gleaming under the harsh fluorescent lights of the warehouse. Even though the job went smoother than any other raid, the experience left her unsettled. Open questions always bothered her.

"You honestly have no idea what the owl might do?" Shay asked. "I thought I wouldn't care, but the more I think about some of the other guys who died... Did any of them die after they had the owl?"

Peyton looked over his shoulder. "All the more reason to deliver it sooner rather than later and collect our payday. You've already proven it's magical, but there has to be more to it than weird curses on people going after it." He rubbed his neck. "But that might not even be from the owl."

"Tell me your theory."

"It was stolen, right? It's possible someone enchanted it later. Stored magic in it, turning it into an artifact."

"Anything interesting you can find? Any links to Oriceran?"

Peyton shook his head. "Not yet, but I'll keep digging."

"I have a feeling I'm gonna be kicking myself when I find out I can make an immortality potion out of it, but a deal's a deal. The last thing the great *Goddess of Truth* needs to be known for is stealing artifacts she was hired to collect."

A smirk appeared on Peyton's face. Shay resisted the urge to throw something at him.

"You got something to say?"

"It's just interesting. You have limits. Your own version of ethics."

"Did you really think I was a soulless bitch?" The smile

was gone from her face. Her need to protect was still close at hand.

"Not entirely... I mean one minute you're threatening to blow a hole through my forehead, and the next you're worried about people not trusting your word."

"You gave me good reason and business is business." Shay could feel her armor coming back over her. This was going to take time. "Just because I used to kill people for a living doesn't mean I have no code, no standards.

"*And* we're back at awkward. Truth is we don't know each other very well. Not yet, but we may, given time." Peyton risked a smile, hoping to break the tension.

Shay picked up the owl, letting the moment pass. *Don't push it.* "We'll get that delivered to the client's contact later tonight."

"You locked this one down quickly. I'm waiting till after delivery to put the word out. When I do, it'll be really good for our reputation. It shows you're not afraid of a few curses or dead bodies. List it under specialties."

Shay cradled the owl to her chest, impressed with its heft. "I can't tell if that's really a thing on the site."

"It is if you know how to post it. What are you going to do when you actually end up cursed on a job? The more high-end stuff you hit, the greater the risk of that sort of thing."

"Hey, I've been shot, stabbed, nearly blown up, strangled, and a lot of other shit in my life."

"Drowned... Just helping."

"That Witch almost impaled me with an ice spear. Curses are just another kind of injury, but you've got a point, so I've got a job for you. Time to build out our roster of contacts."

"What do we need?"

"Start sniffing around to find a few decent magical contacts that we can turn into regular consultants. People who are reliable but willing to not ask too many questions or probe too deeply. Include someone who could help me out of a jam if I do end up with some weird magical injury. I'm not looking for a field Witch or anything, just someone I can go to on occasion and drop some money in exchange for services."

Peyton pulled out his phone and typed a note to himself. "Consider it done."

"I'm going to go park the owl in Warehouse Five... Don't ask, I'm not helping you find it or what's stored there and I already figured out your tracking goo and neutralized it."

"I feel like I'm your Kato. I'm only making you better."

Shay lowered her chin and gave him a menacing look. "Jump me when I walk in the door and I *will* be looking for a new associate. I'll be back in two hours."

Peyton smiled triumphantly, jumping onto the couch. "You just gave me useful information. I know it's about an hour to Warehouse Five."

"It could be a ten-minute drive that I'm making into an hour, so I can run an errand."

Peyton muttered something under his breath. "Can we at least get stuffed crust pizza tonight?"

"All this time with me, and you're still not a proper pizza connoisseur?" Shay made a pained face. "I'll compromise. We'll hit a place that makes both thin crust and stuffed crust. But I reserve the right to mock you the entire dinner for being a damned philistine."

"Not like you don't do that anyway." Peyton's voice grew distant.

"Oh, don't get all your panties in a twist over pizza. I get it, you weren't raised in a proper pizza-respecting family."

Peyton stepped off the couch and pulled out his wallet, flipping it open. "I know, old school. I have a photo in my wallet." He showed the black and white of his mother and father and three young children gathered around a table. "That's us a million years ago. We were never happy for very long. It was more like moments, but this was one of them. Eating pizza... who knew?"

He flipped the wallet closed and put it back in his pocket, pursing his lips. "I miss their murderous little hearts."

"That's gonna have to be something you learn to live with, Peyton. People like us... we all have places that don't heal entirely. We just get used to the occasional stab of pain and keep going. Be ready when I get back. I don't like waiting." *And I don't like talking about feelings.* Shay shook out her hands. May have to go punch something after all.

"Already picked up on that," he said, loudly. Shay was already sliding into the Spider, opening the roll door, even as she secured the owl in a locked compartment she had specially made into the car.

MILF my ass. More like having an annoying little brother.

The pizza didn't disappoint, and the conversation stuck to

the safe topics, but fatigue eventually came over Shay. She dropped Peyton back to his cubicle apartment at Warehouse Two and headed back to her condo.

A quick shower relieved the tension in her muscles and she toweled off, put on a silk nightgown, and slipped underneath the heavy down comforter.

Her phone buzzed the moment she shut her eyes.

"Of course. The universe is not cruel or kind, but annoying and petty."

Shay leaned over and picked up the phone. There was a text from Greg.

Please respond ASAP. Important opportunity that is time-sensitive.

Shay stared at the phone for a second. No rest for the wicked.

Shay texted back. *What opportunity?*

He finally wants to meet you.

She knew instantly who Greg meant and sat up on one elbow. *Smite-Williams?*

Yes.

Where? Is it secure?

I didn't tell him about the diner, and I've only referred to you by your nickname. He suggested a place. There's an Irish pub called the Leanan Sidhe. He says he wants to meet you there tomorrow night at 7:00.

He wants to meet in person?

He only hires people face-to-face. He's made it clear that part is non-negotiable.

Shay blinked at her phone, surprised. High-level power players used layers of minions and lackeys between themselves and their hirelings. If Smite-Williams wanted to meet in person that suggested a mixture of paranoia, confidence, and old-fashioned arrogance.

Okay, Shay texted back. *Tell him I'll be there.*

Should I come along?

No, she texted back. *I don't need a babysitter, but I'll make sure you get a finder's fee.*

I'll let him know right away. I'll give you more details tomorrow.

Okay. Good night.

Shay put down her phone and pulled up the dark blue comforter. She lay still, wide awake half-expecting another text or phone call.

Peyton's research backed up everything Greg had told her about Dr. Smite-Williams. He sat at the top of the magical artifacts game and had paid to retrieve some seriously impressive pieces. *First red flag.* He had a lot more money than the typical university professor and no visible source for it.

Second red flag. He didn't exactly have a dark reputation. Would the man be happy with someone as ruthless as Shay? She didn't work on a leash, even a long one.

She turned on her side and pulled the covers up under her chin. *Where does all this shit go from here?*

25

The next evening, Shay finished a workout at Warehouse One and showered and dressed in narrow black pants and a pale cream-colored silk shirt. She draped a long gold necklace around her neck and looked in a mirror as she put on a deep red lipstick.

She grabbed her keys and headed out the door forty-five minutes early, giving herself the usual cushion of time to take a circuitous route.

Driving a direct route to meet a contact from her warehouse was a good way to die young. One mistake could result in anything from a strike team to a drone bomb. The cautious tomb raider could become an older tomb raider.

The pub where she was meeting Smite-Williams lay surprisingly close to Warehouse One, only fifteen minutes taking a typical route.

Shay did a quick mirror check looking for tails or suspicious drones as she turned a corner, one hand pulling on the wheel.

Is there such as thing as being too paranoid in a world as crazy as this one? Not since magic returned.

She let out a quiet chuckle. Changing careers from professional killer to tomb raider wasn't earning her fewer enemies. Her own caution developed over a lifetime of violence still served her well.

Even before her first tomb raid, she understood how dangerous her new job would be, but it still struck her as ironic that she was routinely killing more people than she did when she was accepting contracts.

Death never brought her pleasure. It was a necessary part of business, and business was good.

Those Alpha Explorer assholes didn't have to die. They should have played ball instead of going down.

Shay shook her head. "I didn't make the rules. I stay alive by them."

Shay pushed through the dense crowd in the pub, surprised by the number of people inside. A din of conversation and clinking glasses filled the place with a general level of noise. She arched a brow in surprise as she looked for her contact.

Smite-Williams had picked a well-populated meet. Shay preferred the opposite. More people meant more places for a killer to hide and more variables to account for in a fight.

Security by obscurity might not be perfect, but it was more reliable and less likely to result in unintended casualties.

Shay stepped around a couple hovering near the corner

of the bar, waiting for a table. Greg had left her a text that Smite-Williams would be in the back. He was described as a handsome, pudgy man in his mid-fifties.

A balding man in a pale blue sweater and jeans bumped against her as he went the other way, smiling as he said, "Excuse me."

Shay gave him a curt smile and made a mental note of his face, while checking her pockets to make sure nothing was removed or deposited. The crowds made it hard to know if it was a clumsy man or she was just made. She glanced back and saw him sit down at the bar without looking back. *Wait till there's a pattern. Let it go till then.*

A man matching the description of Smite-Williams waved from the back. Two empty beer glasses sat in front of him. He was working on a third, and his ruddy cheeks suggested he was already well on the way to being drunk.

Shay looked him up and down as she got closer. His broad smile and easy-going manner undercut the idea of him being paranoid. The willingness to get drunk while discussing magic artifacts bordered on arrogant, but she didn't give a shit as long as he could still carry a conversation and remember it later.

"You must be Miss Carson."

"Dr. Smite-Williams?"

He made a face. "No one calls me that but my dean, and he's a bit of an ass." Smite-Williams chuckled. "After a few more beers, you can call me Father O'Banion, but for now *The Professor* works. That's what most people call me."

"Friends?"

"Friends and *frenemies*." He smiled showing most of his teeth.

MARTHA CARR & MICHAEL ANDERLE

Shay slipped into a seat across from him, slightly uncomfortable with her back to the entrance. She resisted asking him to change seats with her. "Interesting place for a meet."

"This place? Aye, I all but live here, and the owner is a man that... let's just say I trust him with my life, and appropriate arrangements have been made. As long as we talk in this booth, it won't be an issue."

Shay glanced around, wondering what kind of spell was being used. No obvious signs.

"Like I said, appropriate measures have been taken."

Shay looked back over her shoulder at the bar. Everyone was minding their own business. No one was casing the place or looking in her direction. She turned back, focusing on The Professor. "I hear you're in need of a freelance field archaeologist..."

"That I am. There's a magical artifact that I need you to recover. You've come highly recommended from a number of sources that I trust." His smile slid into a smirk that didn't suit him. "You're new on the scene, aren't you?"

"I get the job *done*. That's all that's important."

"That you do, Miss Carson. Heard that too, which is why we're meeting." He punctuated his sentence with a sip of his beer.

"Glad to..." Shay's face twitched.

Fuck. Missing small details gets you killed.

"Problem?" asked The Professor.

"You know my name." Shay kept her tone even. "You *shouldn't* know my name."

The Professor laughed. "Of course, I do. Don't worry, Mister Abbot didn't pass it along. He kept your details out of it, per his usual and I respect that. Require it even. Doesn't mean I don't do my own research."

He raised his hand, signaling the waiter to bring another beer. "Don't sound so surprised. I'm very good at collecting information, and I don't work with people if I don't know their names and faces. It keeps everyone more honest."

Shay almost laughed. An older Peyton. "Fair enough. It's not how I prefer to do business, but you're the man throwing down the cash."

"And I wasn't asking for your permission. Cheers." He lifted the new glass of beer the waiter put down.

"Bring me one of those." Shay nodded to the waiter. "No, you weren't. Do you want to tell me more about what I already know or get down to business?"

The Professor picked up his beer, letting out a sharp laugh. "Not much for small talk, I take it. Tomb raiders rarely like to talk. Too easy to let something slip. Very well, I've verified that you already recovered the treasure of Oak Island, the Golden Owl of Paris, and I'm pretty sure you pulled something valuable out of Lake Toplitz. You've been scoring some impressive wins."

Shay blinked, resting her hands on the table. "You're *very* well-informed."

He grinned. "I hope someone writes that on my tombstone. My second choice is, *the shell is here but the nut is gone.*" He gulped down more beer, set his glass down and clapped his hands together. "Enough about the past. I care more about the future." He looked up at her, locking eyes. "Well, I care about artifacts from the past, and the particular artifact I need you to collect."

"Which is what?"

"The Rod of Supay."

"As in the Incan God of Death and the Underworld? You play hard."

"Ah, an educated woman, just as I expected. That's delightful. Aye, the same."

Shay nodded, taking her beer from the waiter. "And this is a magical artifact?"

"It is a rather nasty little magical artifact that I need to remove from circulation. It creates something that I think the average person would call a *zombie*."

Shay winced. "Great." A cool smile came over her face. "Don't you think it's a bad idea to give me all the gory details? You're a lot more trusting than a lot of clients."

The red-faced professor scoffed. "A successful job requires the gory details. As I said, I know a lot about you, Miss Carson. I know you get the job done, and I know when a client pays you, you treat him honorably enough. I don't have time to play little games. I'll pay you, you'll bring me the artifact." He shrugged. "It's simple, and I imagine we both wouldn't like what would happen if one of us made a move to screw over the other."

Tension spread through Shay's back and shoulders. His demeanor didn't change, but his casual confidence filled her with unease, as if he didn't care about death. Professor Smite-Williams, she suspected, was a lot more than an academic with a sideline in artifact dealing.

"Yeah," Shay said, wrapping her hands around the cold glass. "It's like you said. I deliver the artifact. I get the money. The terms?"

The Professor took a long drink off his glass, finishing

off the beer. He exhaled, giving a hard tap to his chest with the side of his fist. "Five million for the successful return of the artifact."

Her pulse raced at the mention of the huge payday. *Real money.*

"I have good information on the location of the rod. It'll be simple in theory. Insertion, recovery, retrieval, payment."

"If it's so simple, why don't you go get it?"

"I stay in my lane. It's better that way." He let out a low chuckle. "I need a professional to execute a simple plan because theory and execution are two separate things. First of all, the location of the artifact is under the control of some very unpleasant rebels." The Professor hesitated... a question hanging in his mind. "It's my understanding, Miss Carson that you're good at dealing with angry men holding guns."

"I can take care of myself in a fight."

"Good. The second complication is there's at least one other group interested in the Rod of Supay and they'll soon be on their way to attempt to collect it."

Shay nodded, the plan already forming in her head. "No problem. You understand that if necessary, they'll be removed as contenders."

"Oh, a foolish man who shoots at a beautiful woman deserves everything he gets, but I don't think these men will shoot at you."

She snorted. "Why's that?"

"Because they prefer to use dark magic as a weapon. I presume you've heard of the Brujos Rojos."

"The asshole Warlocks who kidnapped children from

Happy Magic Land Amusement Park in Anaheim?"

"Among *other* things."

Shay nodded, sipping her beer. "Yeah, I've heard of them, but I thought they were killed off."

"Roaches can be quite resistant to pesticides." Smite-Williams shrugged, pressing his lips into a thin line.

"You want me to go after an Incan death rod with a bunch of Warlocks on my ass? And you only pay five million?"

"You won't be working alone."

Shay bristled but waited to hear the rest.

"I'm hiring you because you have a combination of skills that fit well with some of my more dangerous desires, including this one. I can give you the most likely location of the Rod of Supay, but you'll still need to use your skills as a field archaeologist to locate it, on site. I will provide a specialist as backup."

"I work alone." Shay considered passing on the job. First Peyton crowding her life, now this. *But five million.* She worked the muscles in her jaw, feeling herself slip further into a new game where she didn't get to control all the rules.

"Not on this job." The Professor lifted his eyebrows, wrinkling his forehead as he smiled. "There's a man, a bounty hunter. Class *six.*"

Shay resisted the urge to whistle in genuine appreciation. Even if a class six bounty hunter was protecting her ass that didn't mean she wanted to work with him. The last thing she needed was to be in close quarters with an asshole-big-shot-bounty-hunter, second guessing her tactics.

I've taken down worse. "I don't care if he's the toughest badass on the planet," Shay said. "I like working by myself."

"I hope you like taking home five million dollars more. Let me make this clear, Miss Carson." The smile remained fixed on his face. "This is nonnegotiable. You're not losing any money on the ride along. Take it for what it is. A gift of free protection."

"People need protection *from* me."

"Then the bounty hunter will be very bored, I imagine."

Shay gritted her teeth. "If he tries anything stupid, he'll regret it."

"You will come up with a plan to execute. I think you'll find this man avoids obvious stupidity."

"If he decides to go after the Warlocks, that's not my problem. I'm there to get the artifact, not save his ass."

"I wouldn't worry. He has a lot of field experience dealing with threats like the Brujos Rojos, and he doesn't shrink from the extreme and necessary application of violence when it's warranted, Miss Carson. I'm sure you'll find him amenable to your style."

The waiter delivered another beer to Smite-Williams even though he didn't ask for a refill.

He took a sip, drumming his fingers on the table. "He's a man who is *very* good at what he does. Feel free to check into *his* background. He's not nearly as secretive as you. Do we have a deal, Miss Carson? If not, I need to move on to other options."

Shay observed the professor as he drank his beer, the faintest of smiles on his face.

"We have a deal. What's the name of this bounty hunter?"

"Brownstone. James Brownstone."

The next morning, Shay pulled the Spider into Warehouse Two and got out, making a direct line for the office.

Peyton sat at the desk, staring at his computer screen. He was wearing a plaid shirt and plaid shorts – nothing matched. He was going for irony.

"Were you able to check into Brownstone?"

Peyton nodded, still looking at the information on the screen. "The guy checks out. Licensed class six bounty hunter. Like all high-end bounty hunters he specializes in bringing in enhanced threats, primarily magical in nature. This guy kicks serious ass, Shay. He's put a lot of nasty guys into ultramaxes." He looked over her. "People talk about not wanting to meet bad guys in dark alleys. This is the guy that bad people in dark alleys are afraid of."

Shay rolled her eyes and scoffed. "He can't be all that."

"This is all public records shit. As far as I can tell, he's been a bounty hunter most of his life. He was an orphan, grew up being raised in a Catholic orphanage."

"Great, so he's a do-gooder. He'll probably beg me not to shoot the assholes coming after us."

Peyton laughed. "This guy has killed more people than *you*. Look, I know you like the lone huntress thing, but I think this Brownstone could be a good match for you. You can be the brains and beauty. He can be the murderous brawn. He's got a good reputation for getting the job done, and if you can concentrate on retrieving artifacts while he concentrates on taking down mercs or Witches, it's win-win."

Shay pursed her lips, one hip jutting out as she crossed her arms. "Smite-Williams didn't leave me much of a choice."

"Five million is a nice pay day."

"I already agreed to terms. You can relax. I'm heading over to Warehouse Four to do my own research. Head over to Warehouse Three and start prepping gear for me."

"Um, question about that."

"What?"

"Can I get a cooler car than the van?"

Shay lowered her chin. "Make a list of everything you want. This death by a thousand papercuts...." She turned and headed to the car before Peyton could answer.

Several loud beeps sounded from Peyton's computer. Shay halted and spun on her heel.

"What the hell was that? And why isn't it going to my phone?"

"Job offers. I'm trying to prefilter some of them for you. You got a guy in England who wants you to help him find an old druidic necklace. Some woman over in Connecticut who wants you to find... an old family photo? Says it's the key to something." He laughed. "That's probably under some split-level three bedroom." A few more beeps sounded. "The word's spreading."

Shay gave a wicked smile, her hands on her hips standing in the middle of Warehouse Two. "Of course, it has. I'm a complete badass."

"Business is booming, *tomb raider.*"

The past nine months have gone by in a blur of typing. The grey on part of my laptop has rubbed off from all the hours of building out the Oriceran Universe. Some of the keys are worn down and a little bent.

It's moved so fast that I haven't had time to really take in how much things have changed. Five series later – Midwest Witch Chronicles, The Leira Chronicles, The Soul Stone Mage, The Kacy Chronicles and the Fairhaven Chronicles – plus maps, art work, a web site, fan groups – Hey FANS! And lots of you guys too! Open house at a local Vet Center in Austin (two Vietnam vets reunited after 50+ years – that was wild), lunch with Fans at the Jackalope (who knew that place has a lot of photos of topless women on the wall in the backroom...), speeches at writer's conferences, a trip across the pond to England, tons of mugs and stickers and signed books.

And a swearing troll started it all off. Yumfuck Tiberius Troll. New mug out there with him as Batfuck.

Here we go into PART 2 of the Oriceran Universe with a badass new logo. It started with Michael Anderle and his second series as a solo – The Unbelievable Mr. Brownstone. (You know that other series he has by himself – Kurtherian Gambit…). Now there's a spinoff he and I are doing with the main character, Shay Carson in I Fear No Evil series and Book 1 - Kill the Willing. It's going to keep going with Alison in a YA spinoff from Michael and myself later this month – The School of Necessary Magic and Book 1 – Dark is Her Nature.

And of course, Leira, Correk and THE TROLL return in a new series, Rewriting Justice and Book 1 coming in May is Justice Served Cold. Leira's not taking orders anymore. Time for her to figure out what justice means in a world with magic. It's Leira 2.0 with Correk by her side and the troll set loose on the nation's capital. What could go wrong?

I've done all this while maintaining a corporate day job (got a promotion!) and I decided to sell the house I'm in and build a new one. Pre-drywall chat with the builder is this Friday. I think this is where I hear when they think the house will be done. There's a 'coming soon' sign that I can see out of my window where I've been writing. Put down 12 bags of mulch last weekend. This week's chore is packing so it's ready to show (translation: make it look like no one really lives here). The good dog Lois has loved all the coming and going and new people to greet and rub up against, leaving a trail of white fur.

Here's the thing I sometimes get a moment to think about and it blows my mind. I was a poor kid in a minister's family, then I was a single mother with a great kid – the offspring now grown, and I survived a terminal diagnosis followed by several more bouts of cancer – all of it lived out in a lot of apartments in big cities in the US. I look back at my time in Chicago and see so many people crowded in a tiny kitchen around a glass top table, talking and laughing and sharing a dish. It was the best and already a good life. Money never defined it even if lack of it made it a little tougher at times.

The house I'm selling (and bought 4 years ago) was my first house and was a BIG step up. A washer and dryer without a coin slot, a garage of my own (no more running through the rain or trying to remember where I parked last), central air conditioning and my own little backyard. Heaven...

So, here's the cool part. Since I met Michael Anderle and this dream of being a *successful* author has come true, I've stretched out my dreams and grown them bit by bit. I'm moving into a house that has all kinds of upgrades that I'm not used to near a state park not too far from downtown Austin. My dream home.

It's been a journey of ups and downs to get here – wouldn't trade any of it – because it got me here with all of you doing something I love with some wonderful people like Magic Mike and Craig Martelle and Steve Campbell. Now, the good dog, Lois Lane and I are going to move on up...

I'm not unique – just stubborn and willing to keep trying – so if you have a dream, keeping going. Don't give up just ahead of the most amazing parts of your journey.

Makes me wonder what is coming next. I can hardly wait... More adventures to follow. Thank you to each of you who read these books and write to me all the time – I am so very grateful.

AUTHOR NOTES - MICHAEL ANDERLE

WRITTEN MAY 1ST, 2018

First, THANK YOU for reading these author notes!

Right now, I'm sitting in Javier's in the Aria Casino, in Las Vegas, Nevada. I'm sitting in the second booth from the right in the bar area.

It's a circle. Probably sits maybe three (3) comfortably and five squished together. Today, it's just me and my laptop, working on these author notes before I call Martha when I get back to my office.

She is still packing, if you care to know (she messaged me in Slack, so I know this now.) Right after I speak with her, I'll get on a call with Hayley Lawson regarding a project we are working on, and then type out another two chapters for Payback is a Bitch due out in less than two weeks.

I turned in two chapters this morning.

I was working with Laurie Starkey (Protected by the Damned) yesterday. I had a collaborator ask me a question three days ago, and the concept came up yesterday as well that is summed up like this:

"How the hell do you put out so many books, so fast?"

The answer is I work with fast people. Or people that may not be fast, but they ARE productive. They get shit done and they know the value of dreams being realized. In general, most of my collaborators are older (not than me, just in life) and know what it takes to make their dreams come true.

Hard work. Often boring, typing our fingers off, work.

I'd bet (without putting it to a spreadsheet) the average collaborator age is early forties. I'm fifty turning fifty-one this year. Craig is older than me and so is Martha, and Steve (Zen Master Walking ™.)

CM Raymond and a LOT of the Age of Magic / Oriceran folks are younger as is Ell Leigh Clarke and Hayley Lawson.

Hell, even TS (Scott) Paul is only one year younger than me (but he looks ten years younger.)

For many of us, this is our second or third profession. We grew up book readers and book lovers, but not authors.

Except Martha.

She has been working this profession (one way or another) for thirty years. As a fiction writer, journalist, ghost-writer, nationally syndicated columnist and a *believer*.

She mentioned before just how much has been accomplished in the last year, but she isn't scratching the surface very much. She spoke in Las Vegas for the 20BooksTo50k event in November of 2017 on what works and doesn't work when building a Universe. Then, just three months later she was in London at the 20BooksTo50k event there talking about getting through multiple battles with cancer and overcoming to see her success.

This year, after 30 years of hard work in writing, writing is offering her the chance to see the fruits of that labor.

I couldn't be happier for her, and the last two of her wishes.

Grandchildren to spoil, and a good man to share her life with.

Her new home is supposed to be finished sometime late summer or fall, I think. Martha says she wants to make me 'touch' all of the upgrades. (Yes, she means that literally.)

I think I'm going to be busy that half of this year. Maybe by 2019, she will forget ;-)

Next book, I'll write about Shay perhaps, or ask Shay to write my Author Notes, we shall see.

This book, I just wanted to congratulate my collaborator for showing us what true dedication means.

Ad Aeternitatem,

Michael

CONNECT WITH THE AUTHORS

Martha Carr Social

Website: http://www.marthacarr.com

Facebook: https://www.facebook.com/
groups/MarthaCarrFans/

Michael Anderle Social

Website: http://kurtherianbooks.com/

Email List: http://kurtherianbooks.com/email-list/

Facebook Here: https://www.
facebook.com/TheKurtherianGambitBooks/